Dick, Stan Greene

S H A W N   A M I C K
and
T E R R Y   R O G E R S

PAGE PUBLISHING, INC.
Conneaut Lake, PA

First originally published by Page Publishing 2020

ISBN 978-1-6624-0996-7 (pbk)
ISBN 978-1-6624-0997-4 (digital)

Printed in the United States of America

Volume 1
A Study in Greene

Of Buffaloes and Lawyers

Bang! Bang! Bang! The impetuous knock brazenly shook the unsteady window within its weakened frame, waking what could only be described as a time-weathered man, curled upon the old and stained sleeper sofa angled from the impulsively beat upon door.

His eyes opened the curtains to the stage of his reality, neatly accompanied by the flatulent knocking upon his shattered, special-ordered, etched-glass, half-paneled door. Oh, his pride and joy.

Perhaps, the depiction of this man requires more rumination as well. He will be undoubtedly mistaken as the protagonist of this world, and more perspective may be needed to define the true depths of the man.

To continue reading this story in search of divine inspiration could only accurately be described as inanity. Neither am I Homer, detailing in poetic verse an epic tale of unavailing hope or the strength of human compassion and outlining bravery and courageousness only to highlight a peculiar weakness to bring about a desolate end. Nor is this the story of a man being guided by the divine hands of Virgil as he hopelessly descends deeper into the depths of the ten well-known circles of hell in search of a path to God.

If it is truly tales of heroism and grandeur that you seek, place this book back where you found it. Drive your ass down to your local bookstore. Locate its expansive fantasy aisle. It will be the one past the big dragon poster, and search the shelves for The Cruelty of Magic. *Keep looking.*

The pitiful disgrace of a man lying still, hoping that the drums of war pounding upon his door would cease, was just like any other. As with all men who stepped foot in this world, he came riddled with vices that often led derelict men of confusion to be absence of purpose or direction. Rarely would this man's actions originate from a desire toward some greater good of humanity. His mind could barely contain even a tenuous thought toward the well-being of anyone past himself.

Yet I suppose, one cannot deny him the capability of empathy.

Toil and abandonment, both of his own volition and the chaos entangling his life with others, brought the bereft shell of a callous and sullen man we find coiled on this out-of-date, cheaply built sleeper sofa.

Hell, some previous sexual encounters would not feel comfortable even calling him the shell of a man, but I digress.

The accompaniment knocking was not the polite, neighborly "Mind if I borrow a cup a sugar" knock. Anger emanated with each beat strike, flowing like the thousand hooves in a thunderous herd of buffalo upset by the lack of evidence they received after paying their hard-earned money to find proof of their "cheating ass" husband's affair.

"You fucking dick!" Echoed the less than five-foot-tall poise of a dame shadowed through the shattered etched glass window embroidered with remnants of mirrored letters that was supposed to read "Stan Greene, Private Eye."

The woman standing behind the glass physically embodied an embolism, which would explain the lack of oxygen received by her face as she tried to force her way through the hole in the shattered glass panel of the office door.

When he could no longer ignore the ongoing stampede she unleashed upon his door, Stan slowly rose from the mattress. The hat protecting his eyes from the rising sun fell from atop his head, in sync with his feet finding the floor. It landed comfortably next to him on the mattress, as if the hat was in protest and requesting, "Just five more minutes."

The half-burned roach resting on his chest fell similarly to his lap.

The sunlight already forced its way into the apartment, greeting Stan as it peered into the third-floor studio apartment through the open curtains, illuminating the hovel Stan called his home.

Stan did not return the greeting hospitably. He groaned as he stretched out his back. A singular crack for each and every year, plus the hard sorrows Stan delved his body into over the course of his life. As his spinal column aligned into place, there was a particular spot, akin to the back of his clavicle, that if he could manage to crack, his body would feel a surge of air rush through, awakening every darkened cavity throughout his frame.

Unfortunately, this would not be one of those days.

"My lawyer said these pictures are useless!" The estranged voice of his pending visitor startled Stan in a way the incessant knocking never could. "They prove that he's a cheat as much as this shit office of yours proves you're a fucking success! I know you're in there, so open the goddamned door!" Her green eyes peered through the softball-sized hole in the door's window pane.

Her commands fell faint on his ears as he haphazardly lit the roach he retrieved from his lap. Stan paused for a moment, watching the flame tickle the tip of his almost forgotten friend. When it refused to light, Stan relented, standing from his seated position, stretching his arms into the air as he yawned.

Quickly folding his sleeper sofa into its frame, he quietly replaced the cushions with his hat atop them. He hoped this might prevent the age-old rumor from spreading further—that he lived within his office.

It did not.

Stan fell upon the sofa cushions and leaned over his bent knees using his hands to wipe the fatigue from his face. His long and thinning hair hung to his shoulders in a way that made it seem as if he might be the long-lost estranged son of Lord Eddard Stark. He tried to adjust it blindly with finesse in an attempt at improving his appearance.

It failed.

Placing his hat upon his head, Stan walked over to his coat rack. He slipped his arm into the patched sleeve of the indiscernible-colored trench coat. Perhaps it was a khaki brown at one point, but it was now discolored and gray, as was the streak that grew prominently in the hair on his head. He would like to think it made him a silver fox, and perhaps it did.

One would not complacently describe him as "handsome" per se, but you also would not enjoy seeing him pop up in your "Mature" filter on Pornhub, either.

"Open up! You act like I can't see you in there!"

Their eyes finally made contact through the cracked and splintered windowpane.

"Would you just—" With a tired, frustrated sigh normally reserved for sleepless fathers roaming the night in search of the small amounts of rest they consume while enduring the shrieking of their child and she that bore it to the world, Stan continued "—I'm coming, okay? I'm coming. I'll be right there."

He barely turned the knob to open the door when his nostrils filled with a familiar fragrance of raspberry and lavender melded together in an unbalanced tango of the senses.

Her face sat contrary to her scent, giving him the distinct impression something had just taken a vile bowel movement beneath her nose. She stood, arms crossed, glaring in disgust of her inhospitable host. Her disgust was not entirely unwarranted, as Stan wasn't known to be a clean man.

"Finally!" She was exasperated, pushing him to the side as she crossed the threshold. A quick preliminary glance around the room revealed his less-than-pristine lifestyle. The half-burned blunt, balled-up pieces of garbage strewn about his floor, and a layer of dust accumulated on the counters and furniture throughout Stan's office. She remained unconvinced that this was not his apartment as it was filled with all the amenities one would imagine befall a middle-aged man absent of purpose in his life, lacking the distinct ability to organize even his silverware correctly.

She threw a file on his desk. "He said it wasn't enough to prove he's cheating. In fact, he said it looked as though they were on a business dinner! I paid you good money to help me finalize this divorce, and I expect you to keep your end of the deal," she said, digging through her obnoxiously purple purse for a cigarette.

"Maybe he's not cheating," Stan said glibly, offering her a light from his match.

"That's not the point, is it, Stan?" The fiery vixen leaped from her seated position to lean over his desk. Stan couldn't ignore her cleavage, adding immensely to her appeal as he lit her cigarette.

"You knew the terms when you took the money. This isn't about the truth." She turned away from him, placing her things back into her purse; the volume of her voice never changed. "Now smoke your fucking blunt. Take a piss or a shit or whatever the hell it is you do when you wake up because I saw you climb off that cruddy little couch." She turned toward Stan, pointing at his bed before trampling abruptly toward the door. "Then…GET! YOUR SHIT! TOGETHER!" She slammed the door behind her as she left.

Her silhouette faded out of the windowpane at the same time another shadow, belonging to a well-postured man, entered into it.

"Excuse me."

Stan listened as a surprised, much lower, and far less seductive voice emerged. The voice stammered to ask the buffalo something else, but she shrugged him off with a surprisingly gruff noise. The silhouettes faded into a single darkness, and one, much more somber shadow prevailed.

A knock, delivered with more respect toward the manufacturer of the door than felt formerly, was followed by a stern but gentle "Hello, may I come in?"

"Jesus, I suppose so." Stan stared at the roach he was conflicted to finish.

The door squeaked open as the nonthreatening stature of a well-dressed man took form from behind the windowpane and entered the well-lit studio apartment.

"Huh," the man said in discovery with a slacked jaw that reminded Stan of precisely how low his ball bag drooped as of late, "you must be Dick."

"It's Stan!" He grumbled, the roach falling out of his hand because of the unique attempt at intimidation he was, unconvincingly, trying to convey by shaking his hand at the man.

"Guess that explains it then. They must have been calling you a dick."

Stan merely replied with the smug look on his face as he began crawling on the floor in search of his fallen comrade. He surrendered to the idea that his missing roach may have landed beneath the sofa and sighed heavily to himself. He knew he would have to eventually dig into that bottomless abyss. However, for the time being, he pulled out the mostly empty jar labeled "Sticky-icky." The gumshoe twisted the top off the jar. Its strong, pungent aroma filled the room instantly.

"You know, I've been in this town since the very beginning, but I'm still not used to seeing it everywhere."

"They don't call it 'The Town Pot Built' for nothin'." Stan recalled smugly as he broke apart the last of his bud on his desk. He sat across the desolate landscape of lost cases and unpaid debts from the thin, well-dressed man. Files from past cases, never resolved, divided the distance between them. Photographs and other pages with Stan's handwritten notes scribbled in the margin dressed the top of the desk like a menagerie of lost faces, each exhibiting its own remnants of debris left from the forgotten packed pipes and hand rolled cigarettes.

"What can I do ya for?" Stan kicked his feet on the desk as if all the years of his life culminated in this one opportunity to knock a few of his files off his desk onto the floor, the filing system of a knuckle-dragging Neanderthal. He showed no worry or care, as if this was a completely natural occurrence.

Making a quick glance at the fallen files and raising an eyebrow toward Stan, he replied, "Ah, straight to the point. My kind of guy. The name's Jimmy Book." The well-postured but nonthreatening man outstretched his hand to shake Stan's with a smile, possibly genuine.

The sleuth simply stared at Jimmy's hand with a blank expression on his face. He was unabashed. A long meerschaum pipe quickly appeared in his hand. Stan cashed the remnants into his opposite hand, casually rubbing the ashes into his thigh.

Jimmy seemed to take the hint. "Right, well…" He brushed his hand off his lapel. "I'm looking for a man that can be discreet. From what I'm told, you're that man."

Stan struck a match off the back of a faded and worn matchbook, its Dirty Vegas logo completely visible from his hand. "'They've apparently said I'm a dick too," he retorted sarcastically as he took a puff from the pipe.

"At this point, I'd say that builds credibility more than anything." The man rebutted as he sat in the dust-covered, rarely used seat across from Stan and crossed one leg over the other with a smile.

"Hmph." Stan smirked, taking the pipe out of his mouth. "All right, so what's the gig?" Stan chuckled, shaking the match. The man's enthusiasm amused him.

"I'm on this case—"

"Case?" interjected Stan with slightly more interest than shown previously; that word meant money to our titular private eye.

"Yes. A case," Jimmy answered quickly. "I'm a local lawyer, and there's this client I've had for many years that believes there is a local distributor that he suspects of questionable business practices." A long look filled the attorney's face. "But it seems nothing can be found on the books."

"So." Stan grunted, leaning forward to grab his potential client's attention. "You'd like me to utilize some questionable business practices so that you can prove that someone else is utilizing questionable business practices?" The smirk that once rested upon the lawyer's face had all but faded since his entry.

"No," said Stan shortly. "I don't need that kind of trouble…" he began trailing off toward the end following the sight of another shadow forming within the windowpane. The mail slot opened, and a bright-pink envelope shoved through. The sight made Stan's stomach drop like the testicles of a middle-school boy looking at a *Playboy* for his first time.

"Great, what now?" Stan thought coarsely. He quickly reached for the matchbook and the pipe once more as he crossed the room to grab the envelope.

Jimmy eyed Stan suspiciously as Stan inspected the envelope lying on the ground, while he created a cloud of smoke to envelop himself.

The arriving envelope radiated with malcontent, in return, with the words Final Termination Notice stamped in red on the front. Stan groaned as he bent down to pick it up, the smoke escaping from his lungs through his orifices.

"It seems to me you could use a bit more of this trouble, you know, to pay your bills," Jimmy said.

Stan gaped at his inherent ward with disgust. Tearing open the envelope, he planted himself back into his chair. "What's the pay?" His feet kicked back up with more angst than before; more files fell to the ground to match those that fell formerly.

Stan's eyes scanned the paper in the envelope for the fiscal damage, and it read "534.76."

"You'll be compensated for your discretion, of course," Jimmy spoke. "How does five hundred fifty sound, appropriate?"

It was the perfect amount, but he came to Stan, not the other way around. "One thousand, plus expenses. So I'd say about fifteen hundred should get the job done."

"Odd." The defender of the law gave the investigator a mocking look. "You were able to calculate expenses with little knowledge of the job." His smile returned to his face. "But fine. I expected you to be a dick about it after what they've said." Jimmy stood from the dusty chair.

"Who is this 'they' you keep referring to?" Stan asked, visibly annoyed.

"It's of little consequence." Jimmy pulled out a thick envelope, white in nature, from his inner coat pocket. "There's two grand in here. I'm sure you'll find that to be enough. I'll be in contact." He simpered. "I see certain supplies in need already." The lawyer glanced toward the almost empty mason jar on the table between them.

"See you tomorrow." Jimmy buttoned his suit jacket, wiping off the dust that had accumulated on his pants, then took his leave.

Stan sat in silent disbelief for a moment, gawking at the money within the envelope sprawled on the files that had not yet fallen onto the floor. He went to kick up his feet once more, but the back of his chair suddenly failed, ejecting him backward upon the floor.

The private eye lay on the ground for a moment staring at the ceiling; his lungs fought for air. He checked to make sure the money in the envelope had not spilled out. Once confirming everything was still safely tucked into its place, Stan released a sigh of relief as he rolled onto his stomach and turned to get his feet beneath him. In that moment, a paper crumbled on the floor caught his eye.

He struggled to stand for a moment, holding on to his desk to keep his balance. Staring at the paper on the ground, he slowly rounded his desk to get a better look. He immediately recognized it as a crumbled-up lottery ticket.

Possibly, it had fallen from that broad's ridiculous purse or even possibly the lawyer's pocket, though the latter was less likely. He flattened the paper and studied the front of the ticket briefly. The numbers on the front reminded him of a hypnotic, almost rhythmic beat. He found another set of numbers, 0519-99-0, handwritten on the back in black ink.

Grape Ape for the Cannibus

Stan sat alone in his office, watching time pass through his third-story window. Amid the cascade of remembrance, the incredulous investigator found both joy and a callous pain. He kindled the flame of his pipe with a mindless puff, clutching the remains of what seemed a bygone age—a desire to serve, the warmth of companionship, a lost and forgotten home. Now he endured in the mid of nothing, save the few precious relics.

If Stan was truly honest with himself, he had no idea exactly how long he sat staring into the unconscionable void before him. It could have been five minutes or even a few hours; it's hard to ascertain the passage of time when you live in the perpetual mental state of wake and bake.

The memories finally culminating in the moment of his present, the gumshoe slapped the pipe into his open palm. He stared into the ashes scattered about his hands. Stan related more to these ashes than any human he had ever met in the life that just passed before his eyes. Ruined, to be cast into the air. Absent in purpose but not presence.

Rubbing the ashes into the outer thigh of his pants, he finished gathering his thoughts. The sleuth found his phone sitting on some files in the center of his desk and his wallet near the desk's edge. Standing from his chair, he walked across the room. He grabbed his coat from the rack and slid his arms into the sleeves as he walked out of the paneled door, shattered and webbed like memories, not incapable of discernment, nor is it truly how it was.

When the door latched, one of the cracks in the spiderweb of the splintered windowpane lengthened, further obscuring his etched name. In that same instant, Stan patted the pockets of his coat and pants in search for his keys. With a held breath and a subtle prayer, he reached for the handle behind his back with his dominant hand. This office door had the tendency to lock on its own, which was great for security most of the time.

This, however, caused an issue for the absentminded investigator on more than one occasion.

"Fuck!" He groaned at the door, peering through the hole in the cracked pane to see his keys lying on top of files newly relocated to the floor of his office. "They must have fallen off my desk!"

Stan cursed to himself amply in the empty hallway. In an attempt to assure himself of his sanity, he took a deep breath and sighed. Slowly, Stan allowed his legs to drag his slacked body, unwillingly, toward the stairs. Each step fell heavier with dread than the last as he prepared the moonlit dance Jack Nicholson desired to see.

The short, portly property owner and superintendent of the finely lit apartment building, Dominick Draper, had quite the nose for money. Stan thought the man sported the snout of a drug hound that recently pounded a line of cocaine when it came to money, regardless of the amount. Out from the shadows, Dominick would appear, as though you'd stolen money from his father a few lifetimes ago.

"My name is Dominick Draper, and you owe me rent. Prepare to be evicted."

The private investigator imagined these words coming from the grubby bastard prior to his eviction; a small part of him hoped it would come true.

Stan rounded the corner of the last staircase before the landing in the first-floor lobby. Across the room, he could hear murmurs echoing from the cracks around Draper's office door.

"I'm going to evict that dick, Stan Greene." Dominick swung open his office door, his cellphone pasted to his ear as Stan entered into his view.

"Speak of the devil, and he shall come," Draper said with a sassy waddle one would think was reserved for the less flight capable of birds as he tapped the red circle on the screen of his phone, placing it into his shirt pocket. He studied the private eye tentatively.

"As I've said, Dom, I'm not a detective anymore." Stan scoffed and rolled his eyes, shaking his head in discord.

Confusion poured over Mr. Draper's face; he shook his head in a response of antipathy toward Stan. "Let me guess, rent will be late?" He closed his office door behind him.

"Actually, no," Stan answered pointedly. "Working on something big. But I seem to have gotten locked out." He tried to make it sound surprising. "Mind helping me get my keys?" Stan asked in a genuine tone, as if it were the first time this week.

"I'm not your personal locksmith, Greene, and if you keep this up, I'll start charging you like one!" Dominick rumbled as he shoulder-shrugged Stan, waddling past him to mount the staircase, the agitation of a branded bull ascending with each step.

"Noted," Stan let out beneath his breath with a heavy sigh, following the shuffle reminiscent of a man slightly taller than Danny DeVito.

When they arrived on the third floor, Draper scoured the hall as he approached the office. His eyes settled on Stan's windowpane.

Draper noticed what Stan had hoped would be entirely unnoticeable—the baseball-sized hole in the windowpane.

"When the fuck did that happen, Dick?" tottered the balding man over his shoulder. "We just got that fixed!" Draper exasperated.

"First of all, I'm fine. Thanks for asking." Stan waved his hands in a grandiose manner. "And second, I'm not a detective anymore," grunted the disgraced private eye.

"As for the window," Stan caressed his finger lightly around the hole, barely large enough to put his hand through, "do you remember that kid you kept getting mad at, the one with the little ball?"

"Yea…" Draper drawled with questioning and unreasonable eyebrows as he unlocked the door with his master key.

"Turns out his father was equally annoyed with his son bouncing it constantly. While I was calmly explaining to him that his wife didn't really go on that business trip. And in fact, she was across town, shacked up in a cheap motel room with another man. When he saw the pictures I took…" Stan's eyes told the story of an innocent boy.

Stan's eyes are to be given the same discretion as a Catholic priest watching your prepubescent children.

"He went into a frenzy." Stan emphasized. "The man grabbed the ball midbounce. And really, I was quite impressed, until he threw it through the window." Stan shrugged, slipping through the doorway accompanied by the melancholy song of his distracting tale. With a swift movement, he retrieved his keys. "Oh, and the kid whined, I knew you'd love that sort of thing," he interjected to gain empathy as he jolted around him once more, jingling his keys hypnotically in the distressed landlord's face. "I swept up the glass."

"Rent is coming, Draper. Don't evict me yet!" Stan echoed as he galloped down the stairs.

The tepid landlord remained in a trance of malice, glaring at the cracked window. Beneath his breath, he muttered something along the lines of, "Fucking dick."

Stan made for the exit of Draper Properties, approaching the double doors to the boulevard like a cowboy walking out of a saloon. Nestled on the east side of town, the building perched upon the bustling corner of Shakedown Street and Ocean Boulevard, stretching into the skyline with the Rocky Mountains etched in the distance. The few tall buildings within this area of downtown were quickly built, though not lacking in craftsmanship. It was prime real estate, within walking distance to the university and most everywhere else worth visiting in downtown Potstow.

The local rags called it the Town Pot Built, the Town That Never Goes Down, a Town So High It Never Falls, the Town with More Hash Stations Than Gas Stations.

The newspapers had a slow news week, and they stretched the stories a little bit.

Potstow was founded by a group of like-minded individuals with the Initiative to pump big money into lobbying for recreational cannabis to be made legal in Colorado. In the process, waylaying lawmakers into letting them privately control the monopoly behind the scenes of the public eye became tantamount.

Though they expected to make a profit, the result of their avarice was something they never thought possible—stacks upon stacks of cold hard cash.

Who would have thought weed would sell in America?

As current banking laws still prohibited the monopoly owners from depositing the physical money earned from the profits of cannabis sales, lawmakers supplemented the bill to allow them to make investments into the public works. This became a safer practice for them to store their profits than foreign banks.

A few lawyers met one night, intending to find other innovative solutions to the influx of cash and, in the process, found a loophole in the state's bylaws. Although they couldn't funnel money into the banks directly, their employees could deposit the cash legally as their payroll as contracted employees.

The money would then be deposited into a bank account linked to the local financial advisory that claimed to be dispersing funds into a wide array of portfolios for each of the employees, which would return to the company, free and clear. Then accounting would send the real payroll to the employees. This process effectively laundered their money legally without having to throw even more profits away toward the frivolous use of illicit means. This extra step would normally cause uproar among the workforce, but this afforded the local businesses to better compensate their employees.

Who could argue with getting more money?

Tax breaks were written to give entrepreneurs the financial freedom to hire these contractual employees and invest into various public works. Through these investments in the infrastructure and the workers themselves, the city sprouted almost instantaneously within the empty southwestern Colorado township once known as Maizefield.

A gold rush erupted that the media dubbed the Green Rush. People flooded into the state to partake of the local fauna and look for work. This caused a job crisis, leading into a housing crisis, then a rather interesting riot that no one really understood at the time.

The only thing people knew for certain about the riot was that everyone, and I mean everyone, was stoned to the high heavens.

People began sleeping on the streets, camping in the parks; the local hostels were full, and the missions stuffed to the brim. Jobs were scarce, and people were filling the state like fleas to a mangy dog. Something needed to be done, and someone had to do it. One of the local entrepreneurs elected to buy a large plot of land for greenhouses to help create jobs and ease tensions developing within the region.

Then the town's future political elite grabbed their shares of those profits and funneled them toward building housing. A mediation station was also built to help control the rioting. Life in town had become a veritable utopia on earth.

A true trickle-down effect flooded industry within the county when the greenhouses led to processing centers, which led to distribution centers of all sorts, and lest we not forget the paraphernalia shops popping up like the flowers themselves.

This economic influx brought with it much-needed jobs to the area. Business breeds business, and the area grew rife with it. Before anyone knew what was going on, the semblance of a town formed. An election was put forth to create a municipal council. Afterward, the newly elected municipal council adopted a decision to apply for corporate cityhood.

There was a typo in the form they submitted to become a city. The letter *n* was left out in the council-approved name, Potstown. It was a clerical error by way of the secretary's office. The upside was, having one less letter made it substantially cheaper for the welcome signs leading into town.

Listening to music has now been strictly prohibited within the clerical offices of the Potstow Municipality buildings.

Stan stepped beneath the marquee of A Stoned Experience, the local rock-climbing shop located just a few buildings down the street from his apartment. He quickly gathered the few supplies he may need in some of his more presently future endeavors. The cashier offered to pack Stan's supplies in a finely stitched leather satchel.

Though he didn't wish to spend the extra cash, the satchel would prove useful.

Plus, he thought the cashier was cute.

Leaving the store, he shuffled his notes back into an envelope after reading them once more. Killian's Distribution was all the way in the outskirts on the west side of town. The Cannibus would get him to his destination, but the ride back would be up in the air. With his personal stash virtually depleted, Stan decided to briefly stop by the corner dispensary, the Blueberry Drop Stop.

All the best strains set among their displays. Green Crack, Grape Ape, Purple Haze, Purple Urkle, The Red-headed Stranger, OG Kush, Afghani Kush, Northern Lights, White Widow, and so many more flavors and extracts were lining their shelves.

Stan's mouth watered at the thought of all the delicious tastes. He pressed his face to the glass of the display with the enthusiasm of a child in a candy store to read exactly what Moon Rocks were.

"Hello, sir!"

Stan was greeted by an energetic young man with slicked-back hair on the top and shaved on the sides.

"Welcome to the Blueberry Drop Stop, where the pot don't stop!" the young man rhythmically shouted from behind the bar.

"You know, it's been a few weeks since I've been in here, but the last guy didn't say that to me," Stan questioned the salesperson with a stink eye.

"Alright, full disclosure. They don't make me say it, but it's catchy. Right?"

"Anyway, how can I help you?" The young man made his way over to Stan with his hand outstretched, awaiting that subtle confirmation of mutual respect you gain by shaking a man's hand.

He did not get this from Stan.

"Well, how can I help you, sir?" He nervously regained his smile, accepting there would be no handshake.

"I'm just looking to refill." Stan less than eagerly answered.

"Ah, but this shouldn't be just a refill, Mister...?"

"Greene." Stan spat rudely.

"Convenient!" he chimed laughingly. "Well, this shouldn't just be about a refill, **Mr. Greene**." The salesman's voice resonated. "This should be an experience every single time you come into the Blueberry Drop Stop."

The kid had a look of thrill that only appears in the eyes of a hunter focused on his prey. "Tell me, **Mr. Greene**, what can your **green** do for you?"

Stan enjoyed the young man's enthusiasm for his job. However, the way he said his name was a different story.

"Jesus, kid. Did they start paying you commission?" Stan grumbled. "Look, I just want to be able to numb myself from the day and forget what time it is. Let's go," he barked with obvious frustration, snapping his fingers, adding, "I have somewhere to be."

"Well, sir. If you would step over here with me, we have a new Break-A-Bud display setup, which allows you to sample most of our more mainline strains for free, and I think I have the perfect one for you." He grinned with almost villainous entertainment.

Stan did as he was asked. He followed the motion of the jubilant cashier's hand and tried out a few flavors at the Break-A-Bud station. To his surprise, he began to actually enjoy himself and started asking for increasingly more samples. Before he knew it, hours flew by just huffing and discussing the various strains.

Eventually, they settled on the recommendation of the salesman—Grape Ape. Though Stan encountered the strain before, he had never actually tried it.

Stan walked up to the counter with the excitement of a twenty-five-year-old man forced to wait over a decade to finally be able to see an Incredibles *sequel, when they knew goddamned-well that no one even wanted to watch neither* Cars 2 *nor* 3.

His eyes trailed along the counter as the salesman rang up the order. Stan placed his hands into the pockets of his coat. A strange texture made him clasp and drag the offending item out of his pocket. In his grasp, he found a winning lottery ticket he had almost forgotten about. He was certain it was worth at least twenty-five dollars.

"Can you cash this for me?" inquired Stan, placing his unforgotten lottery ticket upon the counter.

"Certainly!" The pompous salesmen rejoiced. He scanned the ticket into the lotto machine. "Uh"—he looked at Stan—"this one isn't a winner."

"WHAT?" he shouted, ripping the card out of his hand. "I thought for sure that was a seven." He growled subtly.

"I feel that, man." The man standing behind him in line coughed.

"Oh, do you?" Stan turned around to face his tormentor. "Do you feel that, man?" he mocked.

"I had a big winner. About fifty thousand, I reckon."

Stan could see the tale of woe on the man's face.

"I got jacked on my way to work the other morning. Big guy"—the eyes of the man's face grew to accentuate his meaning—"with a ponytail. He had the strangest accent."

His face distorted further with the weight of his weary tale. "But, man, those big winners are weird anyways. You got to mail stuff in and do paperwork. Not like cashing a simple twenty spot." The dread-stricken man shook his head, accepting his fate.

"If I found the ticket and the guy that took it, what would you give me?" He quickly searched his pockets. "I'm a private investigator." He flashed a worn business card like it was a detective's badge.

"Half is better than all of nothing, man."

Stan's mind began to add up just how much that would be and came to the conclusion—that was a lot of rent.

The investigator felt his inner self jump for joy.

"If you find it…" Reality planted Inner Stan back into his shoes. "…I'll give you half," the hope-filled patron scoffed, reaching into his pocket and handing Stan his own embossed business card. The words "Independent Incorporated" glistened in the light. "Does that mean you're a dick?"

"No, dammit!" The private eye grew weary of exerting the explanation. He snatched the business card before turning back toward the cashier. "I used to be a detective, but not anymore."

After receiving the payment from Stan for his purchase, the clerk mumbled in a horrible attempt to divert Stan's hearing, "Really? Because you seem like a big dick to me."

He was right; Stan did.

"Oh, fuck off," Stan blurted out, grabbing his bag of goodies from the counter. He kicked open the door in frustration, ringing the bell as he left. "I'll find the ticket, and you better pay."

After what seemed like hours, he finally emerged as a new man with a new brand. Stan walked up to the bus stop and collapsed onto a bench. He sat alone, amusing himself with his thoughts, packing his meerschaum pipe once again.

He puffed, watching people pass him on the streets, his mind unmoored to the sonder that swept over him. His mind boiled, unraveling at the basic wonder of consciousness and his appropriation on the scale, comparatively, to what he did not understand.

He came to ponder if, by chance, he had prior relations with the mother of the college-aged girl with the unmistakable assets hanging out her shorts passing by him on her way to class.

The 516 Cannibus screeched to a halt in front of him.

An Officer and This Guy

"Come on, baaaabe!" Will pleaded. "What was the point of moving to Potstow to make a whole lotta money winning these tournaments"— he paused for a moment to aid the impact of his argument—"if I can't even spend some of it on the things I don't like to do."

"Okay. First off, we moved here for your career in E-Sports," Katie paused, "so you could be closer to the stadium. **Not** so you could spend our extra money on a maid instead of helping me clean and straighten up the apartment."

"Now look," she continued with absolution, "it took me a long while to adapt to what you call working when you're streaming, and sure, I get it. And… I, also, understand that after long hours of streaming or a stressful tournament, you might be tired and just want to be left alone." She looked toward Will with frustration mounting in her eyes. "But Jesus Christ, man, you've literally fought a war, taken a shit on a genocidal maniac's throne." Katie paused, adding effect to her delivery. "I don't think cleaning up after yourself is an impossible task."

"Yeah," Will replied with puppy dog eyes, "but I liked shitting on his throne. I hate doing the dishes!" He laughed relentlessly.

"I love you." Katie stepped closer to him, kissing him on the cheek. "But no, we're not getting a maid." She accompanied the kiss with a light slap across his cheek.

"Fine," Will mumbled like a child, pushing his shoulder-length hair behind his ear. Lifting a roll-out TV out of the large box beneath his feet, he stood, looking at Katie, awaiting orders like a dutiful soldier.

"You still want the big one in the bedroom, don't you?" Katie asked with a playful smile because she already knew the answer.

Will grinned back at her. "Mmmhmm." He nodded with glee, widening his smirk.

"Go ahead." She chuckled. He excitedly carried the elongated tube containing their big-screen television back to their bedroom, chanting "Thank you, thank you, thank you" repeatedly as he ran to set up the TV.

Will scuffled in their bedroom. In a few minutes, Katie heard another box open; she knew that meant he was setting up his console in the bedroom.

"Babe!" she yelled. "Come say bye so I can go to work!"

As he jumped up, Katie heard one of the boxes in the room tumbling over.

"It's fine," Will spoke, sounding exasperated while tripping over another box located directly outside the bedroom door. "I'm fine."

Will picked himself from the floor with ease and made his way toward Katie. At the bottom of the steps, he hesitated for a moment. Her eyes glistened watching her childlike fiancé approach; he let that moment embrace him for as long as time allowed, filling his lungs with a long, deep breath.

He was with a woman who loved him entirely, embracing all his flaws, looking at him with a desire in her eyes that made him feel weightless and without burden or doubt. Will's shortcomings emboldened Katie to embrace her own imperfection at times. Within that complete harmonious dissonance, they found a balance within the other they could not find within themselves. They had an inherent desire to cast away their frivolous arguments at a moment's notice, so long as it meant peace and happiness between them; it was that which, in its own, proved their perfection for each other.

She stood in the kitchen dressed in her dark-blue uniform, large police shield upon her chest, about to begin her first day on patrol for the Potstow Police Department. Her crystal-blue eyes enamored Will, revealing the innocent heart of the woman staring back at him. Her curly hair seemed slightly shorter than Will's but still sat at the same shoulder length complemented by its perfect sepia color. She had a few freckles she was self-conscious about; Will adored each of them.

Most would not think to give much caution, if any at all, to Katie. She received many forms of training, from kickboxing, martial arts, and law enforcement combative training to her own regimen that she stuck to religiously.

Will feared no man walking on Earth, but Katie frightened him, intensely. She put such a focus into her combat training Will should be required to hold a permit just to date her.

Her passion, strength, and courageousness personified beauty to Will. For all his faults, she knew only forgiveness and support: a goal Will fell short on more than one occasion. Sometimes, Katie would take time for her understanding to persevere, but she was, and remains, aware that her outlooks and opinions are not final. Her skill for empathy made an impregnable love.

Even when they were angry and fighting with each other, they endured. They compromised to get along with one another. This unbridled dedication led Will to finally propose after returning from his second deployment. The dearth thoughts of a home without her broke him while deployed. He vowed to himself, if he made it home, he would make sure he lived the rest of his life in the company of Katie.

Will gathered Katie in his arms to deliver her desired good-bye kiss. She turned to leave, and he smacked her rear, blowing her another kiss with a wink.

Responding to the smack, she turned her head over her shoulder toward him in time to receive the kiss Will sent through the air. She pretended to catch the kiss on her cheek and laughed at the fool with whom she decided to spend the rest of their entangled lives. Retrieving her coat from the rack, she walked to the front door.

Katie opened the door to their apartment and stepped into the hall. In her peripherals, she noticed a lady standing over by her new neighbor's apartment, quickly stuffing something into her makeup bag and feigning, casually looking into one of the holes in her neighbor's windowpane.

"I don't think he's there. From what I'm told, you'd know if he was." Katie chuckled, adjusting her gun holster around her body before she left, placing one arm through her coat. "The whole floor reeks to high hell! At least that's what the landlord said when we moved."

"Why'd you take the apartment, then?" the mysterious lady inquired.

Katie watched the lady's eyes land upon her detective's badge.

"It's a beautiful apartment." The detective shrugged her reply. "The price was right, and I'm rarely going to be home to see him, anyways." Katie nodded to the door in front of the curious lady across the hall and snickered, turning to walk toward the stairs. Her intuition didn't feel comfortable leaving this lady here, alone. She added, "You comin'?"

"Oh," the lady stammered, "yes, no point waiting for him to return, I suppose." She zipped up the makeup bag, grabbing her suitcase in tow behind her.

They walked side by side, following the staircase winding down to the main floor of the apartment building. The awkward silence built between them as they descended each step.

"Hi, Ms. Edna," Katie greeted the older lady shaking a cat treat can as they passed the second-floor landing.

"So you from Colorado?" Katie asked, trying to make small talk with someone other than her fiancé and other cops. She observed her mysterious companion suspiciously out of the corner of her eyes.

Katie sized up the mysterious lady based on the responses to her general line of questioning—quick to answer questions about the weather but hesitating when the line of questioning edged closer to who and what she was. Katie knew better than to stick her nose where it did not belong; it generally led into more trouble than it was truly worth.

"Well," opening the doors to Ocean Boulevard, the detective said with a smile, "good luck."

"What do you mean 'good luck'?" The mysterious woman gave up her defense; Katie marveled at the first truly natural response she received.

"With whatever you would need from that dick," she quickly added. "If half of the stories they say about him are true. I'm sure you're desperate."

"One at Red Point!" Will yelled across the channel. He crashed his boot along the latch, imploding the locked door in front of him.

"Breach!" T-Dawg commanded. The front man brazenly burst through the entrance, looking to the furthest corner in his line of sight with Will following behind, eyeing the opposite corner—an empty room.

"Clear!" announced T-Dawg.

"Danny!" T-Dawg called out, "frag it out." He spoke in a lower tone of voice, crouching below the window into the next room. T-Dawg used the stock of his assault rifle to break the glass of the window. He motioned for his squad—Will, Danny, and Andre, the medic—to exit the same door they entered.

Once they cleared the doorway, Danny equipped the explosive ordinance. Readying his frag, he shouted, "Frag-out!"

Danny tossed it into the other room, rushing outside with the rest of his squad. They lined along the wall to shield themselves from the back draft.

T-Dawg slammed the door shut behind Danny as he ran past.

The explosion rattled the door separating them from their intended targets. T-Dawg kicked the door open again, proceeding to clear the next room, stepping over the door recently torn from its hinges.

The remains of four people scattered around the smoke-filled room.

"Bad place to camp," Will said.

"How many more?" Andre questioned the team.

"Heat signatures showing at least three more groups," Danny answered. "Showing signatures by Yellow Point."

"Do we have enough? Can we call in aerial support?" Will exasperated.

Danny pulled out his communication device and radioed through a different channel. "Requesting aerial support at Yellow Point. Do you copy?"

Silence filled the line.

"Requesting aerial suppo—" A gunshot rang out; a line shot through the temporal lobe of Danny, grazing Will on the side of his arm.

"Shit!" Andre exclaimed. "They got Danny!"

The fire team took cover behind the building they just cleared.

T-Dawg looked to Andre. "Look, I know you want to try and help him, but we will have to get back to him in a minute. First, we gotta get this sniper." T-Dawg looked at the radio Danny dropped. "Will, can you see the radio?"

"You got it, T."

"I'm going to throw a smoke. Wait till it fumes up and you hear a shot. After the shot, go, and I'll lay cover."

"Done," Will replied. T-Dawg threw the smoke out and put his hand on Will's shoulder, holding him there. Nine seconds into a fully formed cloud, there was a gunshot. "Go!" T-Dawg threw Will toward the radio. T-Dawg lit up the building where the shot originated long enough to get Will back into cover.

T-Dawg ripped the radio from Will's hands. "This is T-Dawg to air support." He rattled off the coordinates of the building located south of him, where the sniper sat. "Blow it to shit! Do you COPY? BLOW IT TO SHIT!"

"Copy," The radio responded.

The moments passed; each felt like hours stretched to darkness watching their comrade, Danny, fade away while they could do nothing to save him.

Danny whispered, "Fly, you fools!" as he passed.

A blast rang from the south as the building collapsed. Air support finally arrived.

"For Danny!" the squad yelled out their air support, clearing out the sniper.

"There's four more signatures showing at Blue Point," Andre announced. "Do we go slow and quiet or fast and loud?"

T-Dawg saw a riot shield lying by a dead body in the road across from them. "Loud as a motherfucker, boys."

Andre grabbed the grenade launcher left behind by Danny. T-Dawg equipped the riot shield, and Will knew what he had to do.

At a single-floor building at Yellow Point, Will and Andre assumed wide flanks—one to the right and one to the left side of the building.

"Ready, boys?" The fire team leader loaded his magazines.

"Let's fuck 'em up," Will bellowed.

T-Dawg held out the shield, walking directly toward the building; he knew the last of the insurgents were inside hiding in. T-Dawg threw one grenade at the entrance, blowing the door off its hinges. Instantly, the bullets began to fly.

Gunfire hammering on his shield, he slowly inched toward the building. Another grenade was let loose, knocking down a portion of the wall. The gunfire continued to pelt onto his shield.

T-Dawg kissed his last grenade before throwing it to the right side of the building, blasting an opening in the wall for Andre to enter.

Andre rained his version of sulfur and hellfire upon the building with his grenade launcher from the flank. The walls in front of them started to fall; bullets pecked into the little supporting wall, separating them from the group of hostiles.

All the while, Will snuck around to the opposite side of the building. Using the explosions from the grenades as cover, he managed to break out a window and silently waited in the shadows.

The hostile group filed into the only undamaged room of the building. Once Will heard the door shut, he tossed one grenade into the room and jolted to get away from the blast.

Before the grenade exploded, a single gunshot illuminated the shadowed window of the remaining room of the building. The bullet found its way centered into Will's heart.

The building exploded as Will's knees fell to the ground.

T-Dawg watched as the soldier, a member of his fire team, and his best friend, was shot in cold blood right in front of him.

He rushed over to Will; holding his head on his lap, he sat on the ground next to him.

"No!" he screamed. "Will! It can't be!"

The pain of losing his friend was too overwhelming to bear.

Slowly, the announcer's voice proclaimed their victory to the spectators. Will's and Danny's avatars materialized next to T-Dawg's for their celebration in the Victor's Circle of Carbon Copy.

"Are you done?" Will asked T-Dawg.

"Look, man, let's not pretend you're not pissed that he fucked your kill death spread."

Will's career as a professional gamer accelerated recently when he and his team leader and close friend T-Dawg signed contracts with a team flying through the ranks known as Duff Nation.

Slayer Monthly recognized Will as the best slayer in North America for the newly iconic game, Carbon Copy, when two spots opened on their illustrious team. The award was based on the game recording his career kill-to-death-spread ratio assessed at the end of each multiplayer game.

Carbon Copy is a virtual reality first-person shooter focused heavily on tactics executed at precisely the right time by other team members, which is how Duff Nation earned a reputation for being the most well-organized team in gaming history. The team consisted of all members with previous military history; they were led by their newly appointed fire team leader, T-Dawg. They kicked ass.

Will took off his virtual reality headset, but his microphone was still in the fire team chat. "What are you guys getting into tonight?"

"I gotta take the lady out for dinner. Take it easy, guys," Danny uttered, quickly leaving the chat.

"I'm off to work," Andre replied before following suit.

"What about you, T-Dawg?"

"Natta, I just feel like getting lit as fuck," T-Dawg replied.

"I told you to stop saying that word. It died in, like, 2018 or some shit," Will said in an exhausted tone.

"Litty," T-Dawg elongated, laughing while smacking whatever he was near, reveling in the fact that he was annoying Will.

"I'll come over, and we can smoke out, man," Will tiresomely replied. "See you in a bit."

"Yep" was all Will heard before T-Dawg left the party.

Will gathered his things to walk out of his apartment into the hallway. He stopped to take another look at his neighbor's door. While moving, he accidentally put a hole into his neighbor's windowpane, directly beside the preexisting one. By deus ex machina, there lay a nearby broom and dustpan to clear the scene.

"Convenient," he had thought to himself as he swept the remnants in the hall.

He looked into the disheveled office through the two holes. To his knowledge, the resident had not returned yet.

Will walked down the steps to the parking garage, jumping into his new sporty biodiesel he purchased a few days ago; he loved the blue shade to it. A sticky note on the steering wheel read "Ur a dork" with a cute smiley face drawn upon it. He beamed at it with happiness, leaving it in place.

Will drove down the road, taking in the quiet town of Potstow. There were no sirens blaring in the distance or people racing past him as he drove a little over the speed limit. It was a quiet town, but that did not make him feel at ease.

Having served for his country himself, he understood and respected the service Katie provided; unfortunately, he was also aware of the risks. Most days, he worried she would be put into a situation where she would have to take a life or, worse, have hers taken from her. He could not bear that to happen to her. What he wanted her to have was a nice, peaceful desk job where he knew she was safe, but he would never ask her to do that. Will knew she loved the excitement and challenge inherent in the job, and he would never try to take that away from her.

He was aware of the possibility he was jealous, missing some of the excitement for himself.

Will pulled into T-Dawg's driveway, wondering whether his neighbor had discovered the new hole left for him in the windowpane of his door. Will realized far too late he should've left a note explaining the occurrence.

"Man," he said to himself, "I just hope he isn't a dick."

The Taking of Cannibus 516

"Behold, the modern wonder of the world, the Cannibus!" the pride-ridden bus driver announced, and the doors sliding open in front of Stan. Smoke poured like a dense fog between the gap.

The aroma landed upon Stan's nostrils, the taste tickling the back of his tongue as he filled his diaphragm with a deep breath. His face filled with elation; the wafting of countless strains danced around him. "I'm home!" hummed the intrepid investigator, crossing the Cannibus's threshold to approach the shape of a man sitting in a large chair within the dense fog Stan knew to be the driver.

"How goes the directing, Dick?" asked the driver as Stan tried standing still to allow his face to be scanned by the bus.

"Detective, Tim, I was a detective, and as I've told you before, I'm a PI now," Stan explained with his usual dismay.

"Yeah, yeah. Go direct your ass into a seat so I can get this race on the way." The driver growled with laughter as he slapped the door shut behind Stan, quickly flooring the accelerator on the Cannibus.

Stan weaved toward an empty seat in the middle of the bus. The motion of the bus, however, had different plans for him, taking away his balance during the recovery from the pothole in their path. In midflight, Stan reached out to catch a pole. His fingers stoved by their destination, bouncing Stan's face comfortably into a…

Stoved. Is that the correct term?

That looks horrible on the page. What is the correct term?

Stubbed…stubbed, really? That would not begin to describe his pain accurately.

Stoaved? No, that is too much. Stauved? Yeah, stauved. That looks a much more eloquent match for the definition.

Stan **stauved** his fingers off the pole, attempting to catch himself, bouncing his face comfortably into a rather large amount of saggy cleavage.

"Usually, I'd be upset about someone trying to motorboat first and ask questions later, but aren't you just a cutie?" A sensual voice belonging to the set of love pillows on which Stan's face currently rested whispered into his ear.

Stan jammed his fingers on the pole.

That's better.

An expression of horror stretched across his face, revealing his embarrassment in the conundrum of the current situation.

She smiled playfully, making room for him on the seat. Her hand patted next to her in a welcoming manner in response to Stan's confusion about what to say or do.

"I-I'm sorry, miss," Stan stammered, sitting toward the edge of the seat openly prepared for him.

"Aw, honey. Don't be." Her hand slid up his inner thigh, pulling him closer while the surrounding smoke clouds enveloped them. "Don't be shy. You've already gotten further than most men have in a long while." Her other hand caressed the brim on the rear of his weathered hat. After what just occurred, Stan could not complain about the lack of personal space.

Apparently, the term stoved *has a colloquial origin derived from the lever of an old-fashioned wood stove oven's flue pipe getting stuck and being unable to be moved; it is a metaphor for its likeness. What a poetic origin.*

Too bad it looks like shit on paper.

A few years older than him, she was a woman who cared deeply about her appearance. Thick with cosmetics, she wore her blush strong, and her eye shadow was a bit much for his taste. She nailed that cat's eye though; this was undisputable, further accentuating her idiosyncrasies. Stan simply thought her to be a bit older for his taste, so he resisted, at first.

"Look, baby, I'm not here for any commitments. I'm just here for the same buzz you are. Let's just have some fun, huh?" She didn't wait for his response but simply winked at him, her hand sliding higher up his thigh. "What do you say?"

Stan deliberated momentarily and decided. "Fuck it. I've got some time." He relented in making eye contact with her, turning around in his seat slightly to face the back of the bus.

"LET ME GET THAT PIPE PASSED DOWN. WHAT DO WE GOT TODAY, BOYS?" he yelled down the bus to the man bogarting the pipe. Chuckling to himself, the kid passed the bowl toward Stan with the subconscious understanding that he was, in fact, an idiot.

Dispensaries and strain owners could not "advertise" because of the similar bans on tobacco, though some "donated" select strains to the Cannibus that were to be featured on the different routes. Passengers of the 516 were pleasantly pleased with this newly proprietary strain called Monopoly Man. Its owners claimed it could make anyone feel rich after smoking it. Stan found it more mind-numbing than the rest, lacking the full-body high he desperately yearned to avoid contemplating his depressing existence.

Stan's new friend slipped her hand toward her full-intentions. A small bump of the bus resulted in a quick, jerking motion. She smiled. "You liked that, hmm?" She looked into Stan's eyes, biting her lip in a coy fashion, not entirely unattractive to Stan at this point. Reaching his right arm around her, he puffed on the communal pipe with his left hand.

"At this point, I'd say I'm comfortable." A grin formed as he accepted the situation, embraced it even.

You should get your head out of the gutter for a moment. Stan's getting the cowboy from this complete stranger. He does not get much action; let him have his moment.

Focus instead on the vehicle of Stan's pleasure.

The Cannibus was truly a marvel of society's achievements in self-sustainability, running entirely off a hemp-based biodiesel. This public transportation system creates 75 to 80 percent fewer toxic fumes than its technological predecessor. The fuel consists of mostly hemp oil, though the city has multiple suppliers of biodiesel from multiple different distributors. This transportation company, in particular, focused on the use of hemp.

Each piece of the bus was 3D-printed individually in a specialized function, woven entirely from microfibers processed from hemp. And it was not just the frame and body of the bus either; everything from the engine block to the clips and bolts were also printed from hemp by-products. The technological research of the city's university allowed multiple levels of threading within the microfibers. By using other components, they were able to create the entire frame from hemp quicker, cheaper, and more efficiently than other factories, while also producing less environmental waste. The result was a flexible, fluid machine that bent and held to suffice its changing needs.

The small bump shook the cab slightly, though barely more than an excuse for Stan's friend to work her way into third base, resulting from a pothole the size of the tire that fell into it. The rim and axle woven of microfibers allowed for bending, releasing the compression on the frame throughout the entirety of the vehicle as the frame, handling all the stress, conformed to the needs of the rest of the body.

The Cannibus was a form of public transportation providing many types of entertainment for its passengers. The purpose, of course, was to give intoxicated citizens a safe, affordable option, keeping them from getting behind the wheel of a motor vehicle. There were specific stops for the bus, with another arriving usually around fifteen to twenty minutes apart from one another, each taking you spider webbing down the roads of Potstow.

A concern for germs became apparent and held at bay through a few touches of modern technology. First, one would need a bus pass—named loosely, for there was no physical pass but rather a facial recognition software that registered you at the entrance of the bus and that also scans for bacteria related to diseases, searching for especially those that can be spread virally as well as charging your account for the ride.

Then once the bus door is sealed after passengers enter, the bus runs its own airborne detox using a combination of hemp by-products and aloe vera extract. After detecting any contaminants, the system vacuum-sealed the cab, dispersing the mixture in the air to clear out any toxins potentially present.

Every time the bus returns to the station, the pipe, known to its passengers as the communal pipe, goes into a detox machine, and a newly cleaned one replaces it. Now these precautions cannot prevent all dangers from happening; they are set mainly as deterrents. There's one major policy in place on the Cannibus that, for the most part, keeps diseases from spreading or any other bad circumstances from occurring.

"Don't be a DICK." It's pretty much the understood rule for riding the Cannibus. Do not be bringing trouble on the bus that's going to mess up the flow for everyone else. It's plastered in bold atop the short list of rules on each wall of the Cannibus, which enrages Stan every time he sees it.

Wasn't that better than reading about Stan getting an old-fashioned tug job?

"How was that, honey?" Stan's concubine questioned.

Stan pulled out his own pipe, taking a long hit. He held back a cough. "Pretty good," he replied, sporting a gigantic smile on his face.

"Hmm, well, here's my number," she replied with a wink, shoving a piece of paper into his hand as the bus came to a halt. "Call me sometime. Maybe I can show you my private eye?" She stood, scooting her cheeks, one after the other, across his face to get out of the seat.

Stan sported a look of concern on his face. He was not unhappy she said that, but he also was not exactly thrilled either. Staring at the number she hastily scratched on a ripped bit of notebook paper, he placed it in the inner pocket of his trench coat.

The 516 continued its way through the town of Potstow. Stan peered through the window to his left, cupping his hands to combat the latest puff from the passenger behind him.

He noticed the hydro lot in the distance. He had not bought a hydrogen car for a few reasons, the obvious of those being his lack of finances. But he also had yet to purchase one because he'd grown fond of the Cannibus.

He knew eventually he would need to visit that lot, or possibly the solar one across the street. The only thing that he was certain was that he wasn't going back to a gas vehicle. It just was not worth paying the extra taxes the city imposed on any of the machines using the archaic technology.

"Ready, boys and girls? Well, I don't give a shit!" With a maniacal laugh, the bus driver sent a flood of gas to the engine as quickly as before, slightly startling Stan as he swayed in his seat.

His reckless driving became mostly unnoticeable after taking off with the design of the bus, but my god, if you watched that man while he drove, you would have to be blissfully ignorant to not question how you were still alive.

One could make a joke about how you would have to be stoned to ride with the guy, but you are much too sophisticated a reader for that nonsense.

"Last stop! Western Outskirts!" The driver slammed his foot on the brakes abruptly, speaking over the intercom.

Stan exited the Cannibus with a variety of scents seemingly lifting him into the air as he fell, missing the last step of the bus. He rolled onto the ground just outside the door. Stan groaned, slowly lifting his head toward his destination before dropping it back into the muck. He noticed a semitruck used for transporting hemp blocking the entrance to Killian's Distribution.

Meanwhile, Tim merely laughed at Stan lying pitifully upon the ground. The driver slapped the door shut, squealing down the road as mercilessly as they had come, chuckling to himself. "Dumbass."

Lost Variances

The rain dropped from the sky, beading across the windshield in its usual steady hypnotic rhythm. The 415 Cannibus arrived to, and departed from, the airport in its usual, punctual frequency. The tourists would board and unboard the cabin with their luggage in tow in their usual impatient fashion.

When constants occur in the cadenced heartbeat of the universe, the strings of reality begin to resonate. This reaction creates a variable within the planar expression of the human construct known as time and space. If this variable were to establish its value, it would bring with it the baggage of understanding and harmony through its eventual simplification upon its intersecting destination. Only through frequency will the variable absolve its destiny to find its solution and resolve within the mundane day-to-day life.

The Cannibus splashed its way down the exit ramp toward the damp tarmac; as the vibrations transferred from one string to harmonize with another, a variable appears on the sidewalk of the Cannibus's destination with her umbrella in hand.

But who played the relative chord?

The variable extends her umbrella in the nick of time to block the maelstrom of puddles that accumulated along the 415's frequent and punctual path to the bus stop.

"Sorry about that, miss," The timid bus driver spoke when he opened the door, stepping off the bus, marching past her toward the luggage compartment. "Here, let me get your bags."

She retracted her umbrella. "No worries. I was ready for ya!" the variable playfully jostled.

The bus driver opened the luggage compartment and turned about-face to step back toward the variable to attend her bags.

Swatting the hands of the driver with her retracted umbrella, she laughed, resonating as nothing less than ethereal. "Don't worry about me. I can help myself." The variable gathered her own luggage briskly, lunging the suitcase and makeup bag into the compartment by herself.

The driver stood in amazement; never had he seen such a delicate flower exist in this putrid, puss-filled world being so full of such spark and vigor. He stood awestruck, mouth agape, as she ascended the stairs without looking his direction. She located a seat, directly behind his, at the front of the bus.

The driver continued with his day, assisting the awaiting passengers and retrieving the tickets from their hands. This queue of passengers followed suit, finding their own empty seats throughout the bus.

After securely fastening the luggage in his usual pattern, the bus driver returned to his seat in his usual manner but continued his trip in a somewhat unusual way.

Trying as he might to keep his eyes upon the roads, they fought his own conscious thoughts, drifting toward the mirror above his sun visor. He looked into the mirrored plane of the Cannibus to find the awe-striking variable, if only for a moment before snapping his eyes and himself back into their familiar path.

His mind, however, wandered into an adolescent fantasy. He thought about the aging of time upon them both as they intertwined themselves into each other—him silently kissing her shoulder and her reminiscing about her day, interrupted by their children running into the room and jumping onto their bed.

"Laughter would be the foundation of their family." He thought this to himself, a smile slowly creeping across his face. He wouldn't dare allow this moment to pass and his lack of action to dictate the rest of his life or their lives together. Mustering all the confidence he could, he brought the Cannibus to a quick halt, resulting in a spilled coffee on his white pants. Yet proving his own courageousness, the driver stood, coffee stains and confidence, in front of the variable.

Oh, I remember the first time I saw Patty.

Mute, he stood there until the uproar of the passengers crawled from the smoke of the bus, clamoring as to why the bus had stopped. Embarrassed at his own zeal and aphasia, the flushed driver sat down to return the 415 onto a less punctual path.

The variable sat behind him, unaware of the actions of the driver, with her legs crossed, watching apprehensively as the communal pipe made its way around the bus. Each of the tourists took their turns, laughing in the same menial manner, as if they actually had to talk themselves into taking a puff from it. When the pipe arrived to her, she waved it off politely at first.

Like the others she observed interacting with the pipe before her, she stopped the long, slender smoking apparatus before it entirely passed her by. For the sake of communion, she allowed herself take a single light hit from the sacred conduit. Then she waved it along, once more, before slowly letting the smoke escape from her orifices, watching it intertwine with the vapor from the rest of the passengers, becoming one beautiful, enigmatic mess. The variable smiled to herself, letting her mind wander to simpler times: times of lust, mystery, and questionable decisions reiterated over and over again.

The Cannibus continued along its path of slight irregularity, joining the interstate outstretching Denver to Potstow, the Sin City of the Mountains, as the variable would cleverly quip. She enjoyed traveling to the area, experiencing the scenery that only the Rocky Mountains of Colorado provided. Relaxing into her seat, she stared through the tinted window at the mountaintops and rolling plains that cascaded the interstate from the distance.

Randomly livestock would enter and leave the scene like props within a Scooby-Doo *background reel.*

Eventually, the variable would be simplified, and the interstate led the constants and the variable, newly quantified, to the fated destination. The bus driver solemnly stepped off his vehicle in the routine way, unlocking the compartment, then turning to direct the passengers behind him into a line along the sidewalk.

The driver attuned to his regular pattern of removing luggage. He reached for the alluring suitcase and makeup bag of the variable, but they were already missing. Looking up, the driver saw the variable, insoluble, had progressed to find a suitor more familiar with complex arithmetic.

He was cursed to never again be stricken with such passion, for a presence known only for a short moment, lingering for all his remaining days. This irregularity, and the peculiarity she embodied, was lost. The bus driver continued his life with this understanding but would rue the day that his eyes trifled with his heart; he wished to never know beauty…so long as he was not meant to have it.

A sad truth most would deny is that great things—beauty, love, success, and many more—are not meant for everyone. Greatness, prominence, beauty—these are all earned and rarely given.

The heavens pulled back their tears. The sun dried the mud and muck from the road. The snow began to fall. Sarahn packed her umbrella back into her elephantine handbag. The handbag resembled a satchel more closely than a poky purse.

Sarahn adjusted the makeup bag on top of her suitcase before extending the suitcase's handle. Draping the satchel over her head and across her chest, she pulled the suitcase behind her as she left the local coffee shop, A Novel and the Bean, with her favorite caramel macchiato in hand.

The faded tan of her drop-waist skirt covered little more than a light veil, complementing her olive-green sweater and matching wool church bowler; with an elegant yet simple bow crystalized in the same permanence of her eyes, she was little more than an illusion. The woman, hiding behind the color-blending hazel eyes, which personified her chameleon persona, played to each of her noticeable strengths with each step.

Sarahn did not work for a living, drudging away, making someone else money. She had no occupation. Though knowledge and skills in all things she does not lack. Some contract work through 1099 employment lead her into some financial obligations remaining unresolved for quite some time. "Freelance Contractor" appeared as her title on all the official paperwork, but eventually, she was audited for a lack of tight accounting.

The IRS agent who came to audit her now does her taxes.

If this were Dungeons and Dragons, fifth edition, she would be a level-twenty rogue half elf named Almië.

She rolled an eighteen during character creation, supplementing that with the racial bonus of plus two on the charisma stat. She was awarded the Boots of Elvenkind early in game, giving her character the distinct advantage in her trade.

In this world, however, she exists as a variable named Sarahn, after a grandmother she never knew on her mother's side. If she has a racial bonus, it would be never having to open a door in her life; her smile opened most doors that stood in her way.

She would pick the ones that did not.

The leather jacket, stopped only inches from the hem of her skirt, just above her knees, draped around the shoulders of her thin, flexible frame, keeping her warm from the chilly mountain air as she walked down E-street in Downtown Potstow.

Though words of beauty would normally be uttered to describe pale resemblance of the soul possessed by Sarahn, it was the confidence she carried perennially that gave her the carnal attraction from those who looked her way. Her face, fair-skinned and thin, was scarred from her active youth, though she rarely hid her blemished cheeks beneath makeup except when in need of disguise, as she thought it gave her character.

Yet her aura could always turn the heads of every male and some of the females along her path when she willed it, her personality as pragmatic and relatable as breath.

When she caught the eye of a random stranger, the boldest would try to approach and spark up conversation while crossing their paths. Those who met her with a "Hey, there" or a "How are you today?" received a like kindness in return, and she simply continued her way. The catcalls were met with an ignoring silence bolstered by a strict, unabated nature in her steps, disarming the callers against the drowning waves of her absent regard toward their existence. Most would just gape in awe as she walked, and to them also, she would pay no mind.

Gazing at her own reflection in the glass of the storefronts as she made her way through the streets of downtown and catching glimpses of a man in a trench coat behind her for a couple of blocks, she turned her head slightly over her shoulder quickly in his direction. When she saw the man's horrendous bowler hat, she realized that she was obviously mistaken.

She thought to herself, *"He would never be caught dead in a hat like that."*

Besides, how could he have known that she was in town today? His mind was probably callously inhibited at the moment. She resolved he had forgotten all about her by now…probably.

She, too, would have liked to have forgotten him. Every haunt of memory gone, absent respite, vaguely deleting even the smallest hint as to whether or not the pain was requited. Against her own desires and wishes, her mind meandered to her fondest memories, when times were simple. The desire between two people existing for the here and now, no thought toward what troubles the future would bring for them. Though the future did progress, with it came sulfur and hellfire.

Could a person choose a single phenomenon in a relationship between two individual human beings where the metaphorical train went off the intended rails? More than likely, it is the culmination of every moment cascading through the myriad of fractals in time that leads to the eventual train wreck.

Potstow allowed Sarahn to travel freely and uninhibited through its streets and alleyways. When she arrived at her intended destination, she received a text. She did not reply but glanced briefly at the message's contents.

She placed her phone in her back pocket with care, eyeing the building she stood before from top to bottom. Sarahn quickly counted each security camera on the outer walls, mentally noting each of their angles, formulating her plan for her eventual entry into the building. She had a specialty for after-hour visits to businesses that accepted her five-finger discount on invaluable objects.

A few blocks later, the man in the bowler hat changed his trajectory, and Sarahn adjusted hers in the opposite direction down a long alleyway that intersected Shakedown Street. She walked until the intersection of Shakedown Street and Ocean Boulevard. Perched upon the corner, she located the building with a sign labeled Draper's Properties.

The building looked unremarkable to her eyes; she counted the few stories tall it stood. "Such a small building, with such a huge heart," Sarahn remarked to herself, crossing the street with her suitcase and makeup bag.

Approaching the double doors to the building, one of them swung open as a tenant exited the building. The sight of Sarahn startled him. "Oh, excuse me," he said, holding the door open for her.

"Thank you," she replied as she passed, feeling his eyes gravitate toward her behind in the process. She crossed the atrium to the stairs located beside the registrar. "Private Eye, Room 309." She smiled to herself, glancing toward the empty desk situated across the room from her before lowering the handle of the small suitcase to carry while climbing the stairs.

She was listening to the songs and smelling the aromas of the building as she elevated through the stairs. An older lady stood on the second-floor landing, shaking a cat treat can. Sarahn passed by silently with a smile. Arriving at the third floor, she dexterously placed the suitcase upon the level floor, sighing deeply in relief as she took the final step, catching her breath a moment before making her way down the left hallway, and following the arrow beneath the sign displaying the numerals "307–312."

Silence painted the hall with bland colors; most of the apartments had full solid doors, apart from one. The sun could have glared through this door as if it were a portal to a heavenly province, etching the name of its proprietor and a large image of an eye in the reflection on the wall. However, it was a cloudy, rainy day in Potstow, with hardly any sun. The window in the door was shattered and cracked with two separate holes, both too small to reach through with her hand.

The letters of the name and title left uneven, sitting on the cracks of the web. She peered behind her, listening, watching for any movement in the halls and rooms surrounding her. Through one of the doors, she heard the muffled sounds of a conversation.

Sarahn gazed through the hole into the office. She scanned around the apartment for any immediate sight of its resident. Stealthily, she unzipped her makeup bag, retrieving a fancy embroidered cloth package from within.

Holding one end of the cloth package, she unrolled her key-etching tool set. Sarahn measured the gauge of the lock and the depth and count of the pins inside the lock mechanism. She etched her measurement on her tool, narrowing down the type of blank key she would need to use. After finding an appropriately sized key, she marked the placement of the pins with her scratch awl. Finishing the last few measurements, she heard the door behind her begin to stir. Quickly, she packed her tools back in the makeup bag.

Opening and closing the door behind her, the tenant glanced at Sarahn. Making herself appear busy, she postured as if looking in through the cracked window for its inhabitant.

"I don't think he's there. Believe me, you'd know if he was," the tenant chortled, adjusting the gun holster around her body before sliding one arm through her coat. "The whole floor reeks to high hell! At least that's what the landlord said when we moved."

"Why'd you take the apartment then?" Sarahn inquired over her shoulder toward the tenant before she could stop herself. Her eyes lingered on the detective's badge nestled upon the tenant's chest.

"It's a beautiful apartment." Her police shield-emblazoned shoulders shrugged. "The price is right, and I'll rarely be home to see him anyways." Nodding toward the door in front of Sarahn, the tenant laughed as she walked toward the stairs. She turned back, adding, "You comin'?"

"Oh, yes," Sarahn stammered. "No point waiting for him to return, I suppose." She zipped up the makeup bag and grabbed her suitcase behind her once more.

They descended the flight of stairs together. On the second floor, the officer greeted the old lady with the cat treats before returning to make awkward small talk the rest of the journey down the stairs, though Sarahn knew why the officer made the effort, having caught Sarahn looking somewhat less than inconspicuous but hardly criminal. Returning at another time seemed like the easiest solution.

The officer opened the doors to Ocean Boulevard and, with a smile, said, "Well, good luck."

"What do you mean, 'good luck'?" The condolence took Sarahn by surprise.

"With whatever you would need from that dick," she quickly added. "If half of the stories they say about him are true, I'm sure you're desperate."

A Few Good Men

Stan sprawled on the grass eroded dirt next to the bus stop in his normal pathetic fashion, as if death called him when he fell from the bus.

No one ever stopped to check on him because he had already begun to smell.

He gathered his senses. Flattening his body before collecting his limbs beneath him like a human earthworm, he began to question the life choices that brought him to this lowly state in the first place.

Stan's mark was a high-level executive of this operation. He would have to con his entrance into the Killian's Distribution to find this mark's whereabouts without alarming the staff he probably surrounds himself.

With a click of the lips, Stan mumbled, "Great." A bellowing sigh followed.

Stan brushed off his tattered jacket, only to convulse into a mix of fear and panic. The dirt rolling off his left shoulder, at a glimpse, looked as though the stash flew out of his pocket, tumbling toward a puddle beside him.

Stan acted quickly!

He shifted abruptly to catch the falling bud with his right hand, losing his foothold in the process. He then realized, as he grasped for air, that the bud had not fallen out of his front pocket. Stan thanked the gods of pot that he and his bud did not fall into the puddle next to him as he fell once more.

He returned to his prior position in dust-covered embarrassment; what happened, however, upon impact of his body to the ground once more, was that one big beautiful, unbroken bud, and two other smaller, insignificant pieces of bud, rolled just outside the pocket of his coat.

In his disorientation, Stan pinched for the fresh-unbroken bud, though it slipped through his outstretched pincer fingers, falling swiftly from his grasp into the near puddle, leaving the traces of its little crystals broken, crumbling on his fingertips.

With a deep breath, Stan spoke to himself, as if he gained some greater understanding of his own actions, "I've gotta stop putting this shit in my coat." Shaking his head, he rose from the ground once more, and opening his leather satchel with one hand, he placed the remaining stash securely within.

Stan recalled bringing with him the dossier of the man he tracked, put together by his formidable wife. He began to pull the file out of the envelope tucked disorderly inside his leather satchel. "Tall, dark, and handsome."

Without even looking at it, the memory of its succinctness emblazoned from the back of his mind. With disgust, he shoved the dossier back into its pocket within the mess of files already building. "Fft…useless." Stan grunted at the anamnesis of how useless this information was.

Yet little did he know how perfectly it summarized the boring man he followed.

Stan scanned the sights the outskirts of Potstow had to offer, walking slowly from the bus stop toward his destination. He noted many construction sites in the distance pursuing some new project. The outskirts were just that—a project with untapped potential, *at least that was how the entrepreneurs saw it.* Metal beams sat stacked around construction equipment, and vehicles scattered about the place.

One was the site for the new Maglev Bullet Train under construction. Its route and purpose were generally unknown to the public, but the speed of transportation was something Western culture had never seen with the use of some propulsion tech that Stan did not really understand, nor did he care. Its speed as a train was still unbelievable, even for his years.

Trucks lined the Industrial Park Road in daylight, remaining to block off certain passages through the night. Currently, there was a truck preventing Stan from entering Killian's Distribution, the locale he needed to seek out his mark.

"Come on! I'm running late as it is! Just get the fuck out of the way!" the driver of a Killian's Distribution truck pleaded.

The guard manning the gate seemed a little slow, or frightened, and was taking longer than usual to open the gate for the driver, a punishment for the driver leaving late for his job. The driver pulled through the gate, becoming detained quickly by the aforementioned hemp distribution truck still sitting in the entrance, impeding his path.

"Come on! Can't I get a break!"

Stan used this moment to slip by the open gate. The guard did not seem to care.

The investigator prepped as he walked up to the front door of the three-story office building. Stan knew he would not be able to get into his mark's office, but he would, hopefully, give himself a chance to talk to his secretary or, possibly, get a look at his schedule without seeming too suspicious.

Stan played out the scenario in his head: *"Hello, miss, my name is Stan, and I need to follow your boss and try to take incriminating pictures of him and possibly make him, and you, lose your jobs."* Stan debated internally for a few moments in a contentious argument with his ego.

Nevertheless, Stan marched up to the door, placing his thumb upon the buzzer.

Brzzzzzpt. "What do you want?" the intercom greeted Stan suddenly. The voice belonged to a woman with the feminine "do not waste my time, and I do not want to put up with your deal" type of tone.

"Uhm, yeah, I'm here to speak with Jacob McKinney." He hoped Jacob was not in the office today.

"You must've just missed him," the intercom interrupted his concerns. "He's on his way to lunch with the craft beer guys."

"Is there any way you could tell me where"—he gulped, the pressure mounting—"they went? It's really important I meet with him." Stan tried very hard to use what he thought would be a good flirting voice.

His mother told him some cockamamie story about his father and the Greene men's charm when he was little, and he still thought it was a relevant factor.

Awkward and forced, the woman on the other end of the intercom took it as nonthreatening, but she didn't answer immediately, which unnerved Stan that his pain and strife was all for naught.

Brzzzzzpt. "Uh, I think his calendar says *The Sativa*, isn't that the new gourmet place downtown?"

Stan heard a voice in the background reply, "No, that's *Indicance. Sativa* is the bakery on Fourth."

"Bakery on Fourth Street? Oh, shit!" A third voice chimed in the background, "You told me it was *Sativa*! He's going to be so pissed."

"Need anything else?" the familiar curt voice of the original greeter questioned Stan. He could hear the third voice talking on a phone in the background, apologizing and redirecting her bosses' anger while restraining her own.

Stan's fear was unjustified and laughable at best. Up till this moment, his mark's staff had no reason for secrecy.

"No, that helps out a lot, actually." Stan wanted to be unmemorable; not even entering the building helped keep that anonymity. "Thanks." He hastily left the foundry the way he came.

One thing Stan enjoyed about Potstow, apart from the Cannibus, the cannabis, and the women, was the creativity of its industries and their horrible puns. One of the most useful to Stan was HyRides.

Both carpool and taxi service, offered at the hydro-car dealership for a nifty tax write-off from the city, was an app anyone could download on their phone for free. If you were in the area of a driver or going the same way as somebody's routes, you would appear on each other's phone and have a chance to look over the person's profile.

Drivers could see comments and reviews from other drivers about the people looking for the rides and vice versa. Stan's driver reviews were a mix of good and bad.

Someone said he tipped well if you counted the weed and change he left behind in the seat.

Stan retrieved his cell phone from his pocket, initiating the app with his index finger. Since Stan always enabled his location sensor on his phone, it immediately connected him to a driver that was close.

They were to rendezvous together at the bus stop he arrived. It seemed simple enough; even Stan understood the system well enough to operate it. Hurrying to the end of Industrial Park Road, he passed a familiar Killian's truck stuck in the traffic jam building up during his absence. Its driver's face was placed on the steering wheel in defeat.

Stan arrived at the end of the road where his HyRides driver already waited.

"You the guy?" the driver asked as he approached.

"Possibly…" Stan paused, eyeing him cautiously. He did not know why, but he immediately disliked him. "What's my phrase?"

"Dude, you're really going to make me say that? That's the safe-guard for women and children."

"How do I know you're not here to kidnap and do hurtful things to me?"

The driver sighed, pulling out his phone. He slowly logged into the driver access system, never removing his gaze from Stan's smug smirk. Clicking on the profile, he read aloud in disgust, "Stan Greene is the best investigator in Potstow."

"Really, dude?" the driver commented in disgust, looking at the mud set like concrete in Stan's hair. "Get in the car. Try not to get your muck everywhere."

"Don't you forget it." Stan enjoyed the little things in life. Thinking a little more highly of himself being glorified by someone else's lips, he sloppily entered the vehicle.

The driver looked at Stan with annoyance. "Right." He was glaring at the trail of mud Stan's shoes brought with him. "Well, thanks for listening." The sarcasm was prevalent in every syllable. "Where to?"

"Indicance, that new gourmet place downtown."

"Could you be vaguer?" The frustrated driver searched the address, beginning the voyage after merging with traffic.

It was a cold, quiet ride. Stan already began to write a scathing review before the driver scolded him for smoking in the car.

"But it's called HyRides."

"Yeah, Hy, as in HY-DRO-GEN." The driver added, muttering, "Fucking dick."

"How did you know I used to be a detective?" Stan looked at him sternly. "That certainly wasn't in my profile." The review only went downhill from there.

"I live in the building over there," the driver innocently spoke, ignoring Stan and pointing to the apartment building on the corner.

After the scathing review and the merciful two stars, Stan readied himself to dismount the HyRides service for fear of being mocked by another driver, twice in the same day. Stan prayed he would arrive at Indicance prior to his target, and to his luck, he did.

Indicance was, like most in Potstow, rife with organics. In this town, it was harder to find a greasy, saturated burger than it was to find something healthy for you. This gourmet restaurant seasoned their pans to perfection with hempseed oil instead of butter. It offered the food a very mature and earthy taste, but it was also rich in heart-healthy, nutritious omega-3s. It was a fantastic place to show someone a great time while in town but a horrid place to take your debit card.

The job paid well, and Stan felt the pressure mount like a weather balloon about to pop. This had been going for two weeks, and he was growing tired of ignoring incessant phone calls on the matter. Stan knew that the pictures he needed would have to be clear and unpixellated. He began to scope out the place as the couple ahead of him was being seated. They were quite busy, as to be expected for the lunch hours, leaving only a few sections available for seating.

"Welcome to Indicance. How can I help ya?" The wholesome voice adorned in black-dress clothes surprised Stan as he readied the camera that would capture his paycheck. "My name's Josh. How many?" he said with a genuine smile.

"Uh, just the one," Stan answered, glancing around to see if anyone looked like they could hear him while he walked closer to the host. "But I do have a special request," he said in a quieter, quite conspicuous tone.

"Well, buddy." He cleared his throat to answer Stan. "Seems you ought to buy someone a meal before you start making 'special requests,' but that's just my opinion." Josh leaned in closer toward Stan so as to make him feel uneasy.

"I, uh," Stan stuttered. "Shit. Sorry, here." He abruptly pulled the picture of the man he was tailing from his pocket with a twenty-dollar bill perched on top of it. "Could you just make sure this guy is seated near me?" Stan's voice shook in embarrassment.

Josh laughed, taking the bill from the picture. "Chill, dude, I still expect to be gettin' a better tip on your way out." He winked. "Take him to table thirteen," Josh said, handing a menu to one of the waitresses.

"What can I get you to drink?" the waitress asked enthusiastically as she directed Stan to his table.

"A Coke is just fine. I'm guessing you can't smoke in here?" Stan inquired, pulling out his pipe.

"Would you care for a THP?" she rebutted, giving him a disapproving glance.

Stan settled for just the Coke. He wasn't a fan of the patches, though he did find the small pun in the name humorous.

Launching the camera app on his worn iPhone, an early model, he tried to line up the shot for a picture of the table across from him, hoping that was where Josh would seat the guy and his friends. As he was aligning his attempt, Josh walked over to him, laughing. "You gonna have enough storage on that thing for a pic, man?"

Stan looked at Josh with a smile; he felt more comfortable this time around. "It's not about the size of your camera. It's how you use it," Stan jokingly replied.

Josh laughed. "Well, your guy and his friends are being seated here next to you. They're waiting for a couple of people in their party to arrive. Don't forget my tip, eh." He chuckled as he walked away from Stan.

The waitress came around with McKinney and his gaggle of sausages. *"Fuck!"* Stan thought. *"I can't ever catch this jackass with a woman."* He began to convulse with his tiny iPhone in hand.

"That's when I said, you know why women like flowers and men? Because they like to watch things die!" The gaggle cackled, and the sight was a monstrous thing. McKinney won his group over with his joke, and even Stan grinned, but their behavior toward the waitress immediately after resulted in instantaneous malcontent from him.

Lunch came and went, with nothing of suspicion for Stan to report. "Just a jackass with his dumbass friends." Stan groaned to himself. He captured a few useless photographs, which was why he started to delete them, among other things, as he got the "Storage is almost full" message from Apple.

They asked for the check; one of McKinney's friends stood up from the table. "Jake! Man, you gotta come out with us tonight. STRIPPERS…music. Some smoke?" he bargained.

His voice already had Stan's attention, but McKinney replied, "No, unfortunately, tonight I have to take this lady out for Tom—"

"MAD DAWG!" The frat-boy hipster in the group laughed and jeered.

"Uh, so yeah, gotta work tonight." McKinney, clearly uncomfortable about the jibe, excused himself from the table.

Waiting for the remaining group to file out, Stan followed suit. He paid his tab and tipped his waitress, catching Josh on his way out the front door. "So how was it?" he inquired with a glib grin.

"The food was great. My work, not so much," Stan said gloomily.

"Well, hey, I'm 'bouta go on break. Wanna burn one?"

"Eh, I've got time." Stan shrugged, following his new friend through the kitchen and out the back door.

As they smoked, Josh questioned Stan about what it was he was doing. Stan pulled a withered business card from his coat, handing it to the inquisitive host.

"A private investigator, huh?" Josh seemed kind of impressed. *He obviously doesn't know just how glamorous the life was not.*

"I wish the dude said more about where he was going tonight," lamented Stan, taking a puff on Josh's joint. "I need that card back. It's my last one."

"What do you mean?" Josh replied, accepting the joint and passing the card back to Stan.

"Ah, this broad wants me to follow that guy in the picture and get him in a compromising position with another broad so she can file for divorce and beat her prenup," Stan explained to his current compatriot. "I've been following him around for a couple of weeks now, and it's just been sausage party after sausage party." Stan shook his head in resentment. Passing the roach, he exhaled a magnificent cloud. "But tonight, he's finally going to be somewhere with a woman."

"You're kidding me." Josh puffed. "Just follow him."

"I don't have a car," Stan replied. "I have no idea where to begin."

"Is it work or pleasure?" Josh and Stan pressed their fingers together to pass.

"Hopefully pleasure, but I've been too lucky today for it not to be work." Stan inhaled.

"Where's he work?"

"Ki-Ki—" Stan coughed. His eyes started to water. "Killian's Distribution."

"All right, check it." Josh pulled out his phone as he accepted back the joint. He searched for Killian's Distribution's phone number in his browser. He dialed; it rang. "Yes, hi. My client is supposed to be going out to dinner with your mister, McKinney, but I forgot to write down where she needed to meet him?" He paused for a moment, and Stan sat in wonder watching through his watery eyes. "Awesome, thanks, sweetheart." Josh placed his thumb on the red circle. "He'll be at the Fourth Floor."

Stan, awestruck, stood in bewilderment. "You're wasted as a host," he blurted out.

Josh grimaced. "Yeah, I've got someone at home saying the same thing. Keeps telling me there is something better out there for me."

"She sounds like a keeper. What's her name?" he asked.

Josh made a habit of laughing at Stan at this point. "Terry." He chuckled once more.

"Maybe I'll meet her one day." Handing back the roach, he gave a small grin.

"Yea, maybe you will," Josh answered with a smile even the Joker would envy.

Dio's "Holy Diver"

The sun had not risen over the horizon on the small snow-covered ranch settled outside of Potstow. In the silent moments before the alarm sounded, a deafening silence struck deeply into the morning as the waning moon sunk into the darkness, ebbed by the pale, sanguine sky. The roosters still slept in their coops, waiting to welcome the sun painting a canvas of abstraction when the radio alarm clock struck 5:00 a.m.

"This is radio Potstow, U94.1, the Stoner. It's the five o'clock hour, and you're having it with me." The young but experienced radio announcer spoke of himself with enthusiasm for the job not found anywhere else at 5:00 a.m. "Jack Nightly in the morning, and now it's time for your wake and bake."

The song started to play with an airy atmosphere. "I would tell you the band and title, but you already know what it is." The instant his voice trailed, the crash of cymbals set the driving bass and guitar line kicked into the medium of the early morning sky. The early motive established itself using the intervals of the root, second, third and seventh in the Aeolian mode of C.

Thomas threw his feet over the bed, stepping into his soft but deteriorating slipper. He stretched his hands over his head and gave a mighty yawn as Dio's voice began the first verse.

Thomas gathered himself to his feet. Continuing his wild stretch and forcing a mighty realignment to his bones; each vertebra popping in succession of the other, before walking into the master bathroom located off "his" side of the bed. Leaving his loving wife, Gracie, holding on to her sleep in the bed behind him for as long as she could, he turned to gaze at his purpose. That was what she represented to him: meaning, direction, and purpose.

Ronnie James Dio's voice entranced the small ranch, letting the music breathe before beginning the second phrase.

The radio proclaimed the resonance of the gods to follow each of Thomas's groggy footsteps, reverberating upon the ceramic tiles of the bathroom. Without turning on the lights, he quickly rotated the knob on the hot water to the tub, which once belonged to his grandfather. It passed down with the house to his father and was now Thomas's daily conundrum to warm the stream of water before he climbed into the shower.

Thomas squeezed toothpaste onto his toothbrush, unconsciously brushing to the driving hypnotic rhythm of the bass and drums.

The toothpaste set his senses ablaze, his thoughts treading toward his upcoming day. He had waited for this particular day with a great deal of anticipation. His plans and schemes were starting to come to fruition.

"It is only time that stands in my way, now," Thomas thought to himself. Dio's voice resurfaced in his awareness atop the forceful motive accompanying the entry of the second verse.

Plots and schemes are always justified in the means. Thomas became begrudgingly aware that his actions, while not despicable, were also less than caring. It was all part of a Thomas that he didn't want to be or become. The steaming water crashed upon his skin, breaking apart millions of reflections; both a sight he grew tired and lamented toward. At the end, he would be the man who would stand where others fell. He would protect the people of Potstow, making the decisions that others could not or were too fearful to do. He would watch his staff live lavishly and enjoy the company of their loved ones. He would see Gracie nestled in nothing less than an unattainable cloud, above all things and everyone else; Gracie would sit happy and as a queen.

Thomas spit his toothpaste into the sink, grabbing a disposable cup placed with care into its dispenser to fill it with water. Turning on the shower, the steam rose from the tub, and like clockwork, he used his cup to begin cleaning the residue left in the sink.

The blessed words of Dio accompanied the kind gesture toward Mrs. Killian.

Thomas had climbed into the tub. He eagerly anticipated the results of McKinney's meeting of the night prior. If his resources were correct, there would be no one else capable of doing the job.

Turning to face the showerhead, he let the water flush from his forehead down to his feet, dulling his attention. After a few intense moments, he spun his back to the shower. The alarm clock continued to ring into the bathroom.

Thomas grabbed his three-in-one—shampoo, bodywash, conditioner—to wash himself, the water rinsing him off as the remnants of Ronnie echoed a hard truth into the ether.

Mr. Killian wiped the soap from his eyes, letting the water drip down his naked body. The darkness of the bathroom draped around him; he left his eyes closed, breathing deep of the rising steam through his nostrils.

By the third verse, Thomas had his fill and shut off the water to the shower. He allowed himself to drip dry only for a moment before stepping onto the ultra-absorbent mat placed outside of the shower to dry himself off with a towel hung, as a kind and loving gesture, for him.

The alarm clock continued to serenade the ranch with the blessed voice of a man taken too early in his life as Mr. Killian made his way to the wardrobe and opened his dresser drawers. From within, he gathered his socks and underwear. Thomas sat on the edge of the bed, pulling on his socks one foot at a time.

The guitar solo barely sang two notes before being rudely interrupted by one Mrs. Killian.

"Bleh," she grumbled, "I hate that song!"

Thomas knew Gracie was not what some people would call an early bird.

"Dio is the devil." Gracie groaned, gathering her blankets.

"Honey, please," Thomas croaked, sliding his foot into one of his socks, "do you really think that Ronnie James Dio believed in the devil?" Mr. Killian responded sweetly as he opened his closet to prepare his suit. "I think he knew better."

Mr. Killian stood peering out the window onto the moon-lit-draped ranch as he reproached his dresser to retrieve his pants. The old barn, once serving as his father's clandestine distillery, sat empty and abandoned. A fence contoured the edges of the property lines of the old ranch as far as his eyes could see in the early morning fog.

He walked over to his closet to retrieve the rest of his ensemble.

"Wear your green one," Mrs. Killian suggested from their bed. "It really brings out your eyes." Her sweet voice caressed his ears from behind. "I think your bowler hat goes well with it." Between a long drawn-out yawn, she insisted, "Black tie." Her command sounded sweet through her yawn as she curled herself beneath the covers once more.

Thomas did as he was told, retrieving the green jacket from its hanger, with a white dress shirt to complement. After adorning himself with the shirt and jacket, Thomas crossed the room once more to the bathroom to fasten his tie in the mirror.

This proved to be a useless act, however.

Thomas flipped the light switch to look at himself in the mirror. The steam still clung to the mirror, clouding his appearance in response. It was as if the universe itself tried its best not to give the most blatant clue to Thomas on the punch line of the joke that was most consistent in his life, while he mindlessly adjusted his black tie using the muscle memory imbued over years of blurred reflected sight.

Thomas had another name, an alias of sorts, one rarely spoken in his immediate presence but often whispered half-heartedly behind his back.

Although in ways he never completely comprehended, the Colorado mountains would combine with the steam from his ritual shower, blurring the image within his mirror. Had it not, he would fully see the long jowls that stress and long nights combined with early mornings bring to a man. This, complemented with the snub-ness of his nose, gave Thomas the unfortunate look of a bulldog.

In his anger, as Thomas was prone to let loose of his self-restraint, his face scrunches, accentuating the imagery.

Alas, Thomas never truly sees himself and completely misses the joke when they call him Mad Dog.

A Duel of Fates

Stan left the restaurant in an elevated mood. His gait was filled with profound purpose and achievement while the drizzled rain led him to take a few questionable alleyways spanning the few blocks between the restaurant and the hemp-brick building denoting Draper's Properties on the front and side.

From the middle of the sidewalk, he looked both ways. Shielding his hat from the wind with his left hand, he jaywalked across the mostly empty street to the sidewalk outside Draper Properties. Stan watched a female in her police officer uniform exit the double doors that served as an entrance of the building.

He ogled and drooled, as one would expect from a starving dog to a steak, trying to wet the only part of him that was dry—his mouth—ready to deliver his best one-liner.

"You're the best-looking dick I've ever seen," he said with an incredulous smile.

"Do you live here, sir?" the officer asked, a contentious look on her face indicating she clearly wanted him to say no.

"Sure do, ma'am." He tipped his worn trilby hat, the water accumulated from the rain dripping around the brim. "Stan Greene, at your service." He twirled his rain-soaked hat in his hand as he bowed in a clear show of comedy, *or an attempt at comedy*, revealing the once hidden muddy hair.

She stopped in her steps in awe of the mess of a man bowing before her. She looked him over, from the frayed and tattered seams of his coat, across the missing buttons of the dust-covered shirt shadowed beneath, all the way to the mud covering the ever-growing bald spot upon his head.

"Well," she said with a sigh, "my Navy SEAL fiancé," accentuating both SEAL and fiancé to hopefully dissuade any interest Stan developed in the six seconds of their meeting. "And I just moved into the third floor of this building and—"

"Third floor, you say?" Stan interrupted. "Why, I believe that makes us neighbors!"

Imagine the most excited face one could muster upon hearing such news; this officer of the law sported its opposite. "Of course, now I realize how I know that name." A smirk appeared in the corner of her mouth. "I think there's a hole in your window." She laughed half-heartedly as she walked away, as though she just won the exchange.

Of course, she had.

Stan climbed the stairs to his office, taking two steps each stride in the last flight with haste, hearing Ms. Edna's door begin to open. The investigator almost arrived at his office door when he heard a voice resonating in the apartment on the opposite side of his third-floor hallway.

"GOD FUCKING DAMMIT!" shouted the voice within the apartment. "WHOSE BRIGHT IDEA WAS IT TO PUT SHOTGUNS IN THIS MOTHERFUCKER?"

Stan could not help but let slip a slight chuckle prior to seeing the horrid state of his office door.

"God fucking dammit!" Stan echoed upon sight of his windowpane with a small new hole accompanying the old.

Stan's voice reverberated the walls within the apartment, startling the owner of the voice within the apartment opposite his office.

Removing his headset from his ears with uneasy anticipation, Will waited for another impending sound. Katie had left the apartment; he wasn't expecting anyone anytime soon. Running toward the living room door, he threw the headset from its position.

Placing his eye to the door, Will took a quick glance through the peephole. He didn't see anyone immediately outside. Will opened the door, finding the wet, muddy-haired man before him in his tattered coat. He thought to himself, *"Yup, this is definitely the guy."*

Standing six foot three inches tall, Will pronounced his stocky build and magnificent mane, looking down at his stumpy counterpart across the hall.

What he saw was a man in need of something, or someone, in its life.

"Oh, hey…" Will greeted his new neighbor shyly, afraid of the reaction he was going to have with the news of his shattered window, even if it was already broken. "You the guy that lives there?"

"I'm standing here, keys in hand," Stan said, brandishing his keys toward Will. "By the looks of it, I'd say I might be." He turned his head from his door for a moment, trying to change the subject from him cursing to himself like a madman. "Sounded like you might be having a difficult time in there, thin walls and all."

"Yeah, I was just playing my game." Will glanced over toward Stan's door. "So, uh, yeah," he stammered. "Sorry about the window to your apartment." Will imagined the etched glass whole rather than the sour sight existing now, heavily spiderwebbed from top to bottom.

Caught off guard by the quick apology, Stan stuttered to reply, "Well, I-uh-it's my office. As you can see, my name is Stan." He pointed at the spot that should have said "Stan"; however, only the "ST" and "N" remained.

Stan stepped out of the way, allowing Will to admire the full glory of the door behind him; he stepped back abruptly when he remembered it was in shambles.

"Sometimes, I may fall asleep there if I'm working late, but I wouldn't call it my apartment." He thought for a moment before continuing, "What happened?"

"Uhm," Will stammered, "I was trying to throw a ball at Katie because she had called me childish." Will stepped out of his apartment to look at the broken glass pane beside Stan. "I'm Will."

Neither person outstretched a hand in acknowledgment. Rather, they stood side by side staring into the cracks each hole delved into the glass pane, as if they were at a museum staring into some profound new canvas of art.

"Katie?" Stan asked. "She wouldn't, by chance, be a cop?" Stan broke the silence, adding a mystical atmosphere, seemingly omnipotent. "Would she?"

"Yeah, she is! How did you know?" Will said in a naive bewilderment, unable to connect the dots of her departure just before Stan's arrival. Then he added, "Did you meet already?"

Stan pondered whether to explain the way he'd embarrassed himself. "For a short moment, we did. She seems nice enough." He tried to divert the conversation away from himself. "But it seems to me, responding to someone calling you 'childish' by throwing a toy at them might just solidify their point, don't ya think?"

"Look, I really wanted the big TV in the bedroom. She said no," answered Will with an inherent droopiness, still standing parallel his first avant-garde masterpiece. "I may have looked a little pouty."

The childish man continued justifying himself. "But to be fair, I had been thinking about it all day. When she saw the look on my face, she just coldly said, 'Don't be childish.'" The voice Will used to mock the love of his life made Stan smile. His tale proceeded. "So I threw the ball that I found in the box I was carrying at her, missed, and now there's a hole in your pane. I'll pay for it, though." Will regretted adding since it already had another hole in it before Will threw the ball.

"Well," Stan leaned against the wall behind him, "I'm sure you noticed it wasn't in the most pristine condition before you came along." He was trying to soften the blow; there was something unconventional about Will that Stan immediately liked. "But that's awfully kind of you."

"Angry clients?" Will questioned, knowing very well it was clients; he didn't see any dames trying to break down his new acquaintance's door.

"Sometimes." Stan stared at the door, letting time space in his mind. "Honestly, every time I fix it, something comes along to break it again." Pulling his pipe from his jacket, Stan asked, "You smoke?" the pipe hanging from his lips, a lighter cupped in his hand.

"Does the pope shit in the woods?" Will replied quickly. "Come on over, my man." He directed Stan with his hands. "It's the least I can do till I get your window fixed."

Will accepted he had probably died in Carbon Copy. He was playing Solo Que and left no one waiting in the lobby for him. The host pulled the door to his apartment shut with a "Fuck it" as Stan entered his suite.

"Your wife said you were a Marine?"

"Uh, fiancé, actually. Though hardly a distinction worth making at this point," Will spoke. "But, uh, yeah. Navy SEAL. They say I served my country, I suppose."

Stan deduced his new acquaintance was probably holding back on the gruesome details.

A high shrill to a low-pitch whistle emanated from Stan, standing stark, immediately noticing the luxury of this apartment in comparison to his own.

"Damn, Dom took damn good care of you. This is much nicer than my place." His eyes landed on the staircase leading to a second floor, his head shaking with bitter annoyance.

"It's a decent place." Will shrugged. "It's got enough space." Will showed Stan to a seat on his couch, retrieving his stash from his bedroom upstairs.

Stan did not sit, however; his inquisitive nature compelled him, roaming like a tomcat drunk and in heat. He was wandering around, glancing at the few pictures and decorating accessories the new couple managed to unpack during their short time in the apartment.

Boxes spread out along the studio floor. Couches sat in the makeshift living room, sitting in the middle of the open floor also containing the kitchen. Their bedroom and other creature comforts made up the attic space of the entire building, Stan assumed.

"It's a rough thing." Stan attempted small talk as he wandered the floor. "Serving your country, being on the front lines like that." He adjusted, allowing the echo to travel up the staircase. "What made you want to serve?"

No reply came until Will arrived at the bottom of the staircase in front of Stan. "Yeah, the military was always busy. Excuse me."

Will pardoned his way past Stan into the space of the living room. "My dad died when I was young, about seven or eight." Will began breaking up his little stash to roll a piece of blunt with his new neighbor. "His brother, my Uncle Jeff…"

Stan sat listening intently, which, he noted, was duly out of character for himself.

"…Used to take me hunting for whitetail down in the North Central West Virginia area." Will opened the blunt wrapper before continuing. "I got this beautiful, clean shot on this twelve-point. When we took it to the local station to get it tagged, turns out, the guy doing it was the coach for the WVU rifle team." He sprinkled the bud into the wrap.

"So the dude keeps in touch, helps gets me a full-ride when I graduate high school. I go to a couple of Olympics. I don't place in anything, but I almost redeemed myself with amazing marks on my sharpshooting." He was rolling the bud slowly to pack it firmly into place.

"After that, military starts coming out of the woodworks: Marines, Army, and so forth." He licks the wrap to hold it securely in place, drying it with his lighter. "They start offering me loads of money, a few promotions. Dude basically signs me up on the spot when he told me they were interested in me for the SEALs."

Lighting his blunt, Will rotated it in his hands horizontally before placing it to his lips. He took a long, deep hit, applying the flame to its end. Holding his breath for a time, Will released slowly, savoring every little moment of it. Will stared at the cherry as it burned, silently for a moment, spinning it vertically in his fingertips.

Stan could tell it had been a while for him; he let him enjoy it.

A full minute of silence spanned before Will continued the conversation without flinching, a smile on his face.

"So," he snapped back into reality and continued, "to answer your question, the action." He took another puff. "I was a big gamer growing up, and I just always wanted that adrenaline rush." He finally passed the blunt to Stan. "The heart pumping, that intensity. I wanted it all."

"Did you see any action?" Stan asked to keep this intriguing conversation going. He puffed, and he puffed, and he passed the blunt to Will.

Will drew through the blunt, contemplating for a moment. *What should he tell Stan?*

There were quite a few missions with covert action, but most of those were still under Top Secret Clearance, and Will seriously doubted Stan had the clearance. "So one of my very first missions…" He paused for a moment, looking over at Stan, unaccustomed to someone older than himself. "Do you remember that Iraqi leader, Hussein?"

"Yeah," Stan answered, receiving the blunt from Will.

"During the scruff when we overthrew his rule, I was in the regiment that took his main mansion." Will puffed once more before passing the blunt, continuing his tale, "We thought for sure his mangy ass was going to be there."

Stan puffed as he listened.

"We go room to room, just 'Clear!' here, 'Clear!' there, a couple of shots in the distance, and, boom, throne room."

Stan took another deep hit, passing it back.

Will received it from him, saying, "My squad got the all clear from HQ, and I'm pissed. I was so ramped up to shoot the fucker, and he wasn't even home. He didn't even think about setting dinner for me and my friends."

"The bastard," Stan replied, holding on to Will's every word.

"Yeah, he was out hiding in some hole in the ground, but at the time, I was there in his throne room, just fuming. Bro"—he took another hit—"I shit on Hussein's throne." He busted a gut laughing, smoke relieving itself through every facial orifice.

"What?" Stan exclaimed, releasing his cloud of smoke.

"You heard me, motherfucker." He laughed again. "I shit on that piece of shit's throne."

For obvious reasons, Stan joined in laughing at this point, unsure if he was just joking or because he was high.

"Wanna see?" Will pridefully offered.

Stan sat there, debating whether he wanted to see any form of representation of another man taking a shit on a tyrant's throne. He came to the most definitive decision of his entire life. "More than anything, Will."

Jumping with glee, like a child getting ready to show his father a report card with straight A's, Will tore through the boxes around the couch. "Where'd she put it? I know she doesn't like it, but there's no way she'd throw it out."

Stan sat smoking on the roach while Will happily unpacked a few boxes, looking for something obviously dear to his heart. He finally found it, approaching Stan with a tumultuous look in his eyes.

He gazed at a picture frame, holding it in both hands securely with the deep pride one has in showing off their child's picture while comparing with other parents. He thrust the green frame beneath Stan's nose, and there it was, a single, small turd sitting on a complementary crème background that Stan recognized from all the pictures in the 1990s as Saddam Hussein's throne.

Will went to hang the picture on the wall behind him. "Yeah, you won't stay here long," Will said, addressing the picture. "Got any plans tonight?" He felt like he dominated the conversation, which, Will noted, was strangely out of character.

Stan checked his watch. "Dammit, yeah." Sighing heavily, Stan remembered the Fourth Floor. "I gotta get dressed and run out to the bar—"

"The bar? Count me in."

Superstition

Sarahn sighed as she lay prone to the roof between the two balusters of the railing. She sat preying, hidden among the shadows a balcony created. In the shade, a clear line of sight at the building sitting parallel across the street appeared. Her eyes wandered toward the analog face of her watch. Intertwined around her wrist, it was an intimate gift that carried heavy weight, both emotional and physical, distributed by the modified band, made of a small leather strip for comfort and lined with reinforced materials, allowing for an almost metaphysical durability.

"Dammit..." she whispers to herself. Returning her eyes to the sights of her crossbow, the conspiring larcenist continued to track the final occupant. A custodian, they clean each of the rooms, one by one, every night. "Hurry up already. I've got shit to do tonight," Sarahn demurred.

Finishing the entire floor, the cleaning lady walked down the long hall to the elevator. Sarahn moved her sights to the roof to prepare her shot. Loaded in the crossbow in her hand was a bolt attached to a fiber woven filament made of compressed hemp. The fine, lightweight strands were deceivingly durable, having a test of 350 pounds.

With the crossbow sights, Sarahn scoped along the streets and the aligning buildings for surveillance cameras, confirming the blind spot she spotted a few days prior. Easing her finger onto the trigger, she took the shot at the wall parallel to herself. It pierced the bricks lightly near the metal door of the roof across the street. The wind rushing between the buildings of downtown Potstow took the bolt slightly off course from her target. However, it landed close enough to serve its intended purpose.

Fastening the filament to the top of the baluster securely, she watched the slack of the line wobble. Sarahn began breaking down her crossbow, carefully placing it back into the opened, molded suitcase behind her. Removing the carabiners from one of the pockets within the case to attach her harness to the track pulley that she mounted on the line, the audacious daredevil stepped her legs over the balusters, holding onto the rail behind her.

Sarahn remained unsure of the zip line's stability; her eyes frustratingly looked to her watch again. The impatient thief sighed once more, taking the leap of faith, streaming across the gap of the building, hoping she remained unseen by both man and machine.

As her feet crossed the precipice of the intended roof, the bolt pulled from the brick wall. She flattened herself, taking a quick deep breath as her forward momentum carried her body to the terrace slab, knocking the breath out of her.

Regaining control of her breath, she lifted herself from the ground and made her way to the bolt, laying a foot away from her. Sarahn grasped the bolt in her hand, triggering a mechanism sending the bolt cascading across the gap once more.

From her belt, she retrieved a one-eighth-inch socket screwdriver and began removing the bolts from the exhaust vent of the heating to the building.

A new technology emerged in the HVAC industry around the time Potstow was built. It created a new efficiency for heating and cooling buildings using ceramics and thermodynamic technology. Unfortunately, in order to control the heating of the building more effectively, they had to use large return and exhaust vents to create within it a low enough pressure to draw the high pressure of the building within. This created a natural flow and helped control temperatures within the building to a more comfortable setting.

Sarahn laughed with glee; the technology created an easy entrance to most of the buildings in Potstow, as well as other eco-friendly places, without detection.

Inside the duct was extremely hot, making it difficult to breathe. Designed to pull areas concentrated in carbon dioxide from the rooms of the building, this would frequently affect Sarahn. Yet she attributed the feeling to the high she received from doing her job.

An accomplished burglar living along the perverse side of the law, for years, Sarahn acquired the items on jobs that most cautious thieves would be smart enough to avoid entirely. This created for her a great reputation but placed her in the sights of many treacherous and vengeful people along the way. Still, Sarahn always accomplished the job, no matter the difficulty.

In fact, the more difficult the job, the more she would be attracted to it.

Sarahn took a deep breath, climbing into the exhaust duct after removing the vent. She searched for the closest vent she could find. Kicking the armored crevasse with all her might, she snapped one of the screws on the vent, opening a small gap into the room.

The heat grew unbearable inside of the large tubular vent. In her chest, she could feel her heart beating faster and faster, the blood rushing through her veins felt like it was bridging across her chest, skipping her head, causing the adrenaline junkie to become increasingly light-headed every passing moment. With her leg, Sarahn made another mighty thrust, prying the cavity for her to crawl into the room. Breathing deeply, she lay on the floor, trying to slow her pulse. When it calmed to a steady pace, she went right to work.

The thief pulled a small mirror from her backpack, extending the rod before she slid the mirror beneath the crack of the door. Searching the ceilings for more security cameras and the hall for any other straggling employees she may have missed, Sarahn glared in darkness with practice to the art.

Confirming to herself that the coast was clear, she slipped silently through the hall. Sarahn approached the door of the mayoral office, her objective just behind this door. With silent haste, she placed her hand upon the door handle, beginning to turn the knob. She was slowly pulling the door open when she heard a funky clavichord playing the aberrant hypnotic rhythm belonging to Stevie

Wonder's "Superstition" emanating from the speakers of a cell phone in the office she prepared to breach.

"Hey!" An unfamiliar voice echoed from behind the door. Sarahn stepped beside the door hinges, ducking beneath the window to the office. "Yeah, I'm just leaving the office now." A shuffling noise broke through the door before it swung open in front of Sarahn. Taking a deep breath through her nose, she silenced herself. "Give me like five minutes, and I'll meet you at the bar."

The voice softened down the hallway; Sarahn took the opportunity to sneak around the door before it latched. She pulled a flash drive from the makeup bag slung across her back, plugging it into the computer.

She had never before been caught.

Well, almost never, but she would not admit to herself that it was her that was caught.

Sarahn sat at the bar, sipping on the drink the bartender made her "on the house." She scoped out the bar looking for Jacob, a contact of hers that had given her jobs in the past.

Interestingly enough, a different contact of hers in town wanted information on the company that employed Jacob.

"Getting two birds stoned at once," she thought to herself with a chuckle.

"Can I get you another one?" an eager bartender asked, removing her empty glass in front of her.

"No, I'm just waiting for someone. He should be along any moment."

The bartender turned his back to her to serve another patron. After a few passing moments, Sarahn noticed Jacob sitting alone in a booth along the outer wall. Standing from her place at the bar to cross the room and join him, she became mesmerized by a flash of brown entering the main door of the bar.

The singular torn and worn trench coat caught her eyes immediately. "Oh my god." She sunk back into her seat, whispering, "Of all the gin joints, in all the towns, in all the world, he walks in here." She sat back down, crossing her legs and smiling.

She looked from his trilby-styled hat, with its frayed ribbon, to his dusty shoes. He was followed closely by an eager-looking and younger man. Her eyes pursued them crossing the floor of the bar, weaving in and out of people, making his way to a booth opposite Jacob's.

Sarahn watched him fiddle with his phone for a few more moments. "Trying the old 'no service' routine," the purloiner commented, shaking her head.

She scrutinized him for a few minutes, concluding he was here to observe Jacob. The pilferer reached into her handbag to retrieve her sunglasses. Placing them securely upon the bridge of her nose, wrapping them around each ear, she paused watching for the man in the trilby hat and his compatriot to be distracted long enough for her to cross the room and angle her approach.

Sarahn approached Jacob's booth. When Jacob's eyes caught her, he stood to greet her. In a seemingly fitted keyhole neckline dress stretching far enough for modesty but not so much as to dull the imagination, she accented the tan bag wrapped around her forearm with fabric seemingly woven from a deep sea. With nothing revealed and nothing hidden, Sarahn captured the wanting eyes of a battalion of heathens within the bar at that moment.

"Hey," Jacob spoke with genuine warmth to his vocal tone, "how are you doing?"

"Oh, I'm fine, thanks," she replied, shaking his hand, gracefully taking a seat with her back to the trench coat-clad man. "Traffic bad?"

"No, I had to swing by the office to grab this." Quickly retrieving a folder from his briefcase, he slid it across the table for her to see. "Could you take a look at these for me?" He tried not to trace her from the ends of her hair to the skin barely made visible through the keyhole, but she caught his failure. She always does.

Accepting the folder, Sarahn flipped through the contents. Inside were blueprints for the Maglev train currently being built outside of Potstow. In the compartment of a car will be an item of interest, a large machine.

Sarahn leaned over the table, looking at the folder, Jacob eyeing her intently. "Seems easy enough," she spoke, looking up to catch Jacob's eyes.

The look on Jacob's face was one of disbelief.

"Excuse me," the waitress interrupted. "We're taking pictures for our social media page—"

"Not interested," Jacob replied rudely.

The waitress turned away; Sarahn watched her return to the table with the man in the trilby hat.

She smiled to herself, removing the sunglasses, placing them back into her handbag. "The job seems simple enough. Smash and grab, right?" she said in a voice full of sarcasm, though her voice turned serious before she added, "But it's going to cost you a lot of money." She pulled a pen out from inside the handbag, writing down a number on a napkin before sliding it over to Jacob.

Jacob took the folder with a smile, staring at the number written on the page. The smile faded, and he quickly stated, "No. No." He was shaking his head. "That's far too much."

Closing the folder delicately with a gentle touch, Sarahn slowly pushed it back to his side of the table. With a smile and intimidating eye contact, she handed the finished conversation back to him. "Well, when you change your mind," she said, "you know how to get ahold of me."

Sarahn stood from the table and shook his hand. "Take it easy, Jacob." She turned around abruptly, making her way to the exit. She made a direct path toward the booth containing the man in the trilby hat and his ambitious friend.

Passing by their table, she couldn't resist the urge to look at his dumbfounded face. Taking a sharp glance over her shoulder to quickly shiv him with her eyes before snapping her face forward, she exited the bar.

He gave her the moronic gape she desired.

She heard his friend utter "That was peculiar." The bouncer opened the door for her to exit.

Sarahn marveled to herself at the look upon his face as she passed.

"He still loves me," she hummed, smiling as she stood on the sidewalk, waiting for her ride.

The thief had stolen the heart from his chest years ago; he had yet to recover it from her satchel of illicit goods.

After only a moment or two in waiting, a black luxury car pulled to the side of the road in front of her. The driver bolted hastily out of his door and around the vehicle to open the door for Sarahn.

"Get in," a gruff and scratchy voice spoke from inside the darkness of the vehicle.

She listened and followed the command.

"What are they doing?" the voice asked impatiently. Its owner sat deep in the shadows. His face illuminated briefly by the lights on the sidewalks, the driver moved the car through the streets.

"They've got plans for some kind of machine that's supposed to be brought on the maiden voyage of the Maglev," she summarized. "It's supposed to be on its way to Oregon."

"Good," the gruff voice murmured, "and did you get the file?"

"Yeah, I was able to retrieve it earlier." She dug the memory card from her satchel, holding it out to him. He stretched out his hand to receive it, but she pulled it from his reach. "Nuh-uh. Money first."

The voice grumbled, pulling out his phone. A moment or two later, Sarahn's phone lit up with a notification.

She smiled, handing the card to her contact.

"You can let me off here," she spoke to the driver.

The driver pulled to the side of the road, jumping out of the car. Sarahn allowed him to open the door for her because she knew if she did not, he would receive grief from her discerning contact.

"Let me know if you need anything else, Faust."

"Unless you can find a lottery ticket that was recently stolen from one of the members of the council," Faust said.

"What's a lottery ticket have to do with anything?"

"Information," he answered in absolutes.

She knew better than to press further.

"I'll see what I can do," Sarahn replied. "Arrivederci." She waved farewell in a way that most others could not—with her waist.

The Old Deal

Faust was the known alias of a local drug dealer; only a few bystanders from the past knew his real name. He picked up the mantle around the same time Thomas began searching for a business loan to create Killian's Distribution. The costs to start a legitimate business were insurmountable. Even still, Thomas deeply desired to get his operation off the ground floor, but the banks failed him.

According to the bank managers, Thomas's business plans were lacking a critical part of a successful business—a way to build profit for the shareholders. "But I am the shareholders!" he would reply in anger and angst, but to no avail. Thomas applied a singular approach to business, one that to most businessmen sounds ludicrous. He believed if you were to pay your employees a wage capable of producing enough money, to not only survive paycheck to paycheck but also help those laborers acquire an amount of wealth themselves, that they would in turn help make the business a profitable machine.

This is contrary to the rest of the consuming society, which stands firmly that hunger is the driving force of sales.

Time after time, they denied him for a business loan, and time was running short. Thomas offered to sign the family ranch as collateral, but their appraisal contended a deflated valuation based on the current use the ranch, or lack thereof. Years after stepping away from the family's cattle and farming of variant forms, the property was now maintained as a homestead, not added onto or improved, simply maintained.

Around the point he came face-to-face with his wit's end, this old friend from the past appeared from the shadows and approached

Thomas with a plan. What was offered at the time had been referred to as a Gentleman's Deal.

Faust and Thomas, although Thomas knew Faust by the name his mother granted him, grew up in similar circumstances down the single-lane road from each other. Both were absent a parent, and the ones remaining had to work long and hard for hours stacked on hours with little to no pay. A hunger dwelt between them for something more, something greater. It rose, festering from callous abandonment to a penurious upbringing. However, like fermentation to wine, aged to perfection, they needed the right circumstances.

These were not the right circumstances.

The insatiable urge to hold, taste, and caress the finer things in life served as a driving force within each of them to go beyond the measures of most—things they couldn't want for a lack of knowing and things they wanted for a lack of means.

They would have all the things.

Thomas and Faust chose their respective and illicit paths to build profitability for themselves and, ultimately, their families.

Thomas took to the drink, not for himself, of course, but for a clientele pursuing a cheaper alternative than what was being offered. At the time, only three alcohol distribution licenses were allocated for the region. A bidding war was instigated by the state between local distributors and corporate franchises; however, it was only the state that won and only the consumers that lost. The more populated regions remained unaffected and granted more distribution licenses capable of satiating the thirsty masses.

In the time before Potstow, the area known as Maizefield became widely known for its resurgence of illegal distilleries and the Rocky Mountain Shine. Thomas's father called it by that name, the most affordable alcohol across the state. When his father owned the old ranch, he struggled to get much to grow on the land and was horrible at raising cattle. He was not known to be much of a farmhand, but he was well-known for his moonshine, and he knew how to make it right. This knowledge passed down, a closely guarded Killian family secret from the generation of Prohibition days, nearly one hundred years before the founding of Potstow.

Faust, however, took to the green, for himself and with others in mind. Before the days of legal weed, Faust became initiated by a local brotherhood. Like Faust, it went by many names, though most knew it only by its exotic emblem. Through anonymous interviews and voice-over videos posted online at a local level, they touted an ideology that the legalization of marijuana encouraged financial flourishment in the area, a message sounding too good to be true.

Behind the scenes, they were less political, using more illicit methods to meet their financial needs. Originally a block kid, perching on the corner of streets under the watchful eye of his superiors, he dealt the product. Over the years, he worked his way up to runner, eventually to the high-level dealer, and embraced the level of intimidation his new mantle brought him.

A younger Thomas, absent the years of strife, exited the local bank with his head held low. For the third time that day, he faced rejection for a loan for which he applied.

It is at this lowly port that the universe would decide to reunite Thomas with his childhood friend.

"Been a long time since I seen you last, boy," Faust gruffly spoke, advancing from the shadows of the alley upon an unwitting Thomas making his latest walk of shame.

Thomas was visibly startled at first, being taken upon rather suddenly. After his eyes affirmed recognition of the man, he embraced his past with an outstretched hand.

"I hear you don't even go by the same name anymore. It's Faust now, right?" Thomas asked in the duration of their handshake with a nervous disposition. He was walking along his path once again, now with Faust in stride beside him.

"That'd be right," echoed the deep voice of Faust.

Faust stood about 6'2", black and skinny, but stout, a shaved bald head with a light beard tied to a thick goatee. He owned large green eyes, as if his insides consisted of the same substance he pedaled.

"I hear you've been having a bout of trouble, old friend." His yellow-green teeth presented themselves with a smile. "Growin' up, I knew you and your daddy ran a good game, but I don't recall either of you ever partaking in what I was offering at the time. You wouldn't happen to have a change of heart, would you?" Faust questioned Thomas auspiciously.

"I'm listening." Thomas stopped in his tracks, eyeing his old comrade with suspicion.

"Well, shit." Faust walked a few steps ahead of Thomas along the sidewalk. Thomas quickened his pace to follow suit. "It's been, what? Four years, at least, since I saw you last." Faust cocked his head back to let his mind wander. "You and your pops were still game back then, but neither of you seemed to have time to visit an old friend that got pinched." With a bated breath, Faust took a step back, crossing his arms. "Almost like I ain't run no deliveries for you back then. Like you forgot we was a kind of family."

"Don't pretend like ya didn't know that it was us, keeping your mother afloat." Thomas stopped in his steps, snarling at the insult. "She doesn't know the game you ran, and she didn't know those cash-stuffed envelopes were from us." Thomas squared to Faust, his finger poking Faust's chest in the beat of his growled words. "But you, god-damned well knew it."

Thomas stared at Faust, eye to eye. "You were family, and of course, you still are." Thomas resumed walking, anger well pronounced in his steps. "We know you got pinched on our run, and we knew you were doing it for her." Thomas shook his head at his old friend, empathizing with the betrayal Faust felt. "We didn't have the pull, or the cash, necessary to get someone out of a situation like that, but, Faust, we fucking made sure she didn't have anything to worry about!" Thomas's anger enunciated itself like steam from a boiling kettle.

"Oh, I knew it was you, and for that I am grateful." Faust's smile curled maliciously. "That's why I'm here, right now." They both stopped along their chaotic paths parallel to each other. Thomas was standing in the sunlight, his face covered in shadow, looking toward Faust. Faust stood to Thomas's side, shadowed by the canopy over-head. A single small beam of light bursting through a crack in the canvas rested on his leg. "Here you are, in dire straits—"

"Dire straits!" Killian replied, offended. "You are mistaken, sir." The small shadow upon his shoe grew as he stepped deeper within it. Thomas adjusted his tie. "I'm just going legit." He continued his walk erect, and proud of the statement.

"Legit, huh?" Faust let out a deep, hollow laugh. "Oh, I know you, Tommy." Faust stepped closer to Thomas and looked down at him; the stance was intimidating. Thomas felt the weight of the past above him, a new heat wave of anger dripping wet from his body. "There's no hiding from me." He looked at Thomas as if staring in an endless abyss of darkness, and he smiled. "I'm here to offer you what they call a once-in-a-lifetime opportunity."

Thomas replied with silence, eager to hear the offer, though he did not want to seem too eager.

"Way I hear it you're leaving the manufacturing and trying to go into distribution. Is that right?" His voice echoed in a low whisper. "Well, I'm trying to make a similar transition."

For all his beguilement concerning money, Thomas never cared much for green. He considered it to be the means to his end, but he did not wish to become forever indebted to Faust.

Time passed, and time did as time does, time after time, and twisted the bond between beast and man.

Thomas found the open road soothing. He loved the sound of the wheels to the road, the loud hum of his truck's engines. He generally kept the radio off, preferring the abstract silence over the latest pop music. The news was depressing, and politics annoyed him. All this, especially of late, with the passing of his father, it all just felt so…much.

Sure, he was a drunk, but what man had lived without sin among virtue?

Everything reminded Thomas of him. Everyone else knew his father for the moonshine runner of a generation, but to Thomas, his father was everything else.

Other than a drunk, failed rancher and supreme moonshine distiller, James Killian was also an accomplished piano player. His catalog drew from an eclectic choice of music. Classically trained, he would play Beethoven, Bach, Mozart, and Mendelssohn. Yet he stayed true to the changing times from a childhood with Elton John,

Cream, and the Beatles; he even enjoyed a lot of the music Thomas grew up with: Rage Against the Machine, Stone Temple Pilots, Smashing Pumpkins. Music inspired nostalgia, reminding Thomas of that one time his dad played that one song.

James also was an accomplished carpenter. All manner of woodwork would bring a tear falling from Thomas's eyes. James, and Thomas's grandfather, built the entire house. He spent most of his time away from the ranch recently. His girlfriend, Gracie, had been quite supportive, allowing him to stay at her apartment to save some gas. He was considering following some of his father's final advice and asking her to marry him.

Of course, he also asked Thomas to go to the titty bar in the following sentence. So take from his wisdom what you will.

Thomas struggled to keep his mind on the task at hand, making his drops. The quicker it was done, the quicker he got paid. After, Faust would take his cut. Killian's Distribution won the bid for the alcohol license, and Thomas intended to build upon his reach. His business was one of the smaller distributors in the northwest region of Colorado. Thankfully, because of Faust's "Gentleman's Deal," he recorded one of the highest profit margins within his region.

With his father's death, Thomas wouldn't trust anyone else with this particular route. His father, renowned as a stubborn bull, drove the route up to the week he died. Thomas reveled in the fact that he wasn't on the job when his heart finally kicked. He thought with a smile, *"That cantankerous hoss would have died halfway through the route and still pulled the truck into the garage at the end of the night before he allowed himself to close his eyes."*

He flipped his blinkers and applied the brakes before turning into Dirty Vegas's parking lot. Thomas liked to arrive here early, but not to indulge himself in the festivities of the night. His father on the other hand, absent of Thomas, made this his final stop. He enjoyed the scenery. Dirty Vegas was a gentleman's club, but gentlemen did not attend, save Thomas.

Jumping down from the driver's seat, he walked to the back of his truck. Mr. Killian lowered the lift, stepped upon it, and hoisted himself to the level of the truck's door. Because of his father's age, they equipped this truck to be more easily accessible than the others. Thomas entered the truck's rear, grabbed the dolly, and pushed it up to a keg marked O'Malley's Porter.

He closed up the truck, using the lift to lower himself and the dolly with the keg to the ground. Thomas took a deep breath before walking around the back. He knocked on the door and waited for a response. The camera by the door focused on his face; Thomas shifted his ugly mug to be recognized. A buzzer rang out, and the door unlocked; he opened the door, pulling the keg in behind him.

"Tommy!" A seldom-heard voice owned by a very stout man with an apelike stature rang upon Thomas's ears as he entered. "It's good to see you." His face replaced delight with sorrow from across the room before he continued, "Sorry to hear about your dad, man. Helluva guy."

"Yeah, 'tis a tragedy."

"Just back that to the corner over there."

"Here?"

"No, no." The gorilla of a man walked toward Thomas, directing him to the appropriate place. "Is there an extra one?"

"No, but I can make sure there is next week." Dragging out his dolly from beneath the keg, Thomas grabbed an empty one instead. The man passed a bank satchel with cash. Thomas wrote a receipt and accepted the cash as tender. He bade his customer adieu and turned to leave out the back.

"Send your sister our condolences, will you?" the man yelled as Thomas was about to close the door. He did not reply to the request, adapting to keep his mind to the task at hand. Walking over to the lift, he raised himself back up to the back door. Thomas wheeled the dolly back into its place and walked to the wheel well of the truck. He entered a combination into a secluded dial and opened a hidden compartment to place the money inside.

The rest of the day went very similar, omitting the need for an extra one and the condolences to his sister. Mr. Killian still had one last stop to make before taking his truck back to the garage.

He backed his truck up to the loading dock. Leaping from his truck, he entered the warehouse. When he entered, the warehouse workers were unloading the empty kegs. They started breaking down the keg's false bottoms and then filled the contents with cannabis. Thomas called out to the workers, "Vegas needs an extra one!" One of the workers gave him a thumbs-up in acknowledgment. Thomas excused himself to the back office and knocked on the door.

"Come on in, Thomas." A voice echoed behind the door. Thomas did as he was bid and entered. "I'm sure you've heard it enough today, but I'm truly sorry for your loss. Your father," he paused as a moment in silence and then continued, "was truly one of a kind."

"Thank you." Perhaps the gratitude was genuine, but Thomas used it as an opportunity. "I know this may seem cold, with the timing and all," Thomas uncharacteristically stammered for a moment, "but have you thought any on our last discussion?" He sat a stack of money on the table between them.

"What do you mean?" the cool, unsurprising voice replied from across the desk. The owner of the voice reached forth a hand, also owned by him, to retrieve it.

"I think you and I can both agree, we're the only ones taking the risk here. If his only job is to sit back and collect a paycheck, I think we just found that raise of income we were looking for earlier. That's sixteen-point five percent each."

The man sitting across from him chuckled before answering, "Always the numbers-man, Tommy. That's exactly what your dad would always tell me about you." A smile spread across his face. "Seems like you're reaching for a twenty-four percent raise with him gone."

Thomas was ready for this response. Thomas sat down with an equally coy smile, replying, "Actually, it's more like three hundred percent to me." He watched to see if his companion could do the math before he continued. "We're businessmen, Francis." Thomas addressed the man by his first name for the first time. "We're building something!" He stood, excitement in his words, inspired to physically elevate himself to match his tone. "What it is that we need to be asking ourselves here is, What does Faust do for us anyways?"

Fourth Floor

The Fourth Floor was a local tavern nestled securely on the fourth floor of the tallest building in downtown Potstow. A marquee hung out the window between the fourth and fifth floors to attract pedestrians from the street, up the steps or elevator into their bar with their drink specials and local band names written seductively by one of their bartenders every day.

It's quite a scene to see if you're ever in downtown Potstow during the midafternoon.

Will pulled his sporty azure car into one of the parking spots near the entrance of the parking garage within walking distance to the bar.

"Okay, so pretend this is my first time, and be gentle with me," Will said, both to express his virginity to the private-eye gig and to be openly ironic about it. "What exactly are we doing here again?"

Stan reached into his satchel to retrieve the sack containing the remaining Grape Ape. "Let's smoke before we go in, and I'll break it all down for you." Stan's meerschaum pipe appears into his right hand by sleight of hand. Grabbing one of the last buds from his bag, he begins to pack his bowl.

"Awesome!" Will jeers.

"Our objective is to capture this man," pulling an envelope from the open satchel, Stan removed a picture of Jacob McKinney from his dossier and placed it on the console between them, "in a compromising picture with a lady who is not his wife."

Will snatched up the picture. "Ah, the tall, dark, and handsome type." This whole process reminded Stan of his days in the bullpen with his fellow detectives.

"Though it sounds like an easy thing to do, it is a task that has vexed me for a few weeks now." Stan felt his jacket for his match-book. "He has only jumped from meeting to meeting"—Stan struck the match off the back of its cover—"rarely leaving the office." Stan puffed on his pipe and passed it to Will. "And the picture needs to be provocative in nature in order to break their ironclad prenuptial." Blowing smoke rings, pondering, slightly surprised with the concise-ness of his debriefing.

"So wait, if he's cheating on her, why don't we just go Eddie Valiant on his ass?" Will replied, slowly puffing on the pipe, stoking the fire within it to burn hot enough to freely puff. "Catch him play-ing patty-cake with Jessica Rabbit."

"That's the issue. The man doesn't play patty-cake, far as I can tell," Stan said in a matter-of-fact tone. "Let alone be anywhere near Jessica Rabbit." Stan accepted the pipe from Will. The sleuth puffed the pipe before continuing. "Other than just being an overall douche, he seems pretty straitlaced. I think it's cashed. Let me pack a little more." Stan ashed the pipe into his hand and rubbed the remnants into his pants. "It's not quite time for him to be here yet, and we need to let him post up first."

"Why's that?" Will questioned eagerly.

"So we can get closer without grabbing attention to ourselves. I've been following this guy for a while. I'm bound to start attracting attention to myself."

They waited for a while before Will caught a glimpse of McKinney parking his car in the garage near them.

"Hey…hey." Will nudged Stan with his elbow. "Is that your guy?" he whispered, pointing at a car pulling in the garage.

Stan slouched down in his seat, lowering the bill of his hat. Will just sat, watching Jacob fervently with an idiotic smile stretched across his face.

Jacob opened the door of his car and stepped out. Adjusting his cuff links and suit jacket, he caught Will's eye. Will nodded upward, never breaking smile or eye contact. Jacob smiled awkwardly, waving in the same manner in return. Closing the luxury car's door, he remote-locked it, making his way to the building across the street.

"All right." Will clapped his hands and rubbed them together. "He's here. Let's follow him in—wait, what?" Will asked quizzically at the mortified look on Stan's face.

Stan shook his head in disgust, beginning to explain the idea of being inconspicuous to Will.

"You mean we don't just roll in and crack heads?" Will said, heartbroken.

"Not in the private-eye business."

They waited a couple of moments before entering the building to avoid another uncouth encounter between Will and Jacob. When they went into the bar, Stan reluctantly allowed Will to sit facing Jacob at a table across the aisle from his booth, while Stan sat with his back to him across the table from Will.

Jacob was still alone in his booth when Stan and Will arrived at their table. The bar was decently busy; Stan worried he wouldn't be able to get a good shot with his iPhone. Regardless, he used the front-facing camera to angle it over his shoulder, trying to line up a decent shot.

"I don't think we'll be able to hear them, but my days of recon taught me how to read lips pretty well." Stan looked at Will, unbelieving. Will tried to reassure him, "For real!"

A few moments went by, and a lady with auburn hair approached Jacob's booth. He rose from his seat and greeted her. Unfortunately, someone moved into Stan's angle. Acting like he was trying to get cell service, he held the phone up, blindly taking shots of the table. He couldn't quite make out her face.

"All right, Mr. Lip-reader," Stan mocked. "What are they saying?"

"Well, so far, it seems like pleasantries. The 'How are you doing. How was traffic?' ordeal. So they know each other?" Will summarized.

Stan stood up, gracelessly shaking his phone. "And?"

"He's pulled out a file folder," Will commentated. "Now he's sliding it across the table. 'Take a look at these,' or it might be 'Take a block of cheese.'" Stan rolled his eyes.

A waitress walked by. "Are you guys doing all right? Having problems with your phone?" she asked, eyeing Stan.

"Yeah, whiskey on the rocks," Stan ordered, ignoring her questioning, trying to get a better angle of the mysterious auburn-haired lady in the booth with his mark.

"Seven and seven for me!" Will cheerfully said. The waitress smiled and winked at Will before caressing her hand over his shoulder on her way to the bar.

"What are they saying now?" Stan queried.

"Not much. She's just been looking at the folder, so far."

"Describe her to me. I can't get a good shot of her."

"Here let me try," Will stated, pulling his phone from his pocket. "She's got reddish hair, wearing sunglasses. It's nighttime, lady. That's just suspicious."

"No need for the social commentary. What else is there? Any tattoos or other identifying marks?"

"No, no tattoos that I can see. She's got a few freckles. I mean, she's cute, like a homely cute. Bright smile that ties her together," Will stated as the overly friendly bartender approached with their drinks. "Hey, do you mind doing me a favor?"

"Sure," she said hesitantly, hoping Will wasn't about to ask some creepy question about her sex life.

"We're trying to get a decent picture of the people in that booth over there." Stan stopped acting like he had no service when the waitress gave him another judging look, his head held low. "Would you mind helping me out?"

It would seem as though Will's father had better genes of charm that had been passed down to him than Stan's father.

The waitress eyed Will's phone for a moment before obliging. She made her way over to Jacob's booth.

Will chuckled. "She just told them she was taking pictures for the social media website… Ooo, he shut her down," commentated Stan's new sidekick.

Stan sat, elbows on his table with his face in his hands as the waitress returned. "Well, that didn't work as well as I had hoped, but I did get a shot." She offered Will his phone back. "Good luck, guys."

"Thanks!" Will spouted positively toward her as she left. "What a sweet girl," he remarked. "Hey, Stan, get your camera back out. Those people finally moved."

Stan angled the front-facing camera over his shoulder once more to try to get a clear shot. The low resolution and scratched screen made it difficult to make out their faces, but Stan took what he thought to be a worthy shot.

"Be cool. She's looking this way," Will alerted, trying to remain incognito, as Stan had explained before they followed Jacob into the building. Stan attempted to make his actions more fluid. In his camera, the auburn-haired lady created a familiar feeling in Stan's gut. Something about her gave him a strange and intimate tingling. "It couldn't be…" he tried to justify, adjusting the zoom with his finger and thumb.

"She's saying something along the lines of 'Seems simple enough,' or maybe it was, 'Seems single and buff.'" Will realized he might be overthinking the whole situation. He made out the next words very clearly. "Going to cost you a lot of money."

Stan sat with a frown on his face, wondering what that would mean.

"Is she a hooker? Is this Jacob into some freaky tricks?"

"That's unlikely. I would have found dirt that apparent," Stan defensively responded. "What was he asking her to look over that was going to cost him a lot of money?"

"She's writing something down," Will deciphered. "He's looking at it, and he's shaking his head saying, 'No, no.'"

"Price too steep?" Will relayed.

"Apparently," Stan answered.

The auburn-haired lady handed the man back his folder, shaking his hand to take leave. She seemingly made a direct path to pass

Stan and Will's table. As she passed Stan, she shot Stan a sharp glance over her shoulder. If her gaze were a blade, the laceration would have been a gut wound—inevitable, felt through each moment. Stan, trying to play shy, only got another brief look at her face before she snapped her face forward, leaving the bar urgently.

"Well, that was peculiar," Will commented. "What was that about?"

"Yeah…" A reverie of the past surfaced in Stan's mind. He delved further into his photographs. "It just can't be…"

Jacob remained in his booth for a few minutes, playing around on his phone before getting up to leave. "Should we leave too?" Will whispered over to Stan, getting better at being inconspicuous.

"You know, I've never had the luxury of having a car before. I normally have to take the Cannibus or get a taxi…sometimes on foot." Stan groaned, thinking of the past weeks. "Let's give it a couple minutes to let him get into his car."

"Do you have one of those tiny GPS locators?" Will's mind raced, tracing all the angles. "We could slip one onto his car."

Stan actually never thought of that, but he wasn't letting Will be aware of it.

"Nah, I can't afford those," Stan replied, reaching into his coat pocket for the envelope containing his deteriorating cash flow. He left a tip for their beguiling waitress and paid for their drinks. "Ready to go?"

Will instinctively backed Stan's six o'clock as they stood from their table to make their way out of the bar. In his services days, he was never number one upon entering the fatal funnel, but he was a solid number two. When Number One entered, busting down the door, Will reacted by following, clearing the rear corner, going the opposite direction of Number One, running along the wall and collapsing his sector to clear the room. This training proved beneficial when playing or streaming "Carbon Copy."

Stan underwent some similar police training; however, he wasn't one of those steroid-raging detectives looking for the thrill in the job. He would rather let the other detectives take down the door and have all the "fun." Because of this, Stan was not ready for the guy waiting for him behind the bar's exit door.

The punch to his nose was even more surprising.

Will, on the other hand, was not taken by surprise. Stan lay among the tiles in front of the stairs leading out of the building, covering what Will suspected to be a broken nose. Will crossed the tall, blond ponytailed assailant square in the jaw with a firm left. While he was dazed, Will angled himself naturally at a forty-five degrees, blocking the blind counter with a wave of his dominate hand, catching the ponytailed assailant's wrist and extending his arm beyond his head in a circular motion. Stepping passed his assailant's side, Will applied additional force to his jaw. This swift motion caused the lumbering invader to lose his center of gravity, falling flat on his back, knocking loose a few papers from his coat pocket. Will hovered over him, holding his arm in an *omote gyaku*, applying pressure to the elbow.

"What the hell do you want?" Will commandingly sounded as his victim yelped in pain. "Answer me!" he said, applying pressure to his arm.

"He's been following—" Will's victim interrupted himself, screaming in reaction to the pressure Will kept applying to his arm, "—my boss. My boss!" His other hand helplessly beat the floor, his thick accent increasingly more prevalent. "I was just trying to scare him and get him to stop following him."

"And you're going to tell your boss you were successful in this. Right?"

"Yeah, whatever you say, man!" the man with the blond ponytail pleaded. "Just let it go! Let it go!"

Will released and kicked the assailant in the side. "Get out of here, Elsa." He looked back to Stan, proud of his reference. "I better not see you again!"

The attacker got to his feet in a hurry. Gathering his wounded pride, he streaked down the four flights of stairs. His shoulder was feeling like it was about to pop out of his socket, his ego hurt, straining for solace.

Will helped Stan to his feet. "Katie would want us to go put in a statement." He looked over Stan's nose, assessing the damage. "But to be honest, I could get in a lot of trouble for attacking him, even to defend you."

"Ugh." Stan tried to spit the blood out of his mouth, clearing his nasal passages. "Ain't the first time someone's broke my nose." He snapped it back into place, the blood flowing harder from his orifice. "Aww, that feels so much better." He breathed in deeply. "I haven't been able to breathe this well in a long time." Stan's eyes caught his iPhone, sprawled next to a crumpled-up piece of paper on the floor. "Shit."

He gathered his phone and the paper, placing the paper in his pocket. The screen was cracked and unresponsive.

"Please tell me you back up your pictures to the cloud."

North Side Story

Among the solus of cascading shade spreading from the one dimly lit bulb shining from over the kitchen sink, Will sat alone in the living room. The television was passing images through the screen; the volume rested at a very low murmur. The local news anchor was barely audible from the sectional sofa where Will routinely perched. If he'd been paying attention to the television, he would have been informed that a big jackpot lottery ticket had yet to be claimed, but Will was not attentive to the message. The benumbed vacuum lining the room mildly compensated his irrelevant television.

Time was meaningless to him, passing around him either far too fast or much too slow in each passing moment. Void of any solace, a month passed within a blink of an eye, each individual moment filled with tension. It was as if he was experiencing the constant sound of fingernails scratching across a chalkboard in his mind; the mites beneath his skin felt like they were trying to crawl out of his pores. The mounting pressure grew, while his stomach sank; an impending dread crept into his chest. His anxiety had not been this active since he was honorably discharged from the military.

The only moments capable of filling the abyss were with his beloved Katie and the scarcity of passing moments he caught Stan coming and going to or from his office.

Regardless of Stan's claims, Will was beginning to have a suspicion that it served as the man's apartment as well.

Footsteps echoing down the hall brought Will leaping to his feet. With haste he meandered over toward the door, his eyes approaching the peephole, as the sniper would his scope.

"Come on," he muttered under his breath. "Come on."

The footsteps quietly tapped, growing louder as they edged their way closer down the hall.

"Come on." His anticipation mounted with each tap. Come o-FUCK!"

Before he could finish his mantra, his front door swung open, busting him in the nose! Katie jumped back in surprise. She stopped home on her break to see how Will was doing. His emotional distance left cause for concern, and she knew what usually followed.

"Oh, shit, baby!" she exclaimed. "Are you okay?"

"Ugh." He grunted through his hands. "I think my nose is bleeding."

"Let me see." She forced Will's hand away from his face to take a better look at it.

"I'm going to tell everyone you beat me," Will said with a grin.

"Yeah, and not a jury would convict me if I did." Her reply accompanied a slap across his cheek. "What the hell were you doing anyways?"

Will hesitated for a moment before answering. "I was hoping you were him."

"Oh, I'm not good enough for you anymore?" Katie handed him a tissue to wipe the blood from his face.

"No, it's not that." Will felt offended by the assertion. "I was hoping I could go back on another assignment with him."

Katie looked at her love with sympathy in her eyes. "Babe, I don't know if that's the best thing for you."

"What do you mean?"

"What I mean is," she gathered a large breath, "you've not been yourself lately ever since you and he went out that night." She let herself trail into silence.

"It's not like that. I haven't been myself in years. And that night with him"—Will tossed the bloody tissue into the trash—"it was the first time I've felt like me that I can remember."

Katie took offense to the statement, as if she lacked the ability to make him feel like himself, or expounded, maybe she never knew him at all.

He continued nevertheless. "There was action. There was intrigue. I felt like I was running on all cylinders for the first time in years."

Katie looked at her fiancé, imagining the tension he was expressing vividly. "If even half of the things I hear about him from the station are true, I'd really rather you didn't. Besides, what does a private investigator need with paramilitary and sharpshooting skills?"

Will looked at Katie blankly for a moment.

"I didn't want to argue about this." Will stomped over to the coat rack with his head held low to the ground, retrieving his coat. "I'll see you later." Throwing the coat over his arm, he left their apartment.

Katie felt like she may have crossed a line somewhere; she just wasn't sure where. She mumbled a faint "Bye" as he closed the door behind him.

Will knew he was being childish, as Katie would often remind him, but felt like he was cutting off a facet of himself. Will, truly, missed the thrill—the universe moving around him, he alone being left behind in the dust.

He muttered to himself descending down each flight of stairs, pausing only for a moment to bid Ms. Edna a polite salutation, to the main floor of the building, as if Katie were participating in the same argument.

Katie sat on their couch, letting out a long sigh. She placed her hands over her eyes and rubbed them for a moment, hoping to wake herself from this bad dream. When she conceded to the reality, she laid her head back onto the sofa, frustrated.

Will reached the bottom of the steps and was greeted by Mr. Draper.

"How are you, Mr. Richards? I hope you and Ms. James have found the place to your liking."

"Uh, yeah. It's fine." Will contemplated for a moment, before bluntly answering Mr. Draper's second question. "So far…"

"Anything I can do to make you feel more at home?"

"Well, have you seen that man from down the hall?" he replied. "Stan?"

"Don't tell me he's been bothering you!" Dom exclaimed. "I'll have him evicted before the end of the week!"

"No, no! That's not what I mean at all." Will thought for a moment before he quietly added, "Stan seems like a decent enough guy."

Mr. Draper scoffed at the preposterous idea.

"Seriously, I've just been wanting to talk to him. If you see him, could you let me know when he's in?"

"Certainly, Mr. Richards, I would be happy to let you know when I smell him."

Will bid his landlord adieu, proceeding to walk out the double doors and down the street in front of Draper Properties. From the street, the living room light shone out the window, creating a silhouette of Katie on the wall.

Will had no intentions of upsetting her; he was trying to follow his moral compass. Though, war and politics eroded the metaphorical line to a very thin veil, the damaged warrior feeling suspended, like a person denying one's own nature was a senseless pursuit. After all, that same ideology led him to find Katie.

Katie wrapped her legs around one of the black counter height swivel barstools placed at the island between the kitchen and living room. The perceptive constable slowly picked at her lunch, remorsefully scribbling a love note to her unfeigned companion upon their magnetic whiteboard, normally adhered to the refrigerator door. She ate what satisfied her hunger, leaving Will enough to eat for when he eventually found his way home, *mysteriously with the munchies.*

Her thoughts settled on giving Will a chance. She could surmise that the true cause for whatever Will was experiencing had nothing to do with her. He was not one for letting her down; rather, he was known for surprising and surpassing all expectations she set of him.

The expectations were set rather high.

Making something out of nothing. Seeing those little things in people that others did not see in themselves. Will saw what most people fail to see, which prevents the stimulation of an open mind.

He saw the why for other people. Right or wrong, he felt their why, and as his admirer, Katie adored that about him.

Maybe, there was something to Stan that did not catch her eyes, or the eyes of most people for that matter. She snickered to herself before taking another bite of her sandwich.

"There would have to be ground rules," Katie thought to herself walking over to the refrigerator to hang the whiteboard. She retrieved the black dry erase marker to add a postscript for her lover detailing the stipulations.

The police monitor on her belt echoed in the kitchen, "All units, please respond, we've got a 10-67 north of downtown Potstow. All available units, please respond."

"This is badge number: seven, zero, six, eight, four. I'm in the area. What's the address?"

The operator gave Katie the address to a homestead in north Potstow. The officer quickly finished her half of the sandwich, grabbing her coat from the door handle before exiting the apartment.

Will took his leave down Ocean Boulevard to the parking garage down the block, then to the parking garages that contained his car. He waved toward the security guard politely in passing. Will unlocked the door, starting the engine with the remote as he approached the driver's seat.

The security guard, gawking, raised the bar for Will, driving by with another wave. Will turned onto the road, finding a route to exit the city as quickly as possible. The lights in the city had other plans, of course. Turning from green to yellow as he approached the empty intersections, he let out a deep groan of dissatisfaction.

Finally, after what felt like an eternity, the light turned green, allowing Will to proceed to the next intersection where the light played its tricks again. After the third game of "red light, green light," Will placed his head in defeat on his steering wheel, flippantly turning the radio on.

George Harrison's "All Things Must Pass" began playing through the speakers.

Will groaned. "Oh my god"

George Harrison's voice serenaded Will; the light changed from red to green. With glee, Will applied pressure to the gas pedal, taking out his frustrations for the night on the road.

Katie shut off the siren on her cruiser as she approached the driveway of the address dispatch relayed to her. The flashing lights of her cruiser outlined the shrubbery along the driveway, illuminating her entrance to the scene of the crime.

She saw a man with his hands burrowed into themselves sitting on the porch and a woman she assumed was his wife with her arms around him, consoling him.

"Dispatch, this is seven, zero, six, eight, four. I've arrived to the scene. There is a man and woman sitting on the steps of the porch. They both look distressed. I'm going to go ahead and activate my body cam."

"This is dispatch. You have already been given a go-ahead by the chief to use the body cam. In fact, he is coming to the scene any moment."

"Of course." She toggled her body cam power switch to the On position. "What's next? I'm going to have to work with that dick Stan Greene too?" The sarcasm seared like a migraine once the possibility became a probability. The annoyed law official etched the outline of her eye sockets with her forefinger and thumb in an attempt to relieve the pain before opening the door to her cruiser.

"Officer, I'm so glad you are here." A third feminine voice entered the stage, approaching from the direction of her own car.

Katie's hand went to her weapon instantly, flipping the button on the holster, though she did not immediately grasp the handle.

She could hear the voice of her father, a retired police officer, echoing one of the last things he said before she moved west with Will.

"What's going on here?" Katie spoke to the arriving starlet.

"Well, ma'am," she replied, "it's truly a tragedy."

"And you are?" Katie interjected.

"Mrs. Vera Montey, and you are?

"Officer James, ma'am."

"Officer James, my husband had to separate himself from everyone. You'll find him out back. When you see the scene, you'll understand." She took a long drag from her cigarette. "It's absolutely heartbreaking."

"And what is that?"

"You see, our children," Mrs. Montey motioned toward the couple on the porch steps, "have been murdered. Emotions have been high, and words have been spoken that a lady such as myself wouldn't utter, even behind closed doors."

Katie fought to discern the veracity of that statement. No coy smile lightly presenting itself on the face of Vera, her fluidity of motion in the face of such horrible news left the officer confused.

Was she genuinely a Southern belle, or did she just want to be?

"Okay, so your children have been murdered?" Katie reeled back, noticing how nonchalant the question may have come off.

"Yes, but they weren't infantile, ma'am." The even-tempered Mrs. Montey took another drag from her cigarette. She continued, "They had recently graduated college and had their whole lives ahead of themselves."

The final syllable trailed with a sweetness; perhaps it was real.

"Right." Katie felt uneasy about her first attestant's vocal timbre. "I'm sure you'll understand we will need everyone to come down to the station to make an official statement."

"Oh, absolutely," she replied coolly.

Katie approached the couple on the porch steps. "Are you okay?"

The couple sat in silence, nodding in response.

A weight hit deep in her stomach; Katie knew she wasn't ready to open the door to the house. Regardless, the impetuous officer stretched out her hand, grasping the handle of the screen door.

The rumbling of gravel fell upon her ears before she opened the door.

"The chief," she grumbled to herself, releasing the handle to the screen door. Katie turned, stepping off the porch to approach her superior.

The police chief stepped out from his Classic 1937 Ford Coupe converted into a biodiesel engine. Katie moved forward to inform him of the situation; however, he stepped around her to hug Mrs. Montey.

"Oh, Vera," the chief spoke to his embraced. "When I got the call, my heart just went out for you. Is there anything I can do?"

"Please, John," Mrs. Montey replied. "Henry is out back. Let me take him home."

"Of course, Vera. We can forgo statements for today."

"You don't understand." Mrs. Montey nodded toward Katie, alerting her superior's attention to her presence. "He doesn't seem to be able to reconcile what happened."

"And how is Catelyn taking it?" John asked.

"They haven't said much to me. I only just arrived moments before you, sir." Katie spoke with authority before Mrs. Montey could answer. "I was just about to enter the building when you arrived."

"Good. Let us jump that hurdle together, Officer James."

"Absolutely, sir. Follow—"

"But first, let me address the Crapers and Mr. Montey in private for a moment. Stay here and wait for the forensic team. From what I've been told, we're going to need them."

Katie did as she was told, though she felt uneasy about the chief addressing the witnesses before her. The chief seemed aware of everything already, and he was physically distraught. They all were.

The chief walked up to the porch and shook one of the hands of each of the couples seated on the edge. Katie watched him situate himself outside of earshot as he spoke. After a few moments, he walked around the house to locate the last missing party—Mr. Montey.

The forensic team rumbled through the gravel as Mr. Montey and the chief reappeared in tandem to the scene.

"All right. Miss James, are you ready to enter the crime scene?"

"Yes, sir."

"Okay, follow me." The chief patriarchally placed himself before Katie; she felt control of the case slipping from her fingertips with each step toward the couples on the porch.

He opened the screen door; Katie noted the blood pooled near the door to her body cam recording.

The chief looked to her and her to him. Both caught their breath before nodding to each other. Then he pushed open the front door.

Romeo and Juliet

Pacing forward and back outside of Stan's new office glass pane, Will was playing through the conversation he desperately tried to plan in his head for the sixth or seventh time. He became distracted by the sunlight refracted through the glass, glistening the unblemished emblem of the huge eye magnified on the wall across the hall, the serif lettering identifying the man behind the glass and his occupation for his dyslexic clientele upon the ceiling and floor.

During his eighth rehearsal, in the back of his mind, he knew full well Stan probably perched behind his desk, smoking from his pipe, watching Will's silhouette move, decidedly frantic, back and forth through the etched glass on the other side. The nervous warrior sighed when he felt ready, placing his hand on Stan's doorknob.

"Okay," Will muttered beneath his breath, before allowing himself into the office. "Here it goes."

Just as Will thought, there squat Stan, pipe in hand, leaned back into his ragged old chair angled toward the door. As always, a skunk-ridden stench laid heavy; smoke drifted lazily around the room.

However, Stan wasn't looking at the door; instead, he was flipping through photographs with his feet kicked back onto his desk. He only nodded to acknowledge his compatriot's appearance.

Will walked into the office, fairly certain at this point it was also serving as Stan's living quarters; he sauntered over to sit in one of the chairs across the desk from Stan, but the compiling dust persuaded him otherwise.

Uncomfortably, Will crossed his arms, adjusting his footing. Stan sat mute, looking at each picture, smoking from his pipe.

"Wanna come over for dinner?" Will broke the mounting silence before adding, "Katie made spaghetti."

Stan silently acquiesced, placing the photographs into a manila envelope on his desk. Rising from his chair, Will took his leave from the office. Still drawing lightly from his pipe, Stan followed Will quietly, locking the door behind him.

Few people can have moments of silence and appreciate the bliss following a realization that you are not responsible for how other people feel in a social setting. When you find someone who can appreciate the euphoria of silence and still want that person to enjoy the absence of things with you, rather than forcing activities or conversation to give the illusion of a good time, hold on to them. You will rarely want to share your silence.

Will graciously opened the door to his apartment in an attempt to welcome his guest, who replied by puffing smoke into his face as he passed. Brushing the smoke away from his face, Will closed the door behind them.

"Have a seat. I'll grab some plates from the kitchen."

Stan did his host's bidding, grabbing a seat at the island, while he finished his pipe. Will appeared on the opposite side with a large brown bowl of spaghetti with two plates and utensils on top. Setting the bowl on the counter, he handed his tenacious friend a set of plate, fork, and knife.

"Okay, so I'm gonna need you to not be mad," Will interrupted Stan, beginning to shove a forkload of food into his mouth. "But I've got a case for you," Will said, Stan sitting opposite him at the dinner table.

"Why would I be mad?" Stan asked with a full mouth, his mind racing through probable outcomes that could possibly make him angry. Then it hit him, swallowing his mouthful of spaghetti. "I'm not looking for the bitch's cat!" Stan raised his voice, slamming his fist on the counter. His fork shook on his plate. "The goddamn thing has been gone for three years, Will! I told her I'm not looking for Mr. Cuddly Fucks or whatever she named that fucking thing!"

"Okay. First, the cat's name was Syd. Sydney Van Wiggleton III when she's being formal. Second, this isn't about Edna from the second floor. So let's just bring that down a notch, all right?" Will pleaded, gesturing with his hands for Stan to retake his seat.

Stan lowered himself to the barstool, but not without a slight twitch in his eye. The mere thought of her asking about that cat again sent him into a blind fury. He was now gritting his teeth at Will, anticipating whatever he planned for him could potentially be worse than the case of Mr. Cuddly Fucks.

"It's not the case that's going to make you mad. It's…" He hesitated, recalling the stipulations Katie put into place before he continued, "…how you got the case that might make you a bit upset," Will said with a nervous disposition.

"Out with it, fuck boy. What did you sign me up for?" Stan replied, jumping up from the table, launching his chair backward and marching around the kitchen side of the island for a beer in Will's fridge.

Will cleared his throat. "Romeo and Juliet."

Stan dropped the freshly opened beer, shattering the bottle. "How the…ya know what? I don't even care how. That's been in the news for the past two weeks. It's exactly what I need right now."

"So does that mean—" Will began.

"Yes. I'll take it. When do they want me?" Stan excitedly asked.

"Now. Katie's down at the station. I can take you." Will rushed for his keys on the counter, slipping on the beer Stan spilled. "Fuck!" he yelled, crashing into the counter. Stan laughed hysterically as he grabbed the paper towels from the table to help clean up the mess.

Leaving uneaten spaghetti is just a waste.

The dynamic duo entered the station to be greeted by Katie in the bullpen. "I assume this means you're willing to weigh in on our case?" She looked to Stan.

"It would be cruel of me, alone, to selfishly profit off my detective skills," his hand reached for a ruffled doobie in his coat's side pocket, "when you guys clearly need my expertise." He placed the joint into his lips.

Katie rolled her eyes, as did Will and the secretary at the front desk. In fact, everyone within audible proximity of Stan rolled their eyes hard enough to look like they were auditioning for the next Exorcist movie.

If Stan's weed had eyes to roll, they would have.

Katie looked at Will. "You told him…" if her eyes were knives, Will would have been killed there, in that moment, in front of all the police on duty "…we needed him?" She crossed her arms, tapping her toes to the tile floor.

"Let's not squabble over the needs of the force," Stan interjected, partly with confidence. However, it was done mostly to calm the fire under Will. "The point is, Scooby and I, we have this handled." He patted Will on the back. "Now fill me in!" The retentive investigator commanded, while he lit the hand-rolled joint hanging out of his mouth. His arm draped around Will, his lips holding the joint with a smile that made everyone around him regret their recent life decisions.

His weed regretted its life decision as well, but no one cares about the poor herb.

Katie informed Stan of all the information and evidence gathered over the course of the case. The local news had been calling it the "Romeo and Juliet" murder—one victim killed by a puncture wound made by a knife and the other originally thought to be an overdose.

Fortunately, the forensic team did not receive the memo sent earlier that day. In it were details that banned the forensic team from processing "needless and expensive tests." Publicly, the forensic team was commended after the testing returned with toxicology positive for ricin.

Shortly after this point in time, their funding gets cut to make space in the budget for a promotion to Potstow's "rising star among the ranks."

"My guy in forensics is trying to put together a 3D model of the knife used," Katie said with a sigh and a shrug. "But it does take time."

Reportedly, there were seven people attending the household that evening: a self-described close friend of the couple, the parents of both the victims, and the victims themselves. Their parents had been brought in to give their statements. The friend had not been located to give his account of the night.

The family members' stories revolved around a similar theme, though the stories start differently, portraying dinner from a different light. They ended precisely the same.

Each said they were outside, enjoying drinks after a long meal together, of which "Romeo and Juliet," as the rags dubbed them, were both in attendance. Everyone claimed they thought the two of them went upstairs to "spend some time together," and the rest of the party just sat outside for a drink. The friend said his goodbyes, exiting the house after everyone else, and had been unreachable since. When they entered the house, they found their children dead.

"Let's begin with the witnesses! I'll need everyone for another round of questioning. I have a keen sense for the smaller details," Stan confidently announced.

"Because you spend every night playing with your small detail." Will laughed.

"If you two are done," Katie said, brushing the smoke from the air, "they are already here, separated inside, different rooms in the back. I'd suggest starting with the father of the girl that died."

"Come, my dear Wilson! We have a case to solve," Stan announced emphatically.

"Will, you know, short for William," Will mumbled as he followed. "I regret every part of what I've done this far in life." Will placed his face into his palms.

Katie grabbed Will's arm. "Will, I don't feel right about this narrative they are telling."

Will kissed her quickly and said, "Don't worry, babe. That's why we're here."

His smile did not satisfy her uneasiness before he turned to walk away.

This wasn't Stan's first rodeo inside the Potstow police department. Normally, he'd be led back in shackles. This time, he was shackle-free, Will following behind, blissfully ignorant of Stan's history with the officers giving them the stink eye as they walked through the department.

They approached the first interrogation room. The father of the deceased girl was anxiously shaking his leg, tapping his fingers on the table. Stan stood, watching him fidget for a moment. Anxiously, the father cast glances at the door, waiting for someone to enter. He kept holding deep breaths, trying to calm himself. Just when he straightened his posture and calmed the persistent quake in his leg, Stan burst the door wide open.

With his lit joint hanging from his mouth and ash flying in every direction, Stan let the lull hold the moment tense, grabbing the seat across from the estranged father. Will placed himself beneath the camera in the corner camouflaging into a nice wallflower.

"So why'd you do it, Craper?" Stan aggressively accused.

Shook with confusion, Mr. Craper stammered his words before nervously asking, "Uh, uhm." He looked to Will in the corner, then back to Stan in front of him. "Can you smoke that in the police station?"

"I'll be asking the questions here, you murderous fuck!" Stan smashed his hands on the table in front of the man. Mr. Craper's body shook from the vibrations traveling through the table his arms rested on.

"Maybe you should dial it down a bit." Will stepped forward, placing his hand on Stan's shoulder when Mr. Craper began whimpering. "He's the first one we've questioned, and we really don't have anything," Will whispered into Stan's ear. Mr. Craper overheard him.

"What is this? Is this good cop, bad cop?" He tried to wipe the tear from his cheek. "Guys, my little girl is…" He struggled to hold his composure, inhaling a long breath. "I promise I'll answer anything to know what happened to my little girl. Please, let's just get this over with," the father said, tapping his fingers impatiently on the table once more.

Stan felt remorseful almost immediately. Taking a deep draw from his slow-burning joint, he leaned back in the chair, sizing up his captive. "What can you tell me about that night?"

"Other than my daughter being poisoned?" Mr. Craper answered in a sarcastic tone. His voice made it clear to Stan the trauma of the night made it hard for him to concentrate on details.

With a disheartened breath, Mr. Craper raised his head from the crippling thoughts running through his mind of whom harmed his daughter. He looked to Stan; Stan, taking another mindless drag, stared right back into his eyes.

"Look, I don't know who really did this. You see, these enemies," Mr. Craper choked, "they aren't real, and my baby girl certainly had nothing to do with it. If you want to find the true culprit of all of this"—he paused for a moment, catching his tongue—"well, they certainly weren't at dinner with us that night."

His tone became unnaturally cool. "The rest of us went outside. My daughter and her fiancé wanted some alone time after a slight disagreement we had with her fiancé's family." He immediately added, "And before you ask, it was not a heated one. We were just trying to figure out who was footing the bill for the concert we were supposed to attend. When her phone rang, my daughter asked if we would 'for the better of the night' all just shelve our emotions, and my wife and I went to the front porch for a drink."

"Well, thank you for your time," Stan said. He and Will exchanged glances; Stan ashed his roach on the table in front of Mr. Craper.

Mr. Craper curled his lips with a fervent look toward Stan.

Stan and Will excused themselves from the room.

"Do you think he's telling the truth?" Stan asked.

"Seems like he has no reason not to," Will spoke. "He's in a lot of pain. I don't think a disagreement over concert tickets would cause some archaic or feudal level of aggression from rivaling houses here. But I think you missed one of those smaller details."

"And what would that be"—Stan cracked a smile—"my dear Wilson?"

"Okay, first, fuck you." Will flipped him the bird, plastering on a clearly fake smile. "And second, pay attention. He said his daughter had a phone call before everyone went outside."

"Good eye, old bean," Stan said through his smirk.

"You're an idiot," replied Will in disgust.

Sticking his head back into the room, he addressed Mr. Craper.

"Do you still have your daughter's phone, Mr. Craper?"

"My wife does. I, uh," Mr. Craper stammered, "I think it's in her purse."

Will closed the door, looking toward Stan.

"Looks like we'll be entering interrogation room 2 next," Stan said, motioning Will toward the room.

Stan approached the door hiding Mrs. Craper, a much calmer presence than her husband. Using a mirror, she started to touch up her lipstick with a darker-red color.

Stan was never great with shades.

Stan entered the room, reaching for another hit, but caught a glimpse of the woman waiting for him and paused. "What can I do for you, boys?" she asked, loudly snapping the mirror shut in her hand and placing it back into her purse.

"We, uh," Stan stumbled, "just spoke with your husband. And he said you…" He stepped closer to the table where Mrs. Craper was seated and looked deep into her—*well, not her eyes.*

"Oh, honey." Her red dress fit tighter than her skin, flowing like an extension of her body with each motion. "Mr. Craper says a lot, and sometimes, he just needs to keep that mouth of his waiting for me." She smiled with a coy look.

Will noticed Mrs. Craper's appearance as well; she had the same hair and bearing of Katie. However, more accentuated outlines crafted the form of Mrs. Craper.

"Your husband, ma'am. He said you might still have your daughter's phone?" Will politely asked.

"Oh." She moaned with exaggeration. "You boys will find out what happened to my baby, won't you?" Reaching into the bag, she pulled out her daughter's phone.

"She didn't keep a lock on it. The children were very open like that," she said in a soft-spoken twang.

They checked the phone log and saw that there was a call from "Sammy<3."

"Who is Sammy?" Stan quickly asked.

"You're going to have to ask the Monteys. He was their son's friend." With a smile, she chewed on her gum.

"I will be sure to do that," Stan replied. "But I'm sure you've heard something about him."

A look of disgust flooded her eyes, accompanied by a scoff. "Look, I already told you, you'll have to ask the Monteys." She averted her eyes and rolled her lips back to the point they almost disappeared. "I don't know who he is."

"Every detail helps," Stan said, raising his eyebrows to Will over his shoulders.

Mrs. Craper scoffed once again. "In the few times we've interacted, he just seemed arrogant and rude."

"Well, thank you for your time." Stan stood from his chair, nodding toward Will. They stepped out of the room with the phone in their possession. Stan turned around to look at his squire.

Will stood next to him, a laconic expression on his face. His mind festered with the malcontent of a seasoned operative, poignant that this would be the deciding case settling his engrossment, or lack thereof, in Stan's affairs. Pressure darkened his intellect. Fading into bleak attempts of conjecture, Will tried to foresee the outcome of this case. Success allowed him to fuel this dependency toward conflict, as the pretension toward strife, and then purpose.

Stan stood opposite him, becoming rubbernecked and elated with a passion he had not felt since the early days on the force. A forlorn drive and ambition, this feeling of resolution, assured that by his hands, he would once again feel the affirmation of being a man: feeling needed and possibly wanted by someone.

For far too long, Stan secluded himself from the outside world, taking these smaller insignificant cases barely sustaining his survival. When he solved this case, it would revise the mark he left on this town. It set him up for a grand entrance to being Potstow's greatest sleuth. The mantle long held, he would fight with rancor and desperation to maintain the title.

An aspiration held by few in Potstow.

"What do you say we get these next two quaking in their loafers, then set out to find this kid?" Stan said in jubilation. Will noticed Stan hadn't reached in his pocket for his pipe as they left the room.

"I'm just your shadow. Either you tell me where to go, or I'm right at your heels," Will sarcastically spouted with a grin.

They entered the holding room of Montey before Stan began his next inquisition; he saw the horror and disparity etched on the man's face.

Carrying a concern unusual for Stan, he walked over to the table where Montey sat, glaring at the man's eyes as he grew closer. Montey did not lift his eyes, nor did he divert his attention when they entered the room. He simply sat somberly in the shadowed, obscured room, staring at the small amount of light illuminating from the lamp perched upon the desk.

Stan sat across from Montey, looking upon his face for a brief moment. Then finally, the palpable grimace broke.

"It's truly a funny thing," Montey said eloquently after taking a deep breath.

"And what's that, Mr. Montey?" asked Stan. Will leaned against a wall in the dark behind him.

"There's no need for the mister, buddy. Just Montey is fine." He callously brushed off Stan's approach. "But still, this all has the feeling of just being the punch line in some sort of cosmic joke." Montey's deranged eyes finally met Stan's for the first time since his ominous entrance. "But do you get it?" he directed back at Stan.

"Well, I can't say I find humor in two dead kids, Montey."

"You don't seem to understand what you've done. You think this is the case, don't you?" The disgruntled father leaned across the desk to his interrogator. "The one to put you back on the map?" He scoffed, leaning back into the shadows.

Will spoke up from the back, "What do you mean?"

"Shadow puppetry," uttered Montey.

Silence. Focus narrowed.

"A form of puppetry that uses cutout figures in a translucent veil of sorts to tell a story through light," he continued.

What's your point?" Stan growled.

"You're the cutout."

In obvious disgust, Montey stretched his arm across the table, grasping the pull cord of the lamp with his hand, yanking it down, leaving the occupants sitting motionless and reticent within the pitch-black room. Stan and Will froze.

"That," Montey said, blanketed in staccato to his awestruck audience through the bleakness of the space. "Did you feel that drunk pensive embrace within that moment, just now, before I spoke, absent even the hum of electricity crossing through the filament of the lamp? How do you measure the depths of silence?

"With pulsating sound," Montey answered his own rhetorical question. "We cannot even appreciate the eloquence of silence without the conundrum of sound." His chuckle approached maniacal. "And the annoyance of it all—that insatiable itch that drives men over the line of sanity! Its presence is the only thing that allows us that moment of bliss in its absence."

Stan and Will remained taciturn in their places.

Montey pulled the cord on the lamp once more.

Stan winced his eyes for a moment, adapting to the light.

"You see, light is the same. We cannot appreciate the light until we've had to suffer the dark." Montey stretched back into his chair with a deep sigh. "You see, Mr. Greene, I know all about you, and you know so little of me. Let me make this clear. My son was my light." He stared straight into Stan's eyes. They were full of woe and regret.

Stan felt like he gazed into a somber reflection, elegantly matching his own.

"In that world of darkness, I did prey." Montey wiped the welling tear from his eye. "It was his birth that finally brought me to the light. He shined bright as the sun to me, and now, all of that has been taken from me, and I once again stalk from the shadows for the rest of my life."

"Montey, I—" Stan was cut off.

"Understand, right!" Montey scoffed. "Or even empathize, maybe?" He glared back at Stan, waiting for another question, but none came. "Most would, or say they would, anyways. Though far too few have truly had their light stricken from this world, taken without a moment's notice. A true 'Candle in the Wind' moment. Too few may have had their hands on the switch, but they don't truly understand." Montey spoke his hand, pulling on the lamp's cable, illuminating the light once again.

"It's just funny how someone has to turn off the lights for you to realize just how dark it can get." Montey brushed his hand toward the lamp, shoving it off the table, where it crashed on the floor. The bulb shattered, leaving the room in darkness, accompanied by a sullen dread.

Stan wondered how he would feel to hear about his own son's death.

Calling their relationship strained would be giving Stan more credit than he deserved.

Even so, the news would obliterate him. Stan stood from the table, motioning Will to follow him out of the room.

"Did you catch anything in that?" Stan asked hopefully.

Will shrugged, carrying a "how the hell would I know" look on his face.

"What?" Stan laughed. "Never had to interrogate someone, Mister Special Forces? I gotta go paint the toilet Potstow green, if you know what I mean."

"All right, I'm going to go find Katie. She told me earlier I'd need to grab the evidence tags to match at the crime scene."

Will started walking back to the bullpen. Sticking his hands in his pockets, he found "Juliet's" phone. He began to scroll through the messages between her and the son's friend, Sammy. After finishing reading about a week's worth of messages, Stan returned from the restroom.

"Ready for the missus?" Stan stretched his hands over his head, tipping his hat from the top of his head.

While Stan adjusted his hat, Will answered, "Absolutely." He followed his associate toward interrogation room 4. "By the way, I read some of those messages, and I think our Juliet was more acquainted to Romeo's friend than we were led to believe." Before they entered the door, Will scrolled through the explicit messages for Stan.

Stan opened the door to the interrogation room, immediately questioning Mrs. Montey. "Let's skip the part where I lose my shit, and you just tell me what I want to know." He slammed his hands down on the table. "Who is this Sammy, and why was he sexting your son's fiancé?"

"Oh dear." Mrs. Montey nervously started playing with her hands and biting on her lip. She stammered, reaching for a cigarette, "Uhm, well, they had dated once before. But it wasn't an issue!" she exclaimed. "My son said they had worked it out, but they were just friends."

"Mrs. Craper tells a different story—"

"Of course she would," Mrs. Montey meddled.

"And friends don't do the things Sammy was talking about doing to your son's future wife, Mrs. Montey." Stan became irritable. "I've had a mom, Mrs. Montey. Certainly, you'd know if there was a chance this kid was jealous she had someone she was about to marry? Any chance, at all, that this kid could have been unhappy about the situation?"

Terror overtook Mrs. Montey; she shifted her gaze around the room, and she began to sniffle. "All I really know about him is that he was a driver for the local taxi service known as HyRides. Do you really think he was capable?" A hopeful tone in her voice rubbed Will the wrong way.

Stan sat back into his seat with a smile. Turning to Will, he said, "We need to find that kid."

"These things happen. The ebb and flow of the universe, testing our resolve. If we are judged worthy, like Job before us, we will be given twofold from the Lord," Mrs. Montey religiously chanted in a melancholy, unexpected tone.

"That's a strange perspective to take about the death of your son," Will the wallflower murmured uncomfortably.

"He's not my only son," she eerily spoke. "There will be a chance for the others to stand before their father's light. It's just the universe balancing itself and all."

Stan and Will left briefly after that. Each stammered to ask another question; both became dumbfounded by the answer they would most likely receive. They silently decided to simply nod and leave the room.

"What the fuck was that?" Will exclaimed once they got outside of the station.

"Yeah, I need a smoke," Stan said, feeling up his jacket for his stash.

The New Deal

"Stephens!" Thomas barked, descending the staircase into the kitchen of his old ranch home. "Bring the car around!"

Thomas couldn't remember a single day in his life without being under the watch of the dutiful eyes of a man named Steven Prescott Finns. Not until his father's death did it occur to Thomas that he did not know the story of how his driver and protector came to be such a huge influence in his life.

Approaching the counter, he retrieved a fresh mug of coffee when he heard Stephen's reply from the patio steps, "Right away, boss." Taking a sip from his coffee, he listened to the scraping of the old barn door opening, Stephens retrieving the car. Taking a bite from a slice of toast without butter, he heard the engine turn over. The car did not move.

Stephens sat in the car with its transmission in drive but his foot holding the brake, watching mindfully at the kitchen window. He watched Thomas wipe his face with his napkin before pulling the car forward, with the intention of arriving at the foot of the patio steps, parking the car, and exiting the vehicle to open the door just as Thomas took the last step. He did not wish to bring Thomas anxiety by sitting outside the porch, waiting for him.

Stephens was rare to let down his employer in this regard.

"What's on the agenda for today?" Stephens greeted, opening the door for a worn and tired-looking Mr. Killian.

Thomas took a deep breath, gaining a very intimidating smile and a look in his eyes that Stephens was not accustomed to seeing.

"Destiny," Thomas proclaimed. "Stephens, ole boy. Destiny."

The words leaped from Thomas's lips, chilling Stephens to his core. He knew the city council had been criticizing Thomas as of late, making him rather desperate for any recourse.

Stephens wanted to ask, How do you suppose to go about that? but thought better of it.

Plausible deniability and all.

He simply offered the door for his employer and briskly returned to the driver side door of the old powder-blue Cadillac Fleetwood, a remnant of better times for Thomas.

If Stephens knew the intent, the malice, the forlorn palliation of a broken Thomas, he would never have chauffeured him that day. He would have never even let Thomas leave the house.

The sun was rising over the horizon behind the car at the precise angle to blind its driver. The driver, deciding to take the long way around the city, felt the intensity of the rage fuming in the seat behind him since they left the house.

Mr. Killian became very animated while they drove by along the flourishing businesses growing on their path. His anger and fury grew into contempt, expressed physically through the muscles in his furrowed brow. The driver would never ask why Mr. Killian was very private in this anger; the driver knew far better than to ask.

The city's growth was supposed to bolster Killian's Distribution to the top.

Growth, prosperity, and riches—these words were used in the promise when they came to petition his vote for annexation. Thomas thought about his employees, his drivers, his secretaries, his board of directors, his family, his Gracie. If Gracie only knew about all the things required for Thomas to secure all the comforts she called home.

The thought of interrupting her ignorance with his financial struggles made Thomas shiver in the back seat. His dark-green eyes darted toward his phone. Thomas snarled, "He's normally awake by now. Where is he?"

His thoughts drifted immediately toward the worst-case scenario possible. *"It was all a sting. They were one step ahead of him once again, ready to pull the rug out from under him. Jacob is in prison, and he hasn't said a word."*

Thomas found his loyalty priceless. Jacob knew that Thomas retained the best lawyers; would build a hard, rock-solid defense; and get Jacob out of the clinker, even if it was the last thing Thomas would do. His faith was well-placed.

Thomas could not watch Jacob be punished for Thomas's crimes; he would never allow that for anyone. Thomas's body itched with the waning, fading chances of success, and then he understood. Devoid of hope, fell thoughts took hold within the recesses of his mind. His back fell into his seat, amid of the chasms of disparity between him and the likelihood of achieving his goal.

"Great, just what I need now," Mr. Killian mumbled; the driver knew better than to do anything but ignore. Thomas placed the phone back into his shirt pocket just as it began to ring. Jacob McKinney glowed from the phone's screen. A sigh of relief released the unflattering furrow existing in his brow when he answered his phone.

"Yeah," Mr. Killian barked, keeping the conversation brief, in case the scenarios played out similarly in his head.

"I hope I caught you before you made it to the office," McKinney responded.

"En route."

"Well, the meeting with the craft beer guys went great—"

"Of course it went great. They're going to be making bank on us selling their product. I don't care about the craft beer guys. Of course, they were going to say yes regardless of the terms. They don't have to deal with the ridiculous taxes the city imposes on us!" Mr. Killian's anger broiled beneath the surface.

Jacob detected Thomas's anger, even in the absence of video.

"**My** desire is to know about **her**." His voice calmed, emphasizing the words; he returned to his curt nature. "Did she think she could do it?"

"That was why I wanted to catch you before you made it to the office. She does, but she said it's going to cost a substantial amount. With our current situation, I didn't think—" Jacob was cut short.

"I don't pay you to think! Let me worry about **my** situation. Get back ahold of her and tell her money is no object!" Thomas's voice skewed harsh, sounding like a rough growl.

"Sir, I'm just concerned, where are we going to get that kind of money?" Thomas knew Jacob's apprehensions originated from a place of concern, not just for his job but also for a man whom he held great respect. Thomas could not care less.

"Let me worry about where we will find the money. We just need to get out ahead of them. Before they try something else. They've been trying to run me out of town, and I won't have it." Mr. Killian's voice howled like it belonged to another. "I was here first, and I'll be damned if they end this with the upper hand."

In times like these, Thomas missed the analog days. The amount of frustration exuded from slamming down the phone, even car phones, once helped him vent his anger and surmounting rage toward the system built to weigh against him. Jacob understood his boss hanging up the phone brutally; he inherently comprehended the weight on Thomas's shoulders. Though he rarely voiced it anymore, *Thomas appreciated this, compensating Jacob handsomely for it.*

"Sir, we're getting close to the office," the driver informed his boss.

"Stephens, I need you to take me somewhere else, but I need you to forget where you take me."

"I've already forgotten, sir." Stephens nodded, turning the rearview mirror to look into the mad eyes of Thomas. "Tell me when to turn."

"Take this left up here." Thomas growled from the back seat. Stephens followed his boss's command like a well-trained dog. "There will be a right up ahead, down a gravel road. Take that."

This road brought up memories for Thomas. He had not been out this far in years. The fields surrounded the road, aged and hardly recognizable, as was he. It was covered with cannabis, growing as far as the eye could see. Thomas found it ironic the use of the land did not change. Instead of growing large houses hiding what was growing inside of them, these areas were now openly growing right in plain sight.

Thomas, never against legalization, hated what legalization had become—to him, at least. The sight fell deeply upon Thomas, anger festering from it, peeling back a seemingly healed wound.

Stephens tried to not ask questions, as he always did, following his boss's commands swiftly as the words would leave his lips.

"That charred building there, on the right."

Stephens quickly pulled the car into the small parking lot outside the charred remnants of a building. Thomas looked out the windows of his luxury sedan.

"Dammit, of course he's going to make me wait!"

Stephens hoped for his own sake whoever had been inclined to make his boss wait hurried. "Would you like me to turn on the radio?" Before Thomas could make a prudish grunt, Stephens swiftly turned on the volume of the radio, tuning it to the local college station. The static of the radio startled his boss.

"Err… yeah, sure…" grunted Thomas. Leaning back into his seat, he crossed his arms impatiently.

The guitar solo from the Beatles's "While My Guitar Gently Weeps" cut through the static on the radio, and the group was doing their "ohs" when Stephens began to pray for a release of the tension.

The disc jockey abruptly stopped the fading of the guitar solo into nothingness. The boring drawl of the midmorning DJ broke the gaps of empty noise on the air, explaining it was from "The White Album." When a car entered across the parking lot facing Thomas and his loyal driver, Stephens's subtle prayer was answered.

"Finally," Thomas snarled, kicking open his door.

Stephens stepped out of his door and circled behind the car to his boss's door.

He had already missed this opportunity to let his boss out of the car. He would be damned to slight him again by not opening the door for him to get back into his seat swiftly.

Thomas made his way over to the newly present luxury car and entered the back seat. When he closed the door behind him, it began to rain.

Stephens quickly gathered the umbrella from the trunk.

"Thomas, it's been a while. How have you been?"

Mr. Killian looked in his seat at the man greeting him. "I've been much better, Francis," howled Thomas. "It seems as though you're doing better?" Thomas motioned to the cannabis growing all around the charred warehouse where they last met.

"Yeah, legalization and decriminalization have done well for the farmer as of late." Francis smiled heavily, looking upon Thomas. "Hell, we've got so much pot we can't even sell it all, and believe me"—he laughed—"we're still selling it hand over fist." Thomas's companion stared blankly; a thought overwhelmed him so much he brought it to voice. "What do you call an item in an economy that has both a high demand and an almost equally infinitesimal supply." He answered his own rhetorical question, "Cash crops."

"Wait, do you mean you have supply just going to waste?" Thomas asked; his prayers were being answered.

"Well, 'waste,' no. What doesn't get turned into some form of smoke or oil gets harvested and turned into oil, fuel, or textiles." Francis looked away longingly. "It's just a shame to not let it all go to smoke."

Thomas marveled at himself. "I don't mean to seem too forward. I know it's been a while since we've done business together." He embraced Francis on the shoulder. "But I think we can help each other in this regard." Thomas shook his right hand. A grim realization washed over him.

While Thomas shook Francis's hand, he noticed a ring that had not been there in the years previous. Thomas kept his poker face stiff. He did not want this contact to be aware that, now, he knew.

His phone chimed and vibrated.

"I'm so sorry," Thomas apologized, retrieving it from his pocket.

"No worries," Francis replied. "We're both businessmen. I completely understand."

Stephens flashed his badge to the security guard, pulling into Killian's Distribution.

Mr. Killian growled to himself in the back seat, Stephens assumed because another tractor trailer parked overnight, blocking the entrance of his trucks in the morning to get out on time.

He did not see the fencing in the back of the office building that had fallen.

"And the cops won't do nothing about it."

Thomas didn't wait for Stephens to place the transmission into Park before kicking the back door open, stepping to the ground.

"I'm so sorry, sir," Stephens spoke, slamming on the brakes and slapping the transmission while the car ground out of gear.

Thomas pressed forward, unaware of Stephens's apology. He made his way into the back door of the warehouse.

Opening the door, Thomas heard the voices of his board members hush from their previous conversations.

"Hush! It's the boss."

"Yeah, it's the boss."

Thomas entered the warehouse through a pitch-black corridor. He could see light bending from around the corner through the doorway, but it was much darker than normal. The building itself was illuminated by only two lights hanging from the ceiling above the center loading area. Beneath the lighting stood three of his closest men.

"McDaniels." Thomas grunted and nodded toward two of them. "Sully." He nodded toward the other.

"Boss," echoed the chorus of the group.

"Where's Hedeon?"

"Picking up the girl." Sully sported a large smile, continuing, "Apparently, he had trouble."

"You're kidding me."

The front door burst forth, and Hedeon walked through the door with a blindfolded woman, bound and gagged, kicking and fighting, draped over his shoulders.

"I told you to be courteous, Hedeon." Thomas growled. "What the hell do you think you're doing?"

"Boss," Hedeon pleaded, "she jumped me before I even knocked on her door. She bit a chunk of my ear off!" He showed Thomas the opposite side of his face, the blood yet to clot.

"Fuck," Thomas said, astonished. "Why didn't you go with him?" He turned on the other three.

"She's a hundred forty pounds, soaked and wet."

"Didn't realize what was going on."

"Hedeon told me he had it." Their voices grunted, ashamed of their responses.

The woman stopped kicking and fighting against Hedeon.

"Sully!" Thomas barked. "Go get our guest a seat. Hedeon," he bound upon the large man, "set her down. Now tell me, why did you tie her up?"

"I tried to run away, boss, I swear." Hedeon sat down his prisoner and removed the blindfold.

The lady grunted, as if denying his story.

"I'll get to you!" Thomas snarled toward the captive; she went silent. "Go on, Hedeon."

"She just kept at me." Hedeon's accent was protruding as his story prolonged. "I tried telling her you wanted to talk, but she started kicking me in the crotch, started trying to tie me up. After, we fought some more. I had to take her with me before the cops were called."

"What a mess you've made." Thomas shook his head disapprovingly, rubbing his brow with his forefinger and thumb.

Sully arrived with the seat. Placing it behind the guest, he forced her into it.

She grunted and fought to stand but relented when Sully moved her back into the seat.

"Now for you." Thomas howled toward his unwilling guest. He walked over to remove the gag from her mouth.

The lady took this moment to spit into the face of her kidnapper's conspirator.

Mr. Killian wiped the spit away and replaced the rope gag.

"You've caused quite a stir for me lately. My old allies have turned against me, I can only assume extorted by information against them. With you in town, I'm sure it's been you that has been meddling."

Thomas paced back and forth, contemplating the destiny of his unwanted and unwilling captive.

"Now you may ask yourself, 'Well, where does that place me?'" Thomas silenced himself, continuing pacing in front of her. He retrieved a cigarette from his suit jacket, placing it upon his lips.

She sat still, feeling the tense emotion building within her captor.

Thomas turned toward her seat. Pulling a handgun from his side holster, he took aim. He growled. "Well, I'm afraid that places you in the Mad Dog's path."

He pulled the trigger, and flames emitted from its tip.

Stanley Act III Scene I

"To smoke or not to smoke?" Stan sat up in the passenger seat bereft from his seat belt. His hand entered his satchel to retrieve his stash, silently answering his inquiry before his tongue rattled the words. "That is the question."

"Whether 'tis nobler to suffer in this life with the sorrows of outrageous accusations," Stan turned his body toward Will, lifting his eyebrows, accompanied by a tempting smile, "or take arms against this blasphemer theory, of heretical augment?" The private eye boldly spoke and broke up the bud upon his satchel's leather flap. "The high, the cloud, the ambience of ambrosia-scented strain." Using his right hand, he retrieved a rolling paper from his shirt pocket.

"The heartache of the chosen sobriety." The investigator folded a quarter of the rolling paper, lightly pressing in the corners of the fold. "Not to consume or take even communion," Stan shook his head briefly, "though devoutly be wished." He nudged Will with his elbow and a smile, taking a pinch from the satchel.

"To toke," then a second pinch, "to smoke," and followed immediately by a third. "To smoke, perchance grant buzz." Stan looked to Will once more for affirmation. "Aye, the contact." Will shook his head disapprovingly.

Ignoring him, Stan continued, "For such layman conversations may come." He tightened the bud against the hemp rolling paper. "We must lament the insolence of pride." The bud grabbed the edge of the paper, like a child gathering its blanket for bed. "Pause for the cause in tribute to the calamity of this long life." Stan stuck his tongue out of his mouth and ran the light paste across it. Carefully, he finished the roll sealing the joint.

He paused momentarily before retracting his tongue. "For who bears the whips of authority are shackled by the decree of the oppressor." Waving the doobie matter-of-factly at his driver, he stuck the joint within his cheek to moisten it. "Tongues fall from their mouths," he mumbled while rolling his jay to gather spit. When he was satisfied with its dampness, he spoke, "Do their minds follow?" He flicked Will's BIC and dried the paper on its flame. "May they break free from their bond of virtue."

Stan placed the joint on his lips, flicking the BIC once more. "Oh, blessed moment when the flame first takes." He inhaled deeply, applying the flame to the jay's end, pocketing the lighter. He exhaled the cloud of smoke in the car. "So that air itself can erupt with taste."

"This euphoric bliss ascends so high," he offered the jay to Will, who waived to decline. Stan shrugged, taking another hit before shaking his head to resolve. "And wastes your worries with a weary sigh."

Stan sat staring at the spliff he was toying between his fingers lovingly. "Oh, such pleasure," he accentuated, "would need fuel to tinder." Stan placed it on his lips. "The spirit designed with a thirst provoked."

"A veil that Death allowed to linger." The intrepid poet paused. Will assumed he finished, but Stan continued. "Like ashes left laggard in a lapsed mem'ry," Stan mumbled, watching Potstow pass by the windows tinted by the smoke laid heavily in Will's car.

"It makes us rather mourn these ills spoken." His voice was gaining emphasis. "Then bare the blasphemous tongues of our foes." Stan began to take a long drag; as he exhaled, he prolonged. "Thus, conscience makes a skeptic of us all." The gumshoe took a small toke, adding, "And thus truth smothered beneath the rubble."

"Only lethargy empowers the fool," he spoke phlegmatically, "when our foundations falter to discord." Stan held the roach carefully to avoid burning himself while he hit it some more. "To this regard, we caution our action, of vigilantes false identities." When it became apparent he was burning more flesh than bud, Stan stubbed the burning cherry in his fingertips.

Stan stared at the roach in his hand, a mournful look on his face. "Oh, dear, Mary, the nymph in my dreams." He rolled the window down and tossed it out the window as he resolved. "Where all my sins remember'd."

"Good Lord, Stan." Will finally broke his silence. He applied pressure to his blinker.

This signaled his future tangent, like a civilized human being.

He pulled into the driveway at the crime scene. "'Course you'd be most poetic about your weed," he mused.

"Thanks for the ride, boy." Stan stepped out of the car, and with a look toward the victims' house, he added, "Well, well, well."

Police tape roped off the front door of the house displaying "DO NOT CROSS" to all of whom that would approach. Chuckling at the sight, Stan began encircling the house. Will gathered the case notes and house key from Katie; he walked straight to the porch to unlock the door.

"What was all that for?" Will inquired when Stan finished his circle.

Stan ignored him and the police line. Opening the door, he was shocked to see a dry puddle of blood pooled in front of the threshold. He stepped through the doorway anyways, stretching the police tape until it snapped around him, entering into a foyer attached directly to an open concept dining room. A chalk outline lay across the floor near the pool of dried blood in front of the door; another adorned the floor by the dining room table.

Instantaneously, Stan's pipe appeared in his hand. Landing his steps lackadaisically, he ventured over to an empty counter space. Will followed as if he was playing crime scene hopscotch. His eyes darted around the room at the exhibit numbers strewn across the house, cross-referencing them to his notes. He blindly bumped into Stan as he pulled his stash from his pocket.

"Watch it, you loaf!" Stan growled. "Gonna make me spill my stash."

He calmed his tone once he saw that none of it was lost. He took a bud from his bag, breaking it upon the empty counter. "Strange, the son was stabbed right in front of the door." He packed the broken bud into his pipe. "Yet not one of the family members talked about it." Stan flicked a lighter and puffed from his pipe, resuming his walk to the dining room.

Another chalk outline of the daughter's body lay by the end of the table. Stan pulled out the seat next to it, allowing himself to sit.

"Shouldn't you be wearing gloves?" Will asked.

"Probably," Stan spoke, then smoked. He eyed the table as curiously as Will eyed him. "Something's missing here." Stan pointed with his pipe to an empty spot on the table where the evidence tags were set before returning the pipe back into its rightful place upon his lips. Dashing his thumb across the lighter's flint to take another drag from his pipe, he looked to his hand in confusion.

"You'll not damn me to the tenth circle of Hell," Stan threw Will's lighter at him with force, "you cambion."

Will laughed. "Dude, there's only nine circles of Hell."

"It's elementary, my dear Wilson." Chuckling, Stan cashed his pipe into his hand, placing the ash into the empty spot on the table. "At the depths of the ninth circle of Hell, sits Lucifer, freezing in the lake of fire, in his mouths the greatest betrayers to mankind." Delving his hand into his stash, Stan retrieved a small bud to situate in his pipe. "Well, what only a few scholars, such as myself, know is at the pits of the ninth circle lies Lucifer's little bum, of which houses the domain of the tenth circle of Hell, for the ultimate betrayers of mankind—lighter thieves." Igniting a match, he lit his pipe.

Will fumed at his response but decided better than to argue over the details of the afterlife. "So she got a phone call. Asked the families to stop bickering. Left the table to take said phone call," he summarized.

"Then returned to the table where she fell over, convulsed, and vomited until she died," Stan said, pointing to the chalk outline near the table. "It's all too peculiar." Stan leaned the chair back on its hind legs, rocking himself in thought as he lit his pipe to smoke. Stan lifted his head toward the back door. "The Crapers said they went outside after the phone call, right?'

"Yeah," Will confirmed.

Stan stood from his seat and carefully made his way past the pool of dried blood, through the kitchen to the back door. He chopped with his pipe hand through the police line. Standing on the back patio in silence, he took in the scene. "Katie said they haven't found the murder weapon for the son." Stan rubbed his eyes, then his chin. "There's no smearing in the blood and no trail of blood from the weapon." He took a deep hit, letting out a bellow of smoke while he continued, "It's almost as if the weapon never left the scene."

"Look, Katie isn't that bad at her job. She was the first on the scene." Will spoke angrily in defense of his fiancé. "I'm pretty sure she would've noticed the knife sticking out of his body."

"I know, I know. I meant no offense by it," Stan said defensively before he toked again. "We just gotta find that kid, Sammy. He's the missing link to all of this."

The name reminded Will of the text in the victim's phone, received a month ago. "Speaking of Sammy, he sent our Juliet a text about meeting her out back. Maybe there's something out there that ties it all together."

Stan thought it a fool's errand but, nonetheless, appeased his friend's wishes, stepping off the patio to take a brisk look around in the yard. Will walked around the back side of the house, while Stan absentmindedly wandered toward the tree line beyond the backyard, smoking his pipe, deep in thought.

It all seemed a little too wrapped with a bow, delicately written as a part of a narrative, but the evidence did not match the story.

Stan drifted farther into the woods, absentmindedly thinking about the crime scene and the interrogations, trying to make sense of the narrative.

He was eventually brought back to awareness when he stubbed his toe on a decrepit old brick wall barely sticking up out of the ground.

"Hey! Where'd you go?" Will yelled from the patio at the house.

"Out here!" Stan replied as he sat on the small wall, rubbing his foot from the pain.

Will followed Stan's path through the woods behind the house. "Holy shit!" Will yelled, catching up with Stan on his wall. "You think they went in that?" He pointed to a tree house nestled cozily, high in a tree above Stan.

Stan tilted his head with a look of bewilderment at the small cabin nestled above him. "Maybe." Sticking his pipe in his pocket, he brushed off the dirt accumulated on the back side of his coat. "Only one way to find out."

The tree house appeared to be intended for much younger kids than the victims and looked untouched by the passing of time—a relic of childish glamour no one ever wanted to harm. Inside that relic, however, told a different story. There was a small air mattress and sleeping bag, perfect for stargazing while lying across the floor. The small campsite was lined with the usual decor associated with "getting off the grid." A river ran not far from the camp, a firepit with logs, unburned, waiting for a fire.

Amid the childish allure and bohemian adornment tattered across this utopian refuge, there lay a knife, splashed in blood, on the floor of the tree house.

"Better call Katie," Stan said with glee, placing his pipe to his mouth in satisfaction. "I think we just cracked the case."

A Scandal in Potstow

"Yes, Jacob, I understand." Sarahn laughed mockingly over her phone. "Your wife hired a private investigator, and he's got something from that dinner the other week.

"No, I really don't want my face plastered over divorce court either," she responded condescendingly toward the mansplaining she was receiving on the phone. Lowering the phone from her ear, she shook her head in annoyance, looking up the Draper's Properties sign.

"Yes, I have heard of this dick, Stan Greene.

"Look, Jacob, you're just going to have to let me take care of it. You're just going to have to pay me my usual fee."

This statement annoyed Jacob, but he agreed before abruptly ending the call.

From the sidewalk, Sarahn looked to the third-floor windows. Not a single light was shining across the entire floor. She stepped toward the double doors, her hand outstretched to grab the handle, but the door opened for her.

"What brings you here so early in the morning?" The voice of the short, portly property owner holding the door greeted her.

"Oh, thank you. I actually have a meeting with a certain private eye."

"Well, now I know you're lying."

Sarahn was taken back, rarely having been called out for a lie. "What do you mean?" she said, her voice drenched in disbelief.

"There's no way in hell that dick is awake right now." He laughed, making his way over to his desk across from the stairs.

Sarahn eyed the awkward landlord in a confused manner as he continued his path to his desk, leaving her to her own accord. Sarahn debated whether to continue up the stairs or leave now before she created a further impression.

Both felt like weak approaches, but to continue up the stairs would lead her toward her destination, so up the stairs she proceeded.

The property owner paid her no more mind. She shamefully ascended the staircase.

Mounting the third floor, she made the familiar left turn down the hallway toward the door with the glass windowpane. The window, intact in all its glorious splendor, impeded the darkness coming from the other side.

Sarahn retrieved a key from her pocket and approached the knob. Attempting to insert the key into the hole, she realized the door wasn't closed entirely. She shook her head; replacing the key in her pocket, she let herself through the door.

A snore came from the couch across the room. Sarahn silently shut the door behind her, surveying the room. There was laundry strewn out across the room, from his desk in his office space to the refrigerator in the kitchen.

"Oh, Stanley," Sarahn whispered to herself, finding a candle to illuminate the room.

Stan's snores masked the sounds of Sarahn quickly searching Stan's desk for a file with the photographs in it. Fortunately for Sarahn, she knew and understood Stan's Neanderthal filing system; she searched the uppermost areas for the files most relevant to what he was working currently.

She sat and read over his synopsis notes on his latest case. She shook her head toward his written conclusion. Eventually, she found Jacob's files among the rubble and the photograph Stan was using to sell the charade.

"The waitress." She smiled and looked over to Stan, grunting and scratching his ass unconsciously. "That had to be your friend's idea. You're not personable enough for something like that."

She unlatched her bra. Then she unbuttoned her pants. She stripped off her shirt, wrapping the most harmful picture in the center of all her clothes, folding them around it. She retrieved one of Stan's white dress shirts from the back of his chair, sliding her hands through the sleeves, buttoning only one or two buttons with clear intentions.

Sarahn crossed the room to the kitchen area, embraced by Stan's snores in the background. Moving a pile of clothes from in front of the refrigerator, she opened the door.

The refrigerator was mostly empty, except for bacon and eggs. She sniffed the bacon, questioning its expiration; she stared at the date upon the egg carton inquisitively.

Finding a small griddle near the sink, Sarahn turned it on to medium. She laid four pieces of bacon across the griddle, searing the meat to the pan. Then she cracked an egg beside them.

A sweet aroma filled the apartment, bacon sizzling on the griddle. A few moments passed without the chorus of Stan's snores accompanying the bacon.

"I see you stirring over there, Stanley," Sarahn spoke with her back toward him. "Come, I've made bacon and eggs." She turned, curling an index finger toward Stan on the couch.

Slowly rising from his sofa, Stan lifted his hat from his eyes. He placed his feet on the floor and stared at her.

After a few precious moments, he pulled out his pipe, struck a match across its box's strip, and took a long drag.

"Sarahn." He enveloped himself within a cloud of smoke. "Let yourself in, I see."

"Yeah, you looked like you were having a good dream." She turned her back to him once more to attend the skillet. "I didn't want to wake you."

"And that was before or after you broke in?"

"Oh, do you want me to leave? I do hope you don't need this shirt." She watched his eyes trace her outline to her bare legs. She smiled while she walked across the room and wrapped her arms around his neck.

Stan looked up at her. As she took the hat off his head, he puffed a cloud between them. "That's my favorite shirt. Im'a need that back."

"Just eat your eggs. I've missed you," she added sweetly.

She shoved a plate of food into his hands and started to fix herself one. Making her way back over to the couch with a full plate, she took a seat, placing the plate balanced on the arm.

"So," Stan paused to relight his pipe, his eyes full of suspicion, "what did you and ole McKinney talk about?"

"Always working, are you?" Furrowing her eyes at him, Sarahn shoveled eggs into her mouth, ignoring his inquiry.

"I'm just trying to figure out why you're here. I thought you made it clear enough, you didn't want to see me again."

"Well, I've heard you've become Potstow's favorite patsy," she sung as her refrain. "I just had to come experience that for myself."

Stan eyed the eggs on his plate suspiciously, looking back to Sarahn.

"It's not poisoned." Sarahn spat. "Honestly, if I wanted you dead, it's not like it would be hard. Your door wasn't even closed," she said pointedly.

"What do you want?" Stan asked, ignoring her jibe.

"I need a place to stay for a few weeks," she murmured, crossing her legs on the couch next to him. She enjoyed watching him splash about. "I have business in town."

"And that business being?" Stan asked in an elongate phrase, trying to make eye contact with Sarahn, though she kept avoiding his gaze.

"Nothing that would concern you…" she quickly added, "… yet, anyways," before shoving more fried eggs into her mouth.

"Should I be concerned about becoming your," he paused for a moment to remember her phrasing, "patsy, was it?"

"If everything goes to plan." She looked back at him for a brief moment with an eager smile, as if watching Stan smash upon the jagged rocks at her shore. "Yeah."

He puffed again from his pipe, contemplating her last refrain, further ignoring his eggs.

She watched Stan break off small pieces of bacon with his hand to toss them in his mouth between drags on his pipe.

Sarahn ate the remnants on her plate, while Stan nibbled and puffed from his pipe. Slowly, they began to nestle together on the couch, Sarahn inching closer and closer to him when he became lost in thought. The sun commenced to rise through the window, and Sarahn broke the silence.

"The Greeks believed Apollo would drag the sun and moon across the sky every day," she said quietly. "Fascinating, they thought their gods would care for them so much. Yet now we realize it's the absence of anything at all that is moving, surrounding us, the sun and the stars, and the distance between them all, that is actually holding everything together." She turned to look at Stan to apologize for everything that happened between them. Just as quickly as the urge arose, it passed, and she turned around, with her back to him.

Sarahn felt his arm wrap around her shoulder. She pulled her knees close to her chest, melding into his side, as if two pieces of a puzzle sliding into place for the few brief moments they are out of the box before they are torn apart and placed away from the light in a forgotten closet, rarely opened.

Stan left with his sidekick prior to Sarahn exiting his office. She retrieved all her belongings, reluctantly tossing his lucky shirt on his desk. She burned the illicit photograph into crumbling ash.

"There," she spoke to herself. "Knowing Stan, he's already deleted the digital copy."

The thief took one last look around his apartment before departing. It was like taking a step into a portal in time. Nothing had changed between them; he was still as mysterious and unemotional as ever.

She walked down the steps of Draper's Properties and out the double doors onto the sidewalk of Ocean Boulevard. The sun was approaching a sunset in the sky as she sauntered toward her hotel.

She craved a bath and a nice long nap. A nice hot shower with steam condensing on the tile walls sounded pretty good too. She may be gone from the world for hours, reemerging clean and proper. She laughed to herself, thinking about that wonderful feeling in store for her.

Sarahn entered her hotel's lobby. Stepping into the elevator, she noticed a large man not breaking eye contact with her. Alarmed, she got off with a fellow passenger on the floor below her room. She took the stairs, the final flight.

When she reached the hallway, the large man was already at her door, knocking.

"Please, miss, I'm not here to hurt you." He spoke with a heavy accent. "My boss is just wanting to talk."

Sarahn slowly backed into the stairwell, trying to not gather the large man's attention. "Great, it's the big guy." She cracked the door to scope her prey.

He had at least one hundred pounds on her, and that was his own fault. His morning Snickers Ice Cream Bars and a diet that would make a diabetic's toes curl in ecstasy seem a bit intentional.

Sarahn knew that in order to take him, she needed to do it quickly and precisely. No mistakes. No excuses would be accepted. The thief retrieved the compressed rope from her bag, then stashed the bag in the darkness of the stairwell.

She let out the slack on the rope to each side of her, wrapping her hands once each. She remembered the days in the southern Chinese mountain range training with her Taoist Shifu. The rope dart was a difficult weapon to master; she did not consider herself to be a master in any sense, but it was now or never.

Sarahn swung the stairwell doorway, setting off at a full sprint, dragging the slack through the doorway behind her. The large man only noticed Sarahn after she made it halfway through the hallway between them.

"Oh, there you are, miss," the large man said, unaware of the yellow jacket nest stirring beneath his feet. "Please come with me. Mr. Kill—"

Before he could finish his sentence, Sarahn kicked him square in the nuts, bringing the large man to a kneel. She clapped her hands around both of his ears to discombobulate him.

The large man groaned, continuing to both knees, concussed by the clap.

Sarahn wrapped the large man with her rope as fast as she could, trying to tie his hands behind his back.

Before she fastened his feet to his hands, he snapped back to consciousness, stepping to his feet to place his center of gravity beneath him. He wrenched his arms to break slack into the knot binding his hands.

Sarahn kicked the back of his knees, dropping him to the ground once more. Only one knee gave way to the force; he freed one hand as he knelt. Sarahn threw a strike to his Adam's apple to collapse his windpipe. With his free hand, he blocked and grappled his assailant, tossing her over his shoulder, slamming her to the ground.

"Please, miss. Don't do this," the large man pleaded to Sarahn. "My boss just wants to talk."

Sarahn gripped his arm, rolling her body across his shoulders, locking her legs on his other arm. The man slammed her into the wall, removing the momentum for her throw. Attempting to wrap the rope around his neck, she slid down his back to the floor.

The large man grabbed the rope as she jammed her knee into his back to gain leverage. The large, accented man bounced her loudly from one wall to the other, trying to break her grasp on the rope. When she finally relented, he broke free from her hold, sprinting for the elevators.

Sarahn grabbed her rope, running for the stairwell. Taking a flight at a time, jumping between the rails, she made the lobby doorway. The large man exited the elevator, and their eyes met over the heads of the other tenants of the hotel.

He rushed for the front door, Sarahn gaining distance behind him. Pushing through the door, he darted toward his vehicle down the alley around the corner. He reached his driver-side door and fumbled with his keys. Exasperated, he looked over both his shoulders. It seemed as though he lost her.

Finally gripping the correct key, he sighed as he slipped the key into the keyhole. Unlocking his car door felt like a release of the tension the last ten minutes had surmounted that he desperately desired.

Unfortunately, this peace was provided only because Sarahn was gaining a height advantage and leaped from two stories above him, landing on his back. After cracking his head off the roof of his car, she tried to shake her aggressor.

"Enough!" the large man wailed, gripping Sarahn by her auburn hair. He tore her from his back, slamming her to the sidewalk.

Sarahn screamed out in pain and made a final attempt to subdue her victim. He grabbed both of her hands, lifting her feet from the ground.

"Will you stop?"

She swung her body forward, biting his ear. In his terror, with blood spewing from his face, he slammed her to the ground once more.

Sarahn employed the damsel-in-distress defense and yelled for help. The large man knew he needed to act fast; grabbing her rope, he wrestled and hog-tied her on the sidewalk. He used the excess rope to gag her from yelling. Though she never stopped fighting, he tossed her into the back seat of his car.

"Oh, man! Look what you did." The large man grunted, holding an old t-shirt to apply pressure to his ear. "The boss is not going to be happy about this at all."

The large man stopped the car a few blocks down the road to adjust the bindings of his unwilling guest. After making certain Sarahn could not wiggle herself free, he pulled out his phone and made a call.

"Sully, it's Hedeon. I had some trouble picking up the girl." He groaned. "I think she bit my fucking ear off."

"Yeah, laugh it up, buddy. Tell the boss I'm gonna be late."

He ended the call with Sully and looked to his hostage, who was still grunting and fighting.

"You've made me a joke. Does this make you happy?" Hedeon grabbed a long cloth from the front seat. "I really don't appreciate it." He wrapped the cloth around her head like a blindfold.

Gagged and blindfolded, Sarahn lay in the back seat with her only regret that she was caught.

Perhaps a different approach would have been pertinent.

The car jerked to a stop. They must be near. Sarahn heard the rattling of chains; she felt the car jerk, moving forward again. She heard Hedeon shut off the car and exit the vehicle. Sarahn felt the door at her feet give way.

She grunted apologies through her gag as he threw her over his shoulder.

"Oh no. It's too late now." Hedeon grunted.

She could hear the door open in front of them as Hedeon carried her, bound, into a building with metallic reverberation. A few voices were having a conversation as they entered. Sarahn fought and kicked to get free.

"I told you to be courteous, Hedeon." A voice she didn't recognize growled. "What the hell do you think you are doing?"

"Boss," Hedeon pleaded, "she jumped me before I even knocked on her door. She bit a chunk of my ear off!"

"Fuck," the growling voice responded. "Why didn't you go with him?"

"She's a hundred forty pounds, soaked and wet," A second voice she did not recall spoke.

"Didn't realize what was going on," a third voice responded.

"Hedeon told me he had it." The last voice sounded vaguely familiar.

She stopped fighting for a moment to observe more clearly. Hedeon felt relieved.

"Sully!" the first indistinguishable voice barked. "Go get our guest a seat. Hedeon, set her down."

Sarahn felt the ground beneath her feet. Hedeon removed the blindfold.

"Now tell me, why did you tie her up?" That indistinguishable voice belonged to a man she'd never met, but seeing his face, she knew exactly who he was.

"I tried to run away, boss, I swear."

Sarahn grunted an insult at the large man.

"I'll get to you!" Mad Dog snarled toward her. "Go on, Hedeon."

She passively listened to Hedeon's story of their altercation. Sarahn knew she was in trouble; Mad Dog's anger was renowned. She looked around the dimly lit room for some kind of escape.

"What a mess you've made." Mad Dog shook his head disapprovingly; he began to pace. Sully arrived with the seat, placing it behind Sarahn, forcing her to sit in the metal chair. She grunted and fought to stand but relented when he deposited her back into the seat once more.

"Now for you." Mad Dog howled, walking toward her to remove the gag from her mouth.

Sarahn knew she would pay for it, but Hedeon's blood had salivated long enough. She spat it into Mad Dog's face.

Mad Dog frowned, wiping the blood-soaked spit from his face; he replaced the rope gag.

"You've caused quite a stir for me lately. My allies have been turned against me, I can only assume weighed by information against them. With you in town, I'm sure it's been you that has been meddlin'."

Sarahn watched Mad Dog in silence. She did not dare break his train of thought.

"Now you may ask yourself, 'Well, where does that place me?'" Mad Dog snarled, continuing pacing back and forth in front of her. He retrieved a cigarette from his suit jacket, placing it into the grip of his lips.

"I wish I'd have told Stan," she thought to herself.

Mad Dog turned toward her, pulling a handgun from his side holster and taking aim. He growled. "Well, I'm afraid that places you in the Mad Dog's path."

He pulled the trigger, and flame emitted from its tip.

Janitor

Inequity, rather the vileness of man, is often understood as an absolute. By that I mean, more often than we should, we label certain characteristics as being definitively good or evil. You see, the wickedness within the souls of the darkest in humanity, while generally remaining hidden, forgotten, or seemingly nothing more than a mere remnant thought, does not exist on its own.

Wickedness cannot be exerted unless that being comprehends kindness and knows how to deliver that fell stroke, that pain. Similarly, love does not exude from those drenched in its warm waters but from those society neglect, developing a thirst for empathy.

Undoubtedly, there are those in this world that have accomplished far more unspeakable villainy than any amount of heroism they have rendered; there are some sins eclipsing any amount of beauty or virtue that may have been present at the time.

It is a hard lesson to learn. Sometimes, you have to do something bad so you can achieve something good—the idea of "the greater good." As a society, we are conditioned into this ideal: sometimes, we must sacrifice in order to achieve something greater. Inversely, though also true, that greater something will lead us to lose our greatest possessions.

Understanding we have perpetuated this behavior is key to comprehending the choices others make throughout their lives because while the choice they made at the time may have caused some hurt or pain, their goal may have been something so immaterial and selfless that the final product justified the strife necessary to achieve such wonders.

As a child, his life was bereft of companionship. He grew sullen toward the recollection of his parents, though his uncle existed in a state of duality for him, serving as both the disciplinarian and the sole source of adoration. He looked up to him in ways that he never could his father—a man stuck in a pipe dream and in debt for his gambling. When he turned thirteen years old, his mother lost an extended battle to a mix of early-onset Alzheimer's and schizophrenia. The latter was well-known, having been treated for most of her adult life. The former, however, brought about an unexpected form of medication, causing a bad reaction with the medication his mother was already taking.

A period of shadow dwelled over their home toward the end of his mother's life, eight months of not knowing what state of pain his mother would be in when he returned home from school. She lived in misery because there was little to no chance of light or happiness coming at the end of her life. Being a day trader in stocks and other funds, his father sustained a meager life at home to care for her, and maybe that, too, played a role in the end.

The agony of his mother jaded him to sorrow when the time passed, and the conversations with his father dwindled into nothing. He went to school and played his games, continuing his existence in some sort of way.

There were days when he thought his mother would know who he was—the child speaking to her. He wanted her to know he loved her, and so did his father, and he probably didn't mean the things he screamed in the night, the things he said to her or to the darkness when he thought no one was around. He just wanted her to know, even though she couldn't always remember, that he would, and his father would, or they'd at least try, to remember the time before all this began.

One day, the kid returned home from school and endured the afternoon he would never forget. He walked through the door and into the kitchen, as he always did, for the PB&J sandwich his father always had waiting for him. Next to the sandwich this time was a soda, which he was nary allowed, save one for dinner. By the soda was a note.

Dear Son,

Your mother had a great day today. She woke up after you left for school and remembered who both of us were! She spoke of how much she missed you and loved you and me too. She spent so much of today happy. I know you won't be able to understand some things that have happened, and I don't know that you ever will. What I need you to do now is call Uncle Tom and ask him to come over. Tell him, "Dad said he was gonna go, like he told you he was." He will know what it means, and he will come and get you so you can spend the day together. Your mother and I both love you more than anything, son. Never forget that. Be good for your uncle.

I'll be with your Mom.

Love, Dad

He always had love for his Uncle Tom. It strengthened when Tom arrived that day. His uncle rushed through the door to find his nephew still enjoying the sandwich and his soda, a fear in his eyes in that moment when Tom saw his nephew, a fear that he had seen something he should not have to see.

"Have you been in the kitchen since you got home, son?" Tom asked in exasperation.

"Hmm," the kid mumbled, chewing the large amount of peanut butter on the sandwich he was enjoying, just like his father knew he liked it.

Wrapping his arms around his nephew with a sense of urgency, Tom circled his arm around to the back of his head, pulling the boy close, peanut butter still in mouth. "Everything's gonna be okay, son.

I promise." He wiped the tears forming in his eyes, holding the boy close to him before his nephew could discern the tears. "I'll be right back, and don't you move. I know your daddy's rule. And if you're really good, I'll get you another soda before we leave." The young boy smiled.

That was the day he moved in with his Uncle Tom and saw there were two versions of him: the loving and fun uncle he had always known and adored and the boss everyone followed dutifully.

At first, he would get to play billiards with his uncle on the pool table he loved. He also knew that when his best friend Johnny got home from practice, he would get to play basketball in Johnny's driveway with him. He always loved going over to his Uncle Tom's because it meant he would get to spend time playing games with his uncle and Johnny.

After a few days of being able to enjoy himself through the rest of the school week hanging out with Johnny and playing games after school, Tom had a sit-down with his nephew on Sunday, after church, and they talked about what happened.

Prior to the sermon at the end of the church service, Tom spoke with the pastor, requesting he lead an upbeat service, one with contemporary music played by a band who attended the church that his nephew always loved to hear, and also that he speak on heaven and how things happen to us we might not understand. And so he did.

Isaiah 25:9: "In that day they will say, 'Surely this is our God; we trusted in him, and he saved us. This is the LORD, we trusted in him; let us rejoice and be glad in his salvation.'" This was the centerpiece of the sermon, and the pastor, at Tom's request, spoke to the congregation of the hard times that befall the faithful. Though sometimes we may not understand why things happen the way they do, it's best to understand that things happen for a reason, and through times of hardship, we must lean on those we love.

After the sermon, Tom and his nephew were approached by the pastor, and he reached out with both hands to comfort a not-yet-grieving small boy who had a shine when standing next to his uncle. "I would like you to think of the church as another home for yourself, son. Know that in your time of need, myself and this beautiful congregation are here for you." He spoke with elegance shrouded in a deep voice, a voice that feigned comfort. For Tom expressed why he needed this service for the boy but not the means of his father's passing.

The news gradually spread around as it does with smaller communities. The suicide of his father eventually made it inside the church. No one wanted to go out of their way to say anything, but Tom's nephew saw the looks of the congregation and knew something changed.

Entering high school, he started to ask more questions and became more concerned with his father's passing after one of his English courses required he read Dante's Inferno. The young man was not aware of what his belief system's rules against suicide consisted of; rather, he never had a conversation, a real conversation, about the topic.

The few times he asked his uncle anything having to do with the subject, it got brushed off, and he would hear the same tired line—"Some things aren't for us to know, boy, but what I do know is that your daddy loved and cared for you, and who would punish him for that?" Having only attended church with his uncle, he could never simply ask the pastor like he wanted.

After class that day, he lingered after the bell to talk to the teacher.

"Mrs. Ayers, I wanted to talk to you about the lesson today," the kid asked nervously as the teacher readied her papers.

"Absolutely." She raised her brow. He had not shown much interest, at least verbally, toward her class thus far. "What would you like to talk about?"

"Well, it's just…" He had no idea what to ask in order to get the answers he wanted or needed. "The seventh circle is for people that kill themselves, right?"

"Well, yes. But it's more complicated than that. It's for violence, against yourself and others."

"Yeah. It's just hard to understand this stuff," the student asked nervously, pulling a chair from one of the desks to the front of the room, up toward the teacher's desk as she grew in confusion at the clear purpose of this conversation.

"What would you like to know?" She crossed her legs and sat back in the chair, eyeing the boy, trying to collect his thoughts and formulate the correct question.

"What really happens to people who commit suicide? Like why are they trees? Trees are nice, right? But the trees get eaten and hurt by harpies, which is weird. And I can't tell if the main guy feels bad for them or not. Does he want to help them? I just don't understand what this is saying about what happens to them." Toward the end of his questioning, his tempo increased; he seemed to be causing himself stress over the conversation. Mrs. Ayers saw this, and she wanted to help.

"Trees are nice, but that's not what's being said there." The boy's eyes became fixated on his teacher. "The trees have leaves of black and twisted branches of contortion. While these trees have a body, it is not one that can heal, and it is devoid of life. The blackness shows that the life is dead. However, we can hear from the cries of those in this circle that they feel the pain of the harpies gnawing on them. But trees only grow outward and upward. They will continue to grow but never heal and always feel pain. Eventually, Dante does feel remorse for them, and he probably does want to help them, but he knows that like the trees enduring the pain, he must continue, onward."

Mrs. Ayers observed the pain in the boy's eyes. "But the important thing to know about all this…is it's just a story. Some people go through pains in life and look for a way out. That doesn't mean they were a bad person. It just means maybe that's what was meant for them. Did you lose someone to this?" She reached her hand out to her student.

"My dad." He whimpered, wiping his eyes.

"And he loved you a lot, didn't he?" she asked with a smile.

"I miss him a lot. But the Bible says he goes to hell. And this says he's in a lot of pain in hell. But he didn't deserve that. He just wanted to take care of me and my mom."

"Well, I'm not one for faith…but I can tell you this. If there is a God, I know he wouldn't punish a father that loved his son and did everything he could for him. A lot of things in this world are just stories for people. Just because you believe in God doesn't mean you also have to think your father is in hell. No God that loves you would ever do that to you. Don't you think?"

He smiled. "Yeah. I guess they do talk about how God loves me a lot. So I guess you're right." He wiped his eyes one last time and rose with a shine in his eyes. "Thanks, Mrs. Ayers. You really helped a lot."

"Anytime. Now go on before you miss lunch." She grinned back to him. He turned for the door, heading to the cafeteria.

On his way out of the classroom, he passed by another kid finishing a late assignment for Mrs. Ayers. He dropped a few things off in his locker when that classmate approached him.

"Hey, kid."

"Yeah." The boy closed his locker, turning toward his classmate.

"Well, the preacher says if you kill yourself, you go to hell. If your dad said he was gonna take care of your mom…then she probably killed herself too, and now they're both in hell together. If you ever want to see them again…" The classmate chortled, degrading the teen to make himself feel superior.

Tom's nephew asked one Sunday if it were all right if he spoke to the pastor about the service. Being months after the events transpired, Tom thought it would be fine and gave his permission. Uncle Tom excused himself outside with a friend, whom his nephew only ever heard called Faust, to discuss a business venture. His nephew knew little of their dealings but saw the man around fairly frequently; he always came bearing a gift and joked about making deals with the boy all too often.

His Uncle Tom said things never go correctly without his supervision. He felt like a lot of his staff were just "dumbasses." This stretched into his life outside of work as well, and Thomas would become furious when things did not go the way he planned them to occur, especially concerning his nephew.

Tom's nephew wanted the same closure he got from his teacher to be parroted back to him by his pastor at the church. However, the boy was met with dismay and sorrow when the pastor did not hold back what he thought was the truth. That day was the last day Uncle Tom and his nephew went to church.

Staring out into the horizon, the janitor took a long, last drag off his cigarette. He liked to watch the sun fall from the top of his uncle's office building, but the sun had set for some time now. Lamenting his life decisions, he pulled his phone from his coat pocket. With his free hand, he removed his earbuds from their holsters, popping them into what he felt a more proper place for them—his ears. His other hand scrolled longingly through his playlists for the right song.

"'Road trip,' no." His thumb glides across the glass. "No, 'Mario's Psychedelic Adventure' isn't quite it either." The janitor lulled aloud. He was looking for just the right list of songs to help him forget about the vomit he'd be cleaning on the first floor. "Fuck Work" gracefully illuminated the bottom of his screen. The cymbal crashed; the bass started grooving. The janitor callously snubbed out his cigarette and attempted to slide it into the receptacle.

The cigarette failed and fell to the ground with the others.

He gathered his things together, crossing the roof to the doorway leading downstairs, eluding the "Remember to lock the door" sign. Descending the stairs, he listened to the bass line to the *Talking Heads's* rendition of Al Green's "Take Me to the River."

The third floor was an easy job for him, although the large conference room carpet held the filth his uncle's employees' drug behind them. He would vacuum it occasionally, briefly. Tonight, however, was not that night.

The janitor rounded the corner, placing his pack of cigarettes on his cart. David Byrne harmonized in his ear like the heavenly angel he is, the custodial employee unable to stop himself from doing a spin as he dumped the trash from Jeanie's desk.

Jeanie worked for his uncle for years. He thought she was a sweet old lady, but he knew better than to touch anything on her desk.

The chorus approaching, the janitor raised his hand to sing with David. He looked up above the elevator at the "3" illuminating on the wall, and with the mention of the song title he shuffled into the conference room.

Atop the occasionally vacuumed carpet sat a large rectangular table with rounded and ornate corners, complete with grand, ornate woodwork the janitor recognized as his grandfather's handiwork. A gift, he supposed, given to his uncle at the peak of his success, prior to his grandfather's untimely death.

The janitor made his way emptying the various trash cans and ashtrays spread around the room. Pushing his cart out the door of the conference room, he grabbed his rag and returned to wipe the table down. Singing and dancing as if no one was watching, the janitor jumped on his cart as it streaked across the hall past Jeanie's desk to his uncle's office.

"Ah, ole Uncle Tom," thought the janitor, grooving the door of the office open. Unbeknownst to the janitor, Uncle Tom's office, as well as the rest of the building, was decorated in a midcentury design. Boxed rooms, with drinking glasses, fine furniture, and desks so close the secretaries could rarely, if ever, get a moment of silence. The employees of Sterling Cooper would have felt at home, though lacking the skyline of Madison Avenue.

His Uncle Tom both loved and hated this building. The history he had there was invaluable, but there was a tax on properties that were not, at least partially, made from sustainable resources supplied by the many businesses within town: hemp, algae, even making use of hydro/ solar power gained an exemption.

Inside Tom's office was a large cherry desk. The janitor did not think his grandfather made this one—too much distressing, and the finish was too dark. On his desk lay a large paper calendar, September set in its top corner. The janitor wiped up the debris with haste, emptying the garbage can and wiggling his way to the elevator call button, Byrne's grunts and Woo's supplementing his journey as the song ended.

The janitor relished the wait for the random shuffle to pick his next song. Another cymbal crashed, the hypnotic theme of Kashmir ringing out into the janitor's ears. He grabbed up his mop, head banging and air-guitaring to the rhythm. Robert Plant sang, the janitor stood in front of the elevator doors, waiting for them to open, now lip-synching into the mop. Throwing out his leg, mimicking his stage presence with Led Zeppelin, knocking the piss out of a speaker by kicking it into the fiery crowd, bolstering his adrenaline as he knocked over his mop bucket, suds hammering against the elevator door. Gazing into the soapy water across the floor with the thought, *"It'll dry before I get back up here."* He pressed the button for the elevator, watching the number above the elevator change from 2 to 3. The doors slid open, and our heroic janitor crossed the threshold with his cart, pointing his finger toward the elevator doors as they closed, singing along with the legendary vocalist.

The elevator fell elegantly, as if the descending fanfare lowered it to the second floor, the bullpen. The elevator doors opened with the reemerging motive; the janitor pushed his cart on to the floor. The janitor became instantly angered as the doors opened, the light peering through the crack of the elevator door. *"How hard is it to just turn them off,"* he thought. A rare occurrence, but enough to send him into a fit. Fortunately, Kashmir bled away his frustration. Offices lined the hall to the left and right. Four doors lined up across from each other on each side with male and female bathroom signs at the second set of doors. Secretary desks sat outside of each door.

Bobbing his head to the rhythmic motive, the janitor unlocked the door to the first office on his right. He despised its owner: the tall, muscular Russian named Hedeon. Loyal to the core, Uncle Tom once made a joke about breaking the janitor's arm for stealing a case of beer in his younger days. Hedeon took it a bit too serious; the janitor still had not gotten over it. Lazily, he cleaned up the mess Hedeon left for him, dumping the trash into his cart.

He crossed the hallway to the logistics department, Sullivan's office. The janitor didn't mind Sullivan too much; he thought the guy a bit of a pushover. Nonetheless, he unlocked the door. He began to straighten Sullivan's office, the trash full of empty cigarette packs; the man smoked like a freight train. Plant's voice trickling in his subconscious.

The janitor made his way into the men's bathroom; the playlist moved on to the airy drumbeat intro of "In the Air Tonight." The reverb of Phil Collins's voice matched the echoes expected in a bathroom, as if he were serenading the janitor from one of the stalls. Gently humming along with Phil, the janitor crossed the hall to clean out the females. Out of courtesy, he knocked first but did not leave enough time for an answer before he entered.

He played the drum fill along the stalls of the women's bathroom. Finally, the catchy hook made him give into his craving of singing aloud, staring into the mirror as if it were the sold-out crowd his daydreams brought to fruition.

He made his way out of the bathroom, opening the office door belonging to the McDaniel brothers, Dillon and Liam. Total "yes" men, they're just around because they know how to stroke the boss's ego, and they never referred to him by his horrible nickname, at least to his face. The janitor just flipped on the light and stuck his head in. *"Eh,"* he thought as Phil's voice faded into silence. The door shut silently behind him.

The even thump of the piano entered his brain as "Bennie and the Jets" began its course. He slid his way across the hall, arriving in front of what the rest of the guys dubbed the concierge. His job was to wine and dine the corporate stooges when they came into town. The janitor thought his wife was cute, but she had a resting bitch face.

The final office on the right belonged to Eli; the janitor slipped into the darkness while Sir Elton John made sweet love to his keyboard. Sitting down in Eli's seat, he threw his feet up on his desk and let Sir Elton melt his worries away for a moment. After the piano solo, the janitor finished straightening up the office, the anointed knight fading off in the same manner as Phil.

That was when it hit him; the seven consecutive notes that culminated the beginning of Clapton's rendition of J.J. Cale's "Cocaine" were struck. The janitor leaped with excitement and wielded his mop like an axe as he rocked out in the hall. He began dancing through the aisles made from the desks of the secretaries, swinging the soaked mop and splashing suds all over the desks surrounding him. The janitor was lip-synching and air-guitaring, channeling his inner Clapton as if performing in front of a sold-out crowd in the seventies at his peak.

JANITOR

After the guitar solo, he knocked over his cart with a one-handed swing of the mop, launching his mop bucket across the hall, as if the simple utterance of the song's title threw him, the cart, and the bucket on their path. The janitor took out his earbuds. Staring at the mess he made, the bucket glided into the office door he hadn't entered yet.

The word left his lips and entered his ears simultaneously.
"Shit!"

PTSD

Egregious pains, brought about by the actions of self-righteous men, that malignant tongues find to be unfathomable, indescribable, and otherwise unspeakable but through scrutiny to stave this stigma with the intention of exhortation. Those shattered by this absolute desolation are simply told to "seek help."

I could feel the vibrating blades of the Black
Hawk helicopter whirring overhead.

The squadron leader, T-Dawg, addressed the squad over the noise and vibration. I couldn't hear a single word he said. I knew what the mission was—to survive. Finishing his motivational speech, he ran to the front of the chopper. When he passed me, he smiled, giving me this little thumbs-up; I nodded. Gripping my gun tighter in my hand, I stood and walked to the back of the plane. "ALL RIGHT, BOYS!" I yelled, stretching out my arms to the ceiling of the chopper. Slamming the button, I opened the door. "Tonight's the night. Grab your glass slippers, and get ready for the ball!" A chuckle grew throughout the back of the chopper that created an inverted vibration of the blades and engine, negating all sound. "GO, GO, GO!" The squadron leader yelled to his squad exiting the helicopter, one by one. Then it was my turn to take the step, the big one, plummeting from twelve thousand feet toward the ground. Everything about it makes your body want to convulse as you fall. Being this small, insignificant speck, free falling, a large vastness below you as those twelve thousand feet dwindled within seconds, cutting through the air. The sound deafening every thought, forcing you to experience the present, the here and now. Your body and mind arguing about how to react, what to do next. "Fight or flight?" and in that subtle moment, time is forgotten, and your instinct lets go at that realization. Flight. You are flying. When you open your eyes again, you're coming too close, pulling the parachute at the last moment, as you approach an altitude of six hundred feet. There is a brief moment where you wonder, "Did it work?" As if to answer that prayer from whatever God you believe, there's a tug on your chest and crotch, the air catching the parachute. It's just a nice little reminder you haven't died, just yet anyways. Then you hit the ground, rolling to break the momentum. That's… That's when it all comes back. Detaching the harness from the parachute. Scrounging the ground for my weapon.

I found the handle and gripped it tight. "All right, team." His voice whispered over the comms in the squad's ears. "Meet at rendezvous Point Alpha." You see, with T-Dawg's recent promotion, I'd been asked to help with the scouting mission. As I was the most experienced, I was asked to lead the ground patrol even though I declined profusely. T-Dawg would remain in contact throughout the mission. I simply reported whether the target was at the expected location. Three days we spent on that hillside, waiting. We jumped from the chopper and walked a day just to get there. We watched the comings and goings of the troops stationed there, and we knew there were far more than we could pray to handle. Thankfully, we weren't going to have to deal with them.

The stint was scheduled for five days, and if we didn't make contact, we were to assume that the target would not be returning to that location. He came. Orders were to return with this information, but T-Dawg had different plans. The target was responsible for the deaths of two people in his first squad, and he hadn't forgotten them. He didn't want to take the chance of him escaping again. We knew that one of the guys, with me on the scouting mission, was known for his skill in stealth operatives. We were instructed to wait for the cover of dark and move when we identified an opportunity. Fortunately, one of the guys with me was a damn good sniper, one of the best I'd say. More confirmed kills than most people would get in a career, and he only served three tours at the time. He set up high on this hillside. The kid and I, the sneaky one, we made way for the base and had open comms between us and T-Dawg. We observed where the target entered the building previously, and it wasn't a large base, but there were still going to be people numbering into double digits waiting for us if things went wrong.

We got into the base…and it just went to shit. They were waiting. Thankfully, they were waiting at the back entrance. They didn't expect us to come in where the target did. I remember exactly what the sniper, Harry, said before he went dark. "Guys. Three coming in behi—" His radio cut out, and I knew, and so did Sol, the kid with me. There was so much hiding and waiting for them to walk out in front of us hidden in a locker or a shadow or behind something. Hours went by before we jumped out to get one that was walking by, but it wasn't just one. They took us into the basement of the building and strapped us to chairs. It was just like a bad movie, a scary one. One guy spoke English, demanding to know where our base was, how many we were, every detail they could get. At first, we wouldn't talk. But then they brought in a guy with a surgical mask and a blood-soaked leathercloth, shielding his clothes from what was to come. I watched, one by one, him remove all of Sol's teeth. Blood poured from his mouth. Then his fingernails were slowly pulled off, then his toenails. In their minds, they knew he wouldn't talk. He'd die from the pain and suffering. He was young and eager to die a martyr. They never expected him to talk. They expected me to stop it. They kept cutting, every part of his body cut off or broken in some way before he finally died…suffering beside me. In his last moments, he was shrieking in pain; his scream filled the room with silence in a sullen instance, even from his oppressors. Then there were four. Me, the surgeon, the guy who spoke, and one guy who never stepped out from the shadows. I led him there. I was in charge.

And I never said a word to stop any of it.

"Then you see what's changed."

"No, I don't. That's why I'm fucking here, isn't it?" Will groaned in frustration. "I thought I was past all this? I thought that by 'immersing myself in my demons,' that I would overcome them?"

Dr. Barwell had given Will the advice of total immersive dominance over his mind, forcing him to overcome the things that broke him. Originally, they thought it to be the warfare. So Will invested in VR equipment, becoming one of the most influential players the Carbon Copy community had ever seen.

"But it was never the war, Will. That, we have always seen, you thrive in."

"Then what is it? And how do I fix it this time?" Will pleaded on his knees to the doctor.

"You're not broken because of the war, Will. You're broken because you survived it."

"James!" Captain Morrigan called out. "Get your ass in here!"

"Fucking great," Katie thought to herself, biting the inside of her bottom lip. "What did I do now?"

Officer James scraped her chair across the tile floor, finding her footing. She shrugged her broad shoulders to gain some semblance of confidence in her stride on the way to Morrigan's office.

"Yes, Captain," she said, crossing the threshold of his doorway.

"Close the door." Captain Morrigan spoke without looking up from his desk. "Have a seat." Motioning to the chair across from himself, he cracked his neck.

"Yes, sir." Katie followed the simple orders from her superior.

"As I'm sure you know, we are looking for a sergeant detective to run the bullpen." His deep, authoritative voice lulled Katie into a sense of trust, but something did not sit right with her. "And you've scored the highest out of all the detectives on the exam."

She waited for the tired old rhetoric—that even though she had the seniority, Katie was not wet enough behind the ears. The weary detective leaned back into her seat, picking at the cuticles on her thumbs.

"We, of course, would like to reward those officers that do good work." His voice droned.

Katie was preparing to get married; she would not be able to focus on the job, having to focus on the nonexistent "growing" family that men in her field were never subjected to in the minefield of legal gray areas. Her leg was shaking out of her captain's sight, waiting for the justification.

"The chief is highly impressed with your professionalism in the case." Her captain kept reading the words on the pages in front of him; he never left the conversation for a single breath.

Being female, she was too authoritative. Though somehow, she managed to pander around the egos of all her male peers, whereas she endured the callousness of offhand comments, being the butt of sexual innuendos.

Which she ultimately thought was funny, but it was the principle of the matter.

"On your police cam, he loved your great idea to bring in that consultant."

A pain seared in the back of her head, light stinging her eyes from the lamp, illuminating the desk. She took a deep breath into her lungs. She awaited the pretentious "little girl" comment, with the following assumption that she wouldn't have the stomach for the job.

"Now we appreciate your unbiased attitude on this case."

Katie closed her eyes in anticipation of the impending shaft.

"Truly remarkable." He placed the stapled stack of papers, unfolded onto his desk, shaking his head. "Diligently defending the innocence of this, uh…" Captain Morrigan squinted down his nose through his black rimmed glasses, holding the stack of papers closer he had been flipping through since her entrance. "Samuel Baker."

She opened her eyes. *"What is going on here?"* Katie thought to herself, not wanting to interrupt her captain's booming voice. It seemed like he was getting to the point.

"The prints on the knife came back. The chief got a judge to sign a warrant to remove the small gnome magnet from the apartment door to compare them, and it's a match. Hell, he's gone so far as to fill out this police report for you."

Katie, a bewildered look overtaking her face, forced her slacked jaw close to keep from gaping. She needed to say something. "Wait, when did this happen?"

"Yesterday," the captain replied.

"Okay, and why am I just being told now?"

"Well, there's been a lot of discussion." Captain Morrigan looked up from the police report into Katie's eyes. "About you, Detective James."

She never realized his eyes were brown.

"What about me?" Detective James leaned forward, placing her hands on Captain Morrigan's desk.

"We know of your desire to rise through the ranks and become captain of this department. The chief and I just want to know we can count on you to play ball." He picked up the papers and dropped them in front of Katie. "The chief has taken the liberty of filling out the police report."

She looked at the papers in front of her, Detective Katie James printed as the officer on the report.

"As you're aware, his involvement in the case was minimal, and he'd feel better if your name was on the report because of his relationship with the victims' family."

There it was, the reason for all the pandering, her signature.

"We are preparing to collar your perp. We've called in your consultants. They should be arriving shortly. We want you to run the apprehension."

Katie was shocked. She would be well on her way to achieving her goal; now she could look further—commissioner, possibly.

"All you have to do is sign there on the bottom line, and I'll be sitting across from my second-in-command of the Forty-Second Precinct."

His face held such a plastic smile.

Katie glared at the pages in front of her; a knock came on the captain's door.

Shave and a haircut. Two bits.

The officer tapped on the door before opening it. "Captain, the dick-uh," he stammered. "Stan Greene is here."

Will and Stan skirted around the trumpeting officer into the room. Katie was quickly skimming the report.

"Prints came back on your knife," Katie gruffly announced as Will and Stan strolled into the office of Captain Morrigan. Katie flashed a discontented expression when Stan emerged behind Will.

Katie was not consumed by malcontent or malice toward Stan. In fact, she was enthralled by Will's ability to connect with someone so easily. Though he had his teammates when he played Carbon Copy and he served with T-Dawg, a blurred line that never seemed apparent would always hold them in a different space than Will and Stan.

Stan stood erect with a smile, awaiting confirmation.

"After we had the judge sign the search warrant, we seized a few belongings from outside the apartment of this Sammy kid to run against the prints as you had suggested." Katie frustratingly looked toward Stan. "They are a match."

"We've determined, however, that he was not on the run," her eyes darted in annoyance toward Stan once more, "as previously suggested. Rather, he went home to visit his own parents. We were able to reach his place of employment and found out he put in for vacation over a month ago."

Stan grunted sarcastically. "Like that's a believable alibi. Obviously, this proves it was premeditated."

Katie reacted abruptly. "If he was trying to make an alibi, maybe it should have been for the time of the murders, not the time afterward when we are looking for a murderer."

"Oscar knew what he was talking about. Everything in life can be about sex, except sex. Seems like Sammy had that with our Juliet. Now he needed power," Stan versed, pulling the pipe from his coat, slowly starting to pack it. Katie recollected her jaw from the floor.

"Yeah, he's been doing that recently." Will sighed. "Why can't you pick between vagabond and enlightened poet? You don't get to be both whenever you feel like it." Will smiled. He rather enjoyed the different personas of Stan.

Stan attempted a cackle, coughing in between chuckles. "There's an importance in being earnest with yourself."

"When you two are done," Katie paused for a short breath, "he's due to be home. We've had officers in street clothes staking out his residence. They've noted his arrival to town last night, and now we have a beat cop watching the place in an unmarked cruiser. It was because of you two that we got this far. We figured you should be there for the arrest and, if needed, questioning afterward."

Stan looked pleased with himself, an unlit bowl held to his mouth. Katie assumed he was trying to seem dignified, but she didn't care about Stan. Nothing he did mattered at this moment. She finished skimming the report and sat back into her chair.

She looked to Will. Smiling, he asked, "What's wrong, babe?"

"Nothing," Katie replied, retrieving her captain's pen from his desk. "You're sure this is the guy?"

The captain sat quietly wearing the plastic smile, and Stan retorted. "We basically found the blood on his hands."

Katie stood on the sidewalk outside Indicance with her squad of police officers in the staging area they set up for the arrest. With eyes on Sammy's apartment, they were preparing to apprehend the suspect.

"All right, team, I need this building surrounded. No one gets in. No one gets out without my say so. We do this by the book. No heroes. We work as a team. We work as a unit. You know your positions. Let's move out!"

She looked to her phone; she'd sent Will multiple messages and still had not received a reply.

Beginning to get worried, Katie had too many men working overtime, standing around waiting for Will and Stan's arrival on the scene. For all she knew, Stan was holding up the process simply to get high.

The chief allowed Katie to run the investigation. she felt a great bit of pride in seeing this to completion. Although she worried about Will, it would have to wait, for now.

"Wilson, Martinez. On me!"

With a few backup officers, they made their way to Sammy's apartment complex. They arrived on his floor; Katie pounded on the door. "Potstow PD!"

They heard a crash inside the room.

"Potstow PD!" They knocked once more. "We have a warrant for the arrest of Samuel Baker! We know you are in there. If you do not open up, we will be forced to knock down the door!"

Katie and her police force gave the suspect a few moments to reply. When they received no response, Katie nodded toward the breach team. They lined up without a moment's notice and kicked through the doorframe. Gaining access to the suspect's apartment, they started the search.

In the apartment, a television was blaring in the background. The local news station was reporting.

"And speaking of criminal, the time to claim that big jackpot is coming to an end. If you are holding on to that lucky ticket, make sure you make your way to the state lottery office to cash it by the twenty-ninth. And now, Ashton with the sports."

The team silently cleared each room, Katie following slowly behind the team making their way through the kitchen, toward the living room with the blaring television.

The microwave hung open, the only light illuminating the kitchen. Popcorn covered the floor, an overturned garbage can, and the assorted garbage that escaped it.

Navigating to the doorway, the lead man of the breach team yelled, "PUT YOUR HANDS IN THE AIR, POTSTOW PD!"

"KEEP IT DOWN. I'M TRYING TO WATCH THE NEWS!" a familiar voice shouted from the living room.

Katie rushed to the doorway behind the team as they filed into the room.

"Hey," Stan's voice found its way to Katie's ear's, "relax, guys. We've already got him."

"What the fu—" Katie whispered to herself as her team gave a stand-down order; they began to stand at ease.

Katie entered the room to find Stan sitting on the suspect's couch, propping his legs up on what she hoped was not the unconscious suspect. Will sat on the accent chair slowly, eating popcorn from a bowl, eagerly watching the scene unfold, averting his eyes from meeting Katie's in any way possible.

"What did you two do?" she fumed.

"I thought you said you were allowing us to take care of it," Stan said, retrieving his illustrious pipe from his coat.

"I told him that's not what you—" Katie shot Will a look that shriveled his resolve to continue.

"How did you guys get into the apartment without being seen?" she asked Stan furiously. Will knew better than to answer.

He would have his own line of questioning later, he was sure.

"Well, I wouldn't be much of a magician if I revealed my secrets."

Katie's eyes swelled from their sockets. Will assumed she was trying to shoot lasers and disintegrate Stan into ashes.

Either fortunately or unfortunately, she failed.

When Sammy regained his consciousness, he awoke surrounded by police officers in his living room. His eyes took a few moments to adjust; one of the officers yelled for a medical transporter while he was starting to shake awake.

Sammy pulled at his hands, finding them bound by shackles.

"Wha-what happened?"

"Samuel Baker," Katie spoke, the EMT checking for a concussion. "I am a detective from the Potstow police department. I have a few questions about your whereabouts over the past few weeks."

The EMT gave Katie the go-ahead as Sammy began to comprehend the situation.

"Could you tell me where you were on the night of July 29th?" Katie asked Sammy.

Stan and Will sat quietly in the background, listening to his responses.

When Katie got to the line of questioning involving his knowledge of the deaths of his friends, Will truly believed the look of surprise coming over Sammy's face.

"They're-they're dead?" Sammy's voice cracked. "What happened?"

"Somebody deserves an Oscar." Stan slowly clapped, retrieving his pipe in disgust.

A symphony of melancholy overtook the face of Sammy; his emotions became unclear and tangled. With a quivering lip and broken tears cascading down his cheek, he caught his breath for a moment.

"I loved them both," he pleaded with them. "It's hard not to know with social media these days." Sammy sniffed. "What happens now?"

Katie sat in the chair opposite to him, reaching her hand out to his forearm, attempting to comfort him. "Now we bring you in for processing and everything else." She motioned to the other officers by the door.

Sammy's eyes sharpened; his brow rose with concern, connecting all the dots in his mind. "Processing?" he asked with a frantic air to him.

"We saw the texts," Stan said as he leaned against a wall, lurking behind Katie.

"TEXTS?" Sammy yelled with his eyes burning toward Stan. "YOU THINK I KILLED THEM?"

"Sammy," Katie said softly, "you're under arrest. Please don't make this any harder than it already is."

One of the officers collecting the alleged perpetrator from his living room began to read Sammy his Miranda rights as they walked him from the room.

The murders gained some local notoriety in the news; now that an arrest had been made, Captain Morrigan decided a press briefing was a good move for the case. The chief of police hosted the press conference, using this opportunity for Katie's promotion to sergeant detective. Katie was asked to deliver a speech and present a citizen's award. She read her speech from a teleprompter.

"My fellow citizens of Potstow, as you know, weeks ago, we were stricken with a crime that confounded us all. No weapon, no motive, no suspect, and worst of all, it happened to a family who thought they were giving privacy to their newly announced, soon-to-be new-lyweds. Potstow isn't free of crime, but a lot of us thought we were free of this sort of crime." Katie looked to Stan, perched alongside Will, to the left of Katie's platform. "And I have nothing but gratitude for the two people that helped us solve this mystery. My future husband, Will, who showed the bravery of every veteran, who will never give up fighting for what he believes, and of course, the man we all truly have to thank." She gestured to Stan, slouching, unprepared for the moment. Looking confused, Katie motioned him with a smile to meet her at the podium standing at the perch of Potstow PD, and he nervously obliged. "Stan Greene, everybody!" she announced, reach-ing out to shake his hand. "This man, as you all know, has one com-plicated history with the town of Potstow. Through his tribulations and challenges, he has a seasoned experience no one else can even come close to. It's my honor to present you with Potstow's highest honor, the Golden Leaf."

The chief shot Katie a look as she spun away from the micro-phone. She rolled her eyes, reluctantly returning to add the final line in the teleprompter, "And to name you Potstow's best investigator."

Katie turned from addressing the crowd to where only Stan could hear her, gripping Stan's hand, not out of intimidation or mal-ice but fear. "Please, Stan. He's buried his demons. Help keep him safe from them and himself." Her eyes were coated with a shine only terror emanated.

"We both need him, Katie," Stan reassured her with a smile. "We'll both keep him safe."

Will held his headset in a firm grasp, lifting his eyes to the spec-tators sitting around the arena. He breathed the air deep into his lungs, embracing the calm before the storm.

Potstow had built a state-of-the-art virtual reality E-Sports arena to satiate the young masses. This led to many of the competitors, such as William Richards, moving into the region. Across Colorado, titles developed to revolutionize the structure of competition.

More like monopolize.

Potstow's attraction with its modernized arena led a strict competition among the titles, bringing three of the state titleholders to centralize within regions around the city. Duff Nation was about to compete in the Eastern Potstow regional. The winner of this title goes on to compete in a unifying competition.

Will exhaled, his racing heart beginning to pace itself. He tightened the headset snug on his head.

Twenty-five teams had dwindled in the qualifying rounds and gathered from around the eastern region of America. The standard team setup consisted of four individual classes. In Duff Nation, the fire team leader, T-Dawg, wasn't lacking in brawn, possessing a singular strategic mind for battle. He was the strategist of the group.

In their early days, he and Will served as equals. Though, T-Dawg cared more on the politics of the job than Will; as a result, he climbed to a rank that Will never intended of achieving. When they returned to civilian life, they both decided to pick up Carbon Copy. T-Dawg seemed to naturally be a perfect fit for the position.

The Nation's Demolitions Expert, Danny served this position in-game as well as during his days in service. Adapting to the weapons in-game took him longer than the rest of the team, but eventually, he became one of the most consistent cover-fire experts playing Carbon Copy. His weapon of choice was the light machine gun, Eclipse. He thought the gun was aptly named; with his extended mag attachment, the bullets could blot out the sun. His ability to terrify any opposing team with a host of different explosive weapons ranked second to none.

Simply put, he loved "making shit go boom!"

The medic, Andre, was saving lives on and off the battlefield, whether it be virtual or in a foreign country. Once he finished his final tour, Andre came back to the states pursuing a career as an emergency medical transporter. Andre was well-liked by almost everyone he met. His employer gave him the freedom to come and go as he pleased. He would spend much of his shift with Danny, a police officer, riding in his squad car, carrying with him the same field bag he had when he served, the radio always on so he could get an ambulance when needed if he ever encountered an issue that couldn't be solved with his on-hand preparations. They lived in a neighboring county not too far from Potstow.

The final position was the tactician; it performed various duties associated with timing and placement on the virtual maps. Duff Nation called him the slayer, the man, the myth, the legend. In competitive play, he owned the best k/d (*kill-to-death ratio for the uninitiated*) in the league. He boasted a four-to-one average in competitive play.

Critics claimed a computing glitch boosted his average in casual play. Always the stoic, Will refused to even acknowledge it.

Will was renowned as the deadliest player in North America. When they needed a clutch play, he rarely choked or disappointed the team. Regardless of the gun, grenade, or melee weapons he would be given, the odds were Will was going to win the fight.

The games system analyst indicated Will was weakest against three opponents, rather than two or four.

The team planned multiple strategies, depending on the map they were playing. At times, they had the luxury of receiving prior knowledge of their competition when entering the tournaments. The traditional setup for tournaments in Carbon Copy was a four versus four. This allowed the teams to study their upcoming challengers.

Of course, they could only accurately prepare for their first opponent each tournament. There was always a chance for an upset in the bracket. Practice meant little if they anticipated the wrong victor between the other seeds or ladders in the competitions, *which was a frequent occurrence*. In these cases, they tried to prepare for what they thought would be the more difficult match.

Individually, the members of Duff Nation were titans of the game, known gods among men. As a team, however, they lacked a certain je ne sais quoi. Other teams could outplay their team shooting, creating a few defining losses in their career. Though they each had renown and notoriety in the game, the team never achieved a championship title. They were privately owned, which meant they did not have a sponsor, unlike most of the other professional teams. They freelanced themselves into a spotlight usually reserved for underdogs.

The competitive matches all sported the same game type: insurrection. It pitted opposing special forces against a defending team. The attackers would be equipped with a bomb; they could wipe out the other team or plant the bomb and detonate it within a parliamentary point of contention on the given map the teams were contesting. The only player who possessed revive tokens was the medic, holding three at the beginning of each match. Each role within the game required a defined style of separating them from the other roles. This allowed teams to strategically focus on the medics and removing the possibilities of revival. Winners were crowned based on a best of five.

A large booming voice filled the arena over the intercom: "Ladies and gentlemen, welcome to the Eastern Potstow Carbon Copy championship!"

The crowd erupted with cheers.

"Today is one of magnificence as we have a surprise for all of you here today!" echoed the voice through the stadium.

The cheers shook the arena, several thousands sitting in attendance.

"Carbon Copy has been dedicated to making a warfare simulation as accurately as possible with our game to create a more fully immersive escape from reality into another world."

The crowd's applause grew still.

"But we here at MixMatched Pants have been eluded by a crucial aspect—the thrill of being the best there is, the power from defeating enemies, not by teamwork and strategy but through sheer mano a mano dominance."

The crowd grew restless, clamoring for answers.

"Have you ever wondered what it would be truly like to be on the field of battle, alone, and with nothing?"

Will's eyes sunk, losing his breath for a short moment.

"Now you can! Introducing to Carbon Copy, Battle Royale!"

One's own thoughts could not be heard in the stadium with the praise that followed.

"All one hundred players participating in today's tournament will be stepping into the first ever Carbon Copy Battle Royale match. They start with nothing, fight alongside and against their team and competition, to finish and win with everything. These teams were unaware of this announcement and have had no preparation for this match. After today's competition, the game mode will go live on the servers only hours after the end of this tournament. Sit back, and enjoy the show!"

Stressful excitement filled each of the players attending the competition, including Will's team. However, Will stood absent any visual reaction. Just stood silently with a cold, blank stare.

Will stood in a plane, his heart rate increasing with every passing moment, cold sweats running down the back of his neck. He looked into the throng in front of him to the sea of empty faces, lacking excitement like most of the plane's inhabitants. Consternation was overwhelming and consuming them, but Will felt it the worst. His breath failed to carry his voice; his attempts to call out were met with silence, and an alarming feel of dread engulfed him. He looked down at his arms, stretched out and bare, feeling the sweat running down his skin, but he could not see it. He felt his legs tremble but could not see them shake.

"Three, two, one, go!" A booming voice resounded.

The throng leaped from the plane. Will neared the now opened hull of the plane, his eyes lost to the vision of what lay below. Searching for an area Will thinks he knows well, he jumped. His eyes closed, his jaw clamped shut, holding on to the cord that would release his chute. His idle hands quaked, pulling the cord.

Will landed in somewhat familiar territory. Gathering himself with his boots on the ground, he immediately scanned the building in front of him for weapons and other equipment. He found a mid-tier assault rifle with an extended mag, two med kits, a vest, a helmet, and a single-shot shotgun. He attached the magazine mod to his firearm; he heard steps approaching.

Will crouched in the corner to attach the mod and waited. A man climbed the stairs Will was hidden behind, and with a few quick shots to the dome, the man fell. He searched the remains for any equipment he might find useful, a scoped bolt-action rifle. He ditched the low-ammo shotgun.

He left the building to find someone camping for him to exit. Will took a shot to the chest, but it only damaged the armor. He took cover behind a wall near the door he just left and hid by a crate located beside him. While undercover of the wall, he found two smoke grenades and one flash-bang. With a quick throw, he lobbed one smoke grenade near the exit he originally planned to take and launched a flash-bang over the wall where the bullets originated.

Instead of continuing his planned route, Will ran the opposite direction around the wall, positioning himself on the opposite side, still hidden from the shooter. Will saw a grenade launch from behind the rock where he suspected the shooter was located.

The assailant threw the grenade into the building opposite Will, falling prey to Will's feint; the smoke worked. Will pulled out the scoped rifle and waited until he had his shot. The moment came; Will fired one clean shot to the head and ran to search the equipment.

The bushwhacker was armored but lacked a helmet. Will replaced his armor with that of his opponent, untouched by his clean shot.

Continuing his path, finding six more men along his way, Will heard something across the comms channel. The tactician had muted his mic, thinking he was alone.

"Well, if he had his damn mic on in the pit before we jumped, he'd have known to jump at Red Point. It's gonna be hell to find him now." The familiar, frustrated voice entered his ears.

"Danny. Is that you?" asked Will over the comms channel.

"Hey, buddy!" Danny answered. "Come on, we are in the Workstation. I guess you're close enough in Red Point to hear our comms now. Looks like they are allowing communication for players who are in short range."

"Probably so people can talk shit," said T-Dawg.

PTSD

"FYI. Pretty sure me being a medic doesn't allow me to revive you guys in a Battle Royale. I just heal myself quicker I guess," Andre informed Will.

The team fanned into a wedge-and-file position rather than sticking together, T-Dawg giving the orders as they approached each location and steps while clearing it. Methodically, they entrenched their opponents before they knew what hit them, preying through one team of three, a few solo stragglers, and one team of two.

A circle on the map kept shrinking, making the game-play area smaller and smaller over time, forcing the players into conflict, slowly closing to its final round with only a small portion of the map left.

Only seven people remained.

Three other players also banded together. T-Dawg crested the top of a mountain incline to see what was hidden below with little room for the remaining players to be anywhere else.

The Nation's other members started sweeping the mountainside. T-Dawg was unprepared for the ambush from behind, all three of them rising from the cliff of the mountain, opposite the side T-Dawg climbed. The match was now a three versus three, and they commanded the height advantage.

"I'm going to pepper that mountainside with mortar blasts. Andre, you take this grenade launcher and do the same," Danny said, swapping his launcher for the semiautomatic pistol Andre carried. He was never stingy with loot. This hindered him on some occasions. "Will, go up the opposite side and clear them out."

"Done," Will replied.

The explosive duo bombarded the mountainside with every drop of ammo they had, while Will ran with brazen regard around the other side. Will was about to top the hillside, the comms rang out a "FUCK!" from Danny. "They hit us back with a rocket, man."

Five players left.

"I'm trying to heal. I don't think I've even hurt any of them."

Will slid down the hillside, searching for his quarry.

"Dammit here they—" Danny's voice was abruptly cut off.

Four players left.

170

Comms had gone silent since the other team switched to a private channel for better communication. Will sat, crouched. He listened with his ears, but they heard nothing, save a ringing. Vision blurred and colors blended with color, whiteness mixed with a blackened void; all sight and sound became neither apparent nor missing. His skin moved away from his heart, and the tips of his limbs grew numb; he fell to the ground.

The remaining players climbed the mountain to find him lying prone, not moving at all. They walked up to his body, expecting a reaction, but it remained still. One of them shot Will, cleanly in the head. They then turned on each other, and the Eastern Potstow Championship was crowned for the first Battle Royale in Carbon Copy.

The supporting cast comforted the four players after the defeat. Danny's recent girlfriend of two months came to support him; her name was Karen. Andre's father, Damien, congratulated him on a job well done even though they couldn't clutch the victory. T-Dawg was commiserated by his fiancé, Josh.

This floored Stan in the stands when he saw it.

Katie, with Stan not far behind, headed to Will. Seeing a forlorn look about Will, she knew what happened, even if he would not admit it.

Stan chose to stand by and idle, feeling that for once, in this moment, he'd just remain silent.

About a week passed since the championship. Katie grew tired of seeing the pain set into Will's face after the Battle Royale match. She had not seen the same demeanor since he first returned from his last tour of duty.

Normally, someone would have been ill-equipped to handle that coming week, but she knew. Katie waited until after the match finished, and Will's team, Duff Nation, was knocked out in the semifinals. Will knew he shouldered a large burden of that blame as he did not play to his usual capacity.

In the week that followed, communication lagged between Katie and Will. He began sleeping on the couch, obsessively playing Carbon Copy, but only with T-Dawg. He tried over and over to reimmerse himself in the game in hopes of removing his ailment. He found no success.

Katie cooked dinner and cleaned, letting him know when the food was ready and setting out clothes for him. The doting fiancée made sure his favorite snacks were stocked and left him to his own devices. She knew that given time, he would make the right decision, as he did those years ago.

Katie knew he went out the day before for about two hours; she had suspicions of where he went, but she dared not ask. On the sixth day following the championship, the sergeant detective found Will waiting at the table when she entered the apartment after getting off work.

"Thank you," Will said, slowly raising his head from the table.

"For what?" Katie replied with a smile.

"You know what. And I love you for it." He smiled back, rising from his seat to give his betrothed a delicate kiss.

"I've not been easy to deal with this past week, and you're the only person in the world to know exactly what it is that I need. In fact, I've ignored Stan's texts all week."

"I'm sure he misses you, babe. Why not go spend some time with him?"

*This is what makes Katie who she is. Confounded by fear for Will the past week, she cared more for his happiness than any regard for her own state of mi*nd.

"Eh, I'm sure he does. But he has sent me at least three texts this past week, asking, 'Is T-Dawg really gay?' So I'm sure he's got a lot on his mind right now."

Will laughed, wrapping his arms around Katie. "However, what is important right now is you, and us."

"And you," said Katie burrowing into his chest.

With a deep breath, Will replied to her. "T-Dawg just called."

"Oh, what did he have to say?" inquired Katie.

"Well, with this new Battle Royale tournament, they've decided to unify the regional titles," Will explained. "They're calling it the

'Potstow Tri-regional Squad of Debauchery' and we're back in the running. If we win, we'd be in position to go for nationals."

Katie looked at her intended, worried about what the competition would bring. She dared not tell him it would be all right or that everything would be okay. She knew better than any of that.

"I'll be here, just like last time. We will get through this." She hugged him tightly, a tear rolling down her cheek onto Will's shirt. A tear welled in Will's eye and fell to her hair as he gripped her with equal strength.

Alls Well That Ends Well

Were divinity a matter of verity rather than a supposition imposed by decades, or perhaps centuries, of indoctrination, not from a place of evil or tyranny but from a place of repetition emboldened by previous generations, who rarely thought to question or explore the probability that Nietzsche might be right; maybe then, Stan would have faith.

Stan mostly meandered throughout his life, some points with a directional strut, usually in an unguided flounder. This misdirection often leads him to the needed destination. In many occurrences, he assumed life owed him a few easy ones.

Where the moments of ill-fated hardship befell Stan, he could trace it back to one of his own actions, a few tragedies excluded. Happiness is generally misplaced with Stan; he often bore the seals of melancholy. In fact, lugubrious in nature, Stan's heart rarely reached elation for anything, save two people.

Both would have lasting effects, for better and worse.

Days after the discovery of the knife, Stan received a call on his cracked phone from Captain Morrigan's secretary, instructing him to grab Will and get to the precinct.

When they arrived, an officer greeted them, escorting them to the captain's office. The officer knocked before he opened it the door.

"Captain, the dick...uh," he stammered, looking back at Stan crossing the threshold of the doorway. "Stan Greene is here."

"Prints came back on your knife." Katie grunted to Will and Stan as they filed into the office. Stan noted a look of disparagement on Katie's face when he stepped around his ward.

The intrepid private eye smiled. Stan enjoyed Katie and their playful back-and-forth, but he felt like she flirted with him too much for a betrothed woman.

"After we had the judge sign the search warrant, we seized a few belongings from outside the apartment of this Sammy kid, to run against the prints, as you suggested." Stan watched Katie shoot him googly eyes from across the room. "They are a match."

"We've determined, however, that he was not on the run, as previously suggested." Her eyes met Stan's again.

He thought, *"Damn, your fiancé is right there."* His eyes motioned toward Will, then back to Katie. She continued, unabashed. "Rather, he went home to visit his own parents. We were able to reach his place of employment and found out he put in for vacation over a month ago."

"Like that's a believable alibi. Obviously, this proves it was premeditated," Stan interrupted with indomitable zeal.

Katie shook her head, replying, "If he's trying to make an alibi, maybe it should have been for the time of the murders, not the time afterward when we are looking for a murderer."

From his coat, Stan retrieved his staple pipe. He coughed, clearing his throat before speaking. "Oscar knew what he was talking about. Everything in life can be about sex, except sex. Seems like Sammy had that with our Juliet. Now he needed power." The intrepid investigator broke a bud into his pipe, marveling at the moistness he supposed he created in Katie's uniform pants.

"Yeah, he's been doing that recently." Will stepped in, smiling, reminding his woman of his existence. "Why can't you pick between vagabond and enlightened poet? You don't get to be both whenever you feel like it."

Stan took a deep puff, in respect to his friend. He lightly coughed, enunciating clearly and distinctly, "There's an importance in being earnest with yourself."

"When you two are done"—Katie looked from Stan to Will—"he's due to be home. We've had officers in street clothes staking out his residence. They've noted his arrival to town last night. Now we have a beat cop watching the place in an unmarked cruiser. It was because of you two that we got this far. We figured you should be there for the arrest and, if needed, questioning afterward."

Stan thought to himself, *"This is it!"*

"You're sure this is the guy?" Katie asked.

Stan removed his pipe from his lips in a suave fashion. "We basically found the blood on his hands."

Stan strolled the sidewalk on the opposite side of the road from Indicance, his compatriot Will trailing a few steps behind him. The gumshoe smoked from his pipe, gazing along the street.

"All right, Stan, I think Katie said they'll be staging"—Will pointed at the restaurant—"right over there."

"Yep."

Stan walked into the shrubbery of the apartment building with Will midway across the street. "Hey…wait!"

Will turned, following Stan into the bushes, skirting the perimeter of the building. They approached a railing. One by one, they stepped over.

Stan stopped, looking at the names on the mailbox. "Baker, 2E."

Will walked up the steps, and Stan jumped the railing, once more fading into the shadow of the brush.

"Why do you keep doing that?" Will said in frustration as he followed. His phone rang—a text notification. A message from Katie. "Katie said she's almost to the restaurant. We can run back over there in a jif—" Stan stopped suddenly. Will walked into his back.

"Watch what you're doing!" Stan grunted, digging into his leather satchel. "Where is it? I knew it was going to come in handy."

Stan gasped, grasping a rope with a grappling hook.

"Where'd you get that?"

"That rock-climbing shop with the cute cashier." Stan smiled, a dumb look set on his face. "She sold me this satchel too."

Stan held the rope in his hands, lobbing the hook into the balcony of apartment 2E. Stan climbed, with Will objecting in tow behind him; his phone beeped—another text. Creeping onto the barren balcony, they silently slid open the glass door.

Stan fell multiple times trying to climb the rope, but when the story gets told from his point of view, he would leave out some details.

"Hello?" a voice uttered from the bathroom of the apartment.

Stan dashed across the room to stand outside the door, the handle turned, the voice calling out once more. "Hello?"

The door opened. Stan punched the inhabitant square in the jaw. The suspect collapsed, with his pants following around his ankles. Will's phone alerted him to another text.

Pulling a pair of handcuffs from his satchel, Stan handcuffed the warranted man in a citizen's arrest. He stepped back to the balcony, yelling for Will to make some popcorn.

Retrieving the popcorn from the microwave, Will poured it into a bowl when a knock pounded the front door.

"Potstow PD!" the familiar voice chanted from the other side.

Will lunged for the living room, tripping over the trash can, spilling half his popcorn on the floor. He got to his feet when the knocking resumed.

"Potstow PD! We have a warrant for the arrest of Samuel Baker! We know you are in there. If you do not open up, we will be forced to knock down the door!"

Will made his way into the living room with great haste. Stan grunted. "They're about to breach the door." He pointed to the TV.

"And speaking of criminal, the time to claim that big jackpot is coming to an end. If you are holding on to that lucky ticket, make sure you make your way to the state lottery office to cash it by the twenty-ninth. And now Ashton with the sports."

"Put your hands in the air. Potstow PD!"

"Keep it down. I'm trying to watch the news!" Stan cackled.

Katie pushed her way past the other officers entering the room, her eyes vivid with fire.

"Hey, relax guys. We've already got him."

Stan sat, feet propped on the suspect's side like an ottoman, when Katie stormed into the room. Will sat to Stan's left on a paisley chair, eating popcorn one kernel at a time, looking anywhere but toward Katie.

"What did you two do?"

Stan reached into his coat for his pipe. "I thought you said you were allowing us to take care of it."

"I told him. That's not what you—" Will shrunk under Katie's gaze.

"How did you guys get into the apartment without being seen?" she asked Stan, brazened with anger.

"Well, I wouldn't be much of a magician if I revealed my secrets," Stan smugly replied.

Katie's eyes swelled from their sockets. Will assumed she was trying to shoot lasers and disintegrate Stan into ashes. Either fortunately or unfortunately, she failed.

Sammy started waking from the strike to his glass jaw, noticing the police officers stacked in his apartment. He heard an officer call for an EMT. He tried to stand, discovering the shackles binding his hands.

"Wha-What happened?"

"Samuel Baker," Katie spoke while the medical technician was checking his cerebral responses, "I am a detective from the Potstow police department, and I have a few questions about your whereabouts over the past few weeks."

"Could you tell me where you were on the night of July 29?"

Stan puffed his pipe; Will chewed his popcorn, watching the event unfold.

"They're…They're dead? What happened?"

Stan chortled to himself, unable to believe the tone in the suspect's voice. "Somebody deserves an Oscar." Stan clapped with slow sarcasm.

The perpetrator quivered his lower lip, bursting into tears. "I loved them both. It's hard not to know with social media these days." He helplessly wailed, "What happens now?"

"Now we bring you in for processing and everything else." Katie sat across from him, placing her arm on his, then motioning to the officers by the door.

"Processing?" the realization finally consuming Sammy.

Leaning against the wall behind Katie, Stan said, "We saw the texts."

"TEXTS?" Sammy yelled. "YOU THINK I KILLED THEM?"

"Sammy," Katie said softly, "you're under arrest. Please don't make this any harder than it already is." *One of the officers collecting Sammy from his living room began to read Sammy his Miranda rights as they walked him from the room.*

"Hey, ladies." Stan walked with a swagger to his eager prey lined along the bar—one blonde, one brunette, both sporting blazing ruby-red lipstick, smiling at him from down the bar. "Come here often?" Stan approached the blonde, a yellow sundress passively complimenting her curvy figure, her face framed by a few blond curls.

The blonde in the yellow sundress looked back into Stan's eyes. Her lips whispered in silence a response. A shrill noise entered Stan's perception, as if deafening him from tinnitus.

"The music must be too loud, love." Stan leaned in a little closer, invading her personal space, though the blonde did not give chase. "What did you say?"

"A great secret will be bestowed upon you, Stan Greene," the voice echoed.

"Wha—" The bar next to Stan was absorbed into the background. The blonde's hair and lipstick turned a gothic black. Stan stood with his mouth agape, staring into the blurry void of her face.

"No great knowledge comes without its price. It will claim the treasure you didn't know you owned, Stan." The blurry gothic's voice was distorted from sensual to harsh, raspy tones. "Your path is set in motion. The seal cannot be undone."

The sweet aroma of hickory-smoked bacon consumed his senses. His trilby hat covered his eyes. He heard a pan sizzling from the area he considered the kitchen. Without trying to move quickly, Stan tilted his head on the couch, viewing the kitchen through the small crack between his hat and face. An elegant female stood illuminated by the small candle on the counter. Her auburn hair swirled in a messy bun, she seemed to be wearing one of Stan's white dress shirts. The beauty of the visage made Stan question whether or not he was dreaming.

"I see you stirring over there, Stanley." Her voice fluttered like angel wings to Stan's ears, though he knew better than to allow her allure to draw him in so easily. She was his siren, singing her song from ashore, making Stan's life the boat coming crashing into the rocks. "Come, I've made bacon and eggs." She curled her index finger at him from across the room.

Stan slowly rose from his sofa, lifting his hat from his eyes. Feeling no need to be bashful, he swung his feet to the floor and stared at her, soaking in the moment while it lasted. After a few precious moments, Stan pulled out his pipe, striking a match across its box's strip and taking a long drag. "Sarahn." He bellowed out a cloud of smoke, likely to impress most hipsters and smoke machines. "Let yourself in, I see."

"Yeah, you looked like you were having a good dream." Turning her back to him, she attended the skillet. "I didn't want to wake you."

"And that was before or after you broke in?"

"Oh, do you want me to leave? I do hope you don't need this shirt." He looked down at her legs, stretching on for days, disappearing beneath his white shirt, just above her knees. She smiled, walking across the room to wrap her arms around his neck.

Stan looked up as she pulled the hat off his head. He puffed a cloud between them. "That's my favorite shirt, I'ma need that back."

"Just eat your eggs. I've missed you," she added sweetly.

Shoving a plate of food into his hands, she began to fix herself one. He made his way back over to his couch and took a seat, balancing the plate on the arm. "So," Stan paused to relight his pipe, suspiciously eyeing his lovely intruder, "what did you and ole McKinney talk about?"

"Always working, are you?" She looked at him through furrowed eyes before shoveling eggs into her mouth, ignoring his inquiry.

"I'm just trying to figure out why you're here. I thought you made it clear enough you didn't want to see me again."

"Well, I've heard you've become Potstow's favorite patsy," she sang her refrain. "I just had to come experience that for myself."

Stan eyed the eggs on the plate before him dubiously and looked back to Sarahn.

"It's not poisoned." Sarahn spat. "Honestly, if I wanted you dead, it's not like it would be difficult. Your door wasn't even closed," she said pointedly.

"What do you want?" Stan asked, ignoring her jibe.

"I need a place to stay for a few weeks." She purred, crossing her legs on the couch next to him. She enjoyed watching him splash about. "I have business in town."

"And that business being?" Stan asked in an elongate phrase, attempting eye contact with Sarahn, though she avoided his gaze.

"Nothing that would concern you..." she quickly added, "... yet, anyways." She stuffed more scrambled eggs into her mouth.

"Should I be concerned about becoming your..." he paused for a moment to remember her phrasing, "patsy, was it?"

"If everything goes to plan,"—she smiled eagerly back at him for a brief moment, as if watching Stan smash upon the jagged rocks at her shore—"yeah."

He puffed again from his pipe, contemplating her last refrain, further ignoring his eggs. Although the bacon smelled far too appetizing, he'd been breaking off small pieces to nibble in between puffs. This seemed to satisfy Sarahn. She stopped staring at him like a mother hen to her young, which worried Stan slightly.

She finished her eggs and bacon, and he, his bacon and bowl. They huddled side by side on the couch in silence as the sun rose to meet the morning sky through the window of his office.

"The Greeks believed Apollo would drag the sun and moon across the sky every day," she said quietly. "Fascinating, they thought their gods would care for them so much. Yet now we realize that it's the absence of anything moving and surrounding us—the sun and the stars and the distance between them all—that is holding it all together." She turned around, gazing upon Stan, then quickly facing away from him again.

He looked back at her with wonder; in all her bleak pessimism lay a beautiful innocence robbed. Wrapping his arm around her shoulder, she pulled her knees close to her chest, melding into his side.

They sat together for a few hours in silence while Stan smoked with his arm around Sarahn, wanting time to linger a bit further but knowing the mood would only spoil if it lasted too long. That was when Stan's door burst open. Sarahn seemed unsurprised, whereas Stan seemed overly surprised. He stood to meet the form forcing their way into the office. She wore a hood, hiding most of her facial features. "Oh, I thought you'd be alone," the hooded and scarved figure stated.

"No worries, miss," Stan comforted his new acquaintance. "Ms. Depity and I were just reviewing the notes on her last case." Sarahn smirked toward the back of Stan's head. "How can I be of service?"

"Well," the hooded form hesitated a moment, trying to determine where to begin. She collapsed in the chair in front of Stan's desk. "I've nowhere else to turn. I've been reading the articles about how you solved the 'Romeo and Juliet' murders and thought maybe you could help me." She lowered her hood, revealing her short black hair. "My dearest brother has gone missing, and I fear the worst has become of him."

Stan took a seat at his desk across from his patron, pulling a clear glass jar from his desk. He opened the aroma seal, and the room instantly stank of the pungent fumes of this week's bud of choice. "Do go on." He motioned to his client with his hand to finish her story.

"Right," she said, scrunching her nose toward his jar, continuing through her obvious disgust. "He called me the other night before he went missing, and he just sounded…off."

Sarahn perked up from her seated position on the couch. "What do you mean?" she questioned.

"I don't know how to describe it. His voice, his tone, they were all him, but the words…" she paused in thought. "They weren't his."

Stan took a puff from his pipe. "What exactly did he say?" Stan pondered aloud.

"That he 'wasn't going to be around for a while' and that I shouldn't come looking for him, but, Mr. Greene, you have to realize that my brother hasn't always been on the right side of the law. I think something horrible has happened to him. He sounded afraid. The fear was prominent in his voice."

"Yes, I understand, but what words weren't his?"

"Right." She stopped sniffling and clarified her thought. "He called me Margaret."

"Is that not your name?" Stan asked through the billowing smoke he created.

"No," she spoke, waving the smoke from her face. "Margaret was the name of our sister that died when we were young."

"Interesting." Stan smoked in silent reproach for a few moments, contemplating the importance of this evidence.

"How did Margaret die?" Sarahn questioned unabashedly from the couch, intrigued by the mystery in front of her.

"She drowned."

Stan wasn't one to pass up paying work. "What, can I ask, is the compensation for the job?"

The sister of the late Margaret brightened her tone by the statement. "I have my life savings. I can pay you three grand now, and I can pay you another three at the resolution when you find my brother."

Normally, the fee for this kind of job was not preceded by multiple 'grands' of value. Stan instantly jumped to his feet. "Absolutely, miss. I will find your brother before any nefarious means come of him, I assure you." His client seemed absolutely ecstatic by the news. "Do you know the last whereabouts of your brother, before the call?"

Sarahn sat back into the couch, Stan into his chair, both listening cautiously to the tale given life by the distraught sister.

The formerly hooded dame introduced herself as Marybeth Davis. Miles, her missing brother, was named after the legendary musician. Throughout their lives, they remained unnaturally close as siblings, hardly a disagreement between them. Family meant the world to them, being faced with the mortality of their common sister at such a young age. Marybeth was the one to discover Margaret's lifeless body in the pond on their family's estate. Margaret was always a strong swimmer, and the loss deeply impacted her twin, Miles. Marybeth and Miles found solace in each other, their bond growing with every passing year.

Miles began having dreams as of late, unusually cryptic in nature, where he found himself looking up at a distorted sun, feeling light on breath, trying with all his might to swim toward the light, but something held him, not allowing him to escape. Marybeth feared for her brother as this led him down a path of drug abuse and alcoholism, frequenting a local gentleman's club and associating with what Marybeth described as immoral friends. The gentleman's club was the last known whereabouts of her missing brother.

Marybeth fought back the tears through the story, Stan listening intently. Extending his right hand to shake her hand, Stan used the other to take the envelope full of cash. "I will bring your brother home." He escorted the distressed maiden to his office door with a newly restored pane of glass depicting "Stan Greene, Private Eye" on the outer side. Opening the door, he let her out of his office. "You can rest assured of that, Ms. Miles."

Stan shut the door. Sarahn waited a few moments, listening to the footsteps trailing off down the stairs before letting out a hollow laugh. "Don't tell me you fell for that?"

"Fell for what?" Stan bemused, flipping through the envelope of cash. "She's looking for her missing brother."

Sarahn laughed at him but said nothing more. Stan sat at his desk, smoking in thought for the next few hours, when Will came barging through his door.

"Stan, I think I know what happened to Mrs. Edna's cat!" Will exclaimed, busting through the door, paying no attention to Stan's guest. "I've been hearing some scratches—"

"I've told you I want nothing to do with that damned cat!" Stan stood and pointed at his companion. "Besides, we've already got a case." Stan stood by his desk, straightening files fallen astray.

"Oh, shit!" Will jumped for joy. "Good because I was just trying to get you off your ass. You've been lazy lately."

"Aw, they have you looking for missing pussies, Stanley?"

Will jumped back in surprise when he heard Sarahn's voice enter the conversation. He looked to Sarahn, still sporting Stan's white shirt, then back to Stan. "Is this our client?" His eyes were full of wonder.

"What?" Stan choked. "No, no, this is my old friend, Sarahn. She"—he added an inflection on his next syllable—"made her way to my office last night." Stan shot an accusing look toward his former paramour. "Sarahn, this is Will." He motioned thoughtlessly with his hands toward Will. "This is my," Will hoped he would describe their relationship as partner; he met with Stan's steel tongue when it formed the word "neighbor," instead.

"Nice to meet you." Will reached out to shake her hand but was stopped by Stan walking through his outstretched arm to grab his coat from the rack.

"No time for that now. We must be leaving." Stan donned his coat; the wind created knocked a few papers off his desk to the floor.

"Still wearing that old thing?" Sarahn's eyes looked at all the rips, tears, and failing seams seemingly holding Stan's trench coat together.

Stan grabbed his hat from the couch, making for the door and motioning Will to follow. "I trust you'll be long gone by the time I return?"

She smiled coolly toward him. "Oh, Stanley, you know me so well."

"Just put whatever you're rifling through back when you've finished snooping. I have an order to this chaos."

"I have already. Couldn't you tell?" Sarahn called out and laughed at them. Will and Stan exited the room. They could still hear her chuckling when they met the stairs.

Stan filled in Will with pertinent information on the case as they made their way to the sidewalk in front of Draper's Properties.

"Okay, but I was more interested in the lady wearing your lucky shirt on the couch."

Stan shot his compatriot a fervent glance before entering the blue sports car. "Don't worry about her. She'll be gone by the time we get home." Stan scoffed. "In town for a few weeks on business, what a joke." Will did not pry more; he could tell it was a sore subject for Stan. After a few quiet moments, the private eye added, "And she said I was the one always working."

Will left the parking garage with Stan in tow in the passenger seat of his sporty azure car. Excitement poured out of the two of them, settling on a location to celebrate their latest success. "So where are we going?"

Retrieving his pipe from his jacket, Stan drew a few calming puffs. "Well, I suppose, if we are going to celebrate"—Stan inhaled—"there's only one place in town capable to contain such a fest." Smoke escaped his orifices as he spoke.

Will and Stan smoked his pipe the entire ride to the outskirts of Potstow to a small establishment called Dirty Vegas. Neither of them knew what to expect when they arrived. Very few cars were parked in the small parking lot, but that could be deceptive. Will parked his car in front by the main entrance and shut off the engine.

Exiting the car, they made for the front door. Will buzzed the buzzer, and Stan looked up to the camera, watching the door. A large man swung it open to greet them. "Ten dollars each."

"Ten dollars each?" Stan objected. "It's still early. There probably isn't even anyone dancing anyways!"

The large man looked at Stan. "Hey, man, keep it down." He eyed Will and Stan. "Okay, five each."

Stan begrudgingly doled out the cash, muttering "Highway robbery" beneath his breath, crossing the threshold of the gentleman's club. The large bouncer made his way behind the bar and into the back of the establishment.

When the bartender finished serving one of the few patrons in the bar, she greeted the fresh duo as they approached to grab a seat. "What's your poison?"

"Oxytocin," Stan said.

She chuckled, "Well, you've come to the right place." Grabbing a glass, she threw in three ice cubes, poured a double shot of Jack, and filled it to the top with fountain Coke. "Here, this one's on the house." She winked, then walked away, leaving Will unattended.

"Man, you're just on fire today," Will said.

"What do you mean?"

"First, Sarahn. Now the bartender. I've never seen a single chick look your way, and now twice in a day." Will let out a long whistle.

"Eh, they can smell it." Stan sniffed, motioning his hand by his nose like he was wafting the air. "Other women, once you get it on you, they all want you." He scoffed as he pulled out his pipe. "It'll pass. She'll be gone by the time we return."

"Why do you say that?"

"I have something she's looking for, apparently." Stan took a long draw from his meerschaum pipe. "Honestly, that's the part that's bothering me."

Will motioned the bartender back over when she reappeared behind the bar. "Rum and Coke, please. Why?" he asked Stan before giving the bartender his belated order. "What is she looking for?"

"No idea." He puffed inquisitively.

They sat at the bar, listening into the conversations between dancers and staff. Stan felt he needed to get closer to a set of blonde and brunette dancers to hear what they were saying. Will thought it was an excuse to get a lap dance. Their venture proved enjoyable, though fruitless for information about Miles. Stan felt the scent was lost. He rubbed his bloodhound nose raw. Will and Stan stumbled out of Dirty Vegas, supporting each other at the shoulders.

"Did you see the one in the green G-string? She was my favorite." Stan spoke through a grin seemingly unnatural to his face. Will enjoyed the view, however did not partake in the daily specials listed on the chalkboard. Stan indulged in the sampler platter.

"Yeah, I saw her. She was hard to miss with your face buried in her crotch." Will chuckled, checking his phone. "Katie's going to be pissed when she gets here." He wobbled into a drunken impression Stan frankly found hysterical. "I thought you were 'working'?"

Katie's car pulled into the parking lot, finding her two fools embracing each other in their drunken stupor. "Come on, get in! It's about to rain."

Getting into the passenger seat, Will leaned over to kiss Katie. He was met with a stubborn "Mmhmm," and she did not engage him in her usual loving manner. "And don't make me tell you again," she turned to Stan. "Not in my car!"

Stan sat with his pipe hanging from his mouth and matchbook in hand, readying to tear out a match to light, with a look of shock on his drunken face. "Whaaa?"

Stan and Will stumbled from Katie's car through the double doors to Ocean Avenue and supported each other during their journey to the third floor. Passing Ms. Edna in the hallway, Stan slurred a derogative comment to her. Will apologized for his friend, escorting him the remaining way to his office.

The intoxicated investigator moved his support from his friend's shoulder to the window of his door, fumbling with his keys to unlock the door. Will turned toward his apartment, tripping over the normally well-placed broom, falling backward into Stan. The weight of the fall distributed across Stan's body to his palm. The window, unable to support the shock, shattered beneath his palm.

"Son of a bitch."

Stan sat at his desk, sobering from his drinks, looking at the fresh hole in his doorway. Leaning back into his chair, tossing his feet onto his desk, he knocked a manila envelope off his desk, scattering the developed pictures within across the floor.

"Shit, I thought I mailed those already."

He fell to his knees, scooping the pictures back into the envelope, when it dawned on him. The picture was missing. The only picture worth sending was gone. Stan connected the dots in his mind, realizing what Sarahn had done. The ashes were left as a cold reminder from his paramour of reveries. He looked to his watch. There was still time to catch the 516 to the Industrial Park.

With the entrances blocked, Stan stared down the rusted fence separating him from the foundry, thinking to himself, "Yeah, I'm in shape." Approaching the tall metal chain-link fence, he studied its diamond-shaped holes, thinking that he would be able to easily find a grip as he started climbing the daunting, thirty-foot wall separating him from his mission.

Stan patted his pocket to verify his pipe's security and quickly felt for the freshly purchased bud to make sure it remained sheltered from harm. He then took hold on the fence, still standing on the ground. Slowly, he added his weight. The fence began to bow, as though something was pushing down on him, making it more difficult to hold onto the fence. The fence did not epitomize sturdiness; he was unsure if it could support his weight.

It was a valid concern.

Stan gave a valiant effort. He made it almost fifteen feet up the fence before imagining his bud was falling out of his coat pocket and quickly reaching back to grab it. Forgetting his hold, he came crashing hard on his coccyx. There came a barrage of vulgarity, with Stan biting down on his bottom lip, trying not to scream "My fucking ass!" alerting anyone else to his presence.

He tried again. This time was not nearly so heroic as his first attempt. He'd barely gotten feet from the ground before he stoved his grip, bending his finger backward, causing him to convulse into a small tremor. Meanwhile, he managed to become less concerned with the other hand currently holding him to the fence and, once again, came down crashing.

His fury was raging at this point. Kicking the fence out of frustration, Stan threw punches at it as if it just robbed the sticky-icky jar back at the office, jumping like he was in a boxing match, throwing jabs. Then taking a very short about-face, he jolted and placed some distance between him and the fence. Rage swelled within him, and a fire rose from his deepest pits. He sprinted with all his might toward the fence, launching himself toward it.

The fence bent with his kick until his left foot penetrated the fence, just enough to result in him hanging with metal strands now pinching and stabbing against his skin as he hung there trying to free his foot. After wriggling viciously and a lot of blaming God for his problems, Stan managed to free his leg, which, of course, resulted in him falling hard onto the ground again.

His final attempt, he told himself, "If it doesn't work this time, I'm just going home." He checked the pipe and then the green. He made sure it was all secure in and took a full sprint at the fence. Probably the most athletic act Stan attempted in his recent life, he used his speed from sprinting to launch himself up the fence, each grip afterward a seamless transition all the way to the top. Reaching the top of the fence, he pulled himself up to see the large piece of machinery on the other side. A bed of dirt rested next to it. He considered jumping on top of it so he wouldn't have to climb back down.

Before he could make up his mind, he noticed how badly the fence was swaying now that he was on top of it. As he swung his leg over the top of the fence, that portion of the wall came crumbling down. Stan reached outward, hoping to grab onto something, but there was nothing. Thankfully, he landed in the pile of dirt and just had the wind knocked out of him, with a lot of back pain.

Roger Murtaugh had a phrase to describe exactly how Stan felt as he tried to fill his lungs with air and roll on the ground.

Making his way to the entrance of the foundry, he found the door was locked, which was to be expected. Stan walked around the building until he found the fire escape high above his head. Dread shot through him like the pain in his lower back with the thought of having to climb this ladder. It would have to slide down for him to be able to use it. This thought did not excite him to any effect. He investigated the area for a moment, locating a decent-sized rock. Through either a stroke of genius or luck, he threw the rock at the ladder. He watched in wonder as it worked. The ladder fell right into his reach. In his glee for something finally going his way, for a moment, his shoulder and back pains seemed to melt away. At the top of the three-story building, he collapsed onto his knees and rolled over on his back, gasping for air. As he lay there, he had an inner monologue with himself, questioning, "Maybe this sort of work isn't my specialty."

Stan gained his foothold while trying to focus his breath as he stumbled awkwardly toward the door. He let out a sigh of relief as his fingers revealed the door to be unlocked. "Thank fucking God," he stammered as he entered the building. Stan made his way down the stairs, coming to a secretarial floor with a large conference room. He noticed something on the opposite side of the hallway from him—a cart full of cleaning supplies propped the door to the open conference room.

Stan recalled from the papers that he'd need access to the second floor to find the project manager's office and gather any information of worth. Crossing the floor to open the doors of the elevator, he heard singing coming from behind the cart.

Stan watched as an elated janitor danced with a free spirit. He was kind of impressed with his moves. As the janitor continued singing, Stan pressed the button to open the elevator doors. As they closed behind him, he watched the janitor streaking across the floor, riding his cart. Stan marveled at how close he was to discovery, trying to remember where he knew those lyrics.

The elevator lowered Stan to the second floor, and the doors slid open before him. Stan scanned the walls for a light switch and flipped it on. Stan made his way down the aisle made by desks, his eyes scanning the doors for the writing found on them.

Stan passed the bathrooms, and his eyes caught the name "Jacob Mckinney" etched in the glass. He tried to open the door; it was unlocked. "Lady luck smiled on me twice in one night," Stan whispered to himself as he opened the unbarred door.

The investigator did not know what he was looking for, anything that would shed light on infidelity. Flipping through the papers on the desk, looking for a calendar or a datebook, all he could find was accounting paperwork.

Stan became frustrated. He reached for his pipe and fat sack of herb. Taking a bud, he began to break it over a loose manila folder labeled Díoltas he found on the desk.

Stan absentmindedly grabbed another bud and broke it in a similar fashion as the first. He heard a subtle knock, startling him. Out of horrible survival instinct, Stan blurted out, "Hello?" Quietly kicking himself for his absurdity, he silently broke up another bud when no reply came.

A few moments of reserved peace passed to no avail. Stan found nothing on this computer. He looked down at the manila folder he had been breaking his buds upon to the overwhelming pile he created. Grabbing his pipe, he packed it, then started going through Jacob's drawers. Every few folders, he'd take another puff from his pipe and move on to the next.

"Nobody's this clean", he thought to himself, delving into another folder.

He laid his new matchbook from the bar the other night on the table to pinch some of the shredded flower, packing another bowl in his pipe, when a commotion happened outside of the door. Stan froze in fear, listening to water splashing on the floor outside the door, then a thump on the door itself.

The word left his lips and entered his ears simultaneously.
"Shit!"

La Muerte De…

Time. Described throughout existence in numbered and poetic verses, but is it real? Rather, the more pervasive inquiry…does it matter? Events may have correlated this far, and a measure of what has or has not is less than evident. Time is said to flow like a river, but do we wade in the same waters? The present is a misguided phenomenon, and the past is as ethereal as the future, locked in a binding filiation that becomes nothing more than the events occurring. These occurrences, not time itself, are the experiences. Where does the river exist, from the headwaters to the water-fall or its mouth to the ocean?

Where do events, time, or the passing of the long thought river begin, flow, or dare I say it, end?

On the horizon, far too distant for eyes to perceive.

The word left his lips and entered his ears simultaneously.

"Shit!"

Panic swelled in the pits of Stan's core at the thought of some-one gathering on the other side of the door. He scanned the room for a place to hide. On the left, a space between the bookcase and the wall. With any luck, his tattered coat could make him look like a coat rack, his legs draped in the shadows. He glanced back at his pile of weed scattered across the folder on the desk.

The janitor stared at the door like it proclaimed the obscen-ity itself, questioning the validity of his anxiety. Had he heard any-thing at all? Cautious of the soapy water and the cursing door, he approached carefully.

He pulled the trigger, and flame emitted from its tip.

Thomas lit his cigarette from the revolver-shaped lighter, drawing air through its filter, deeply engrossing the toxins into his lungs.

"But what to do with you?" Mad Dog growled. A long silver cloud of smoke escaped the weeping orifice.

Sarahn clenched the gag in her mouth, mumbling her intentions without enunciating a single syllable.

"What?" Mad Dog snarled. "What did you just say? Remove her gag."

Hedeon removed the gag from an angle, keeping a safe distance behind his captive.

"Faust wants the ticket," Sarahn repeated, unabatedly stretching her jaw muscles.

"The ticket?" Thomas asked. "What ticket?"

"That big jackpot winner. Genius here"—she nodded toward Hedeon—"stole from the councilman. I was trying to get it back?"

"What good is a stolen lottery ticket?" Mad Dog rounded on the large cowering man.

"It's not the jackpot that makes it valuable." Sarahn smiled. "It's what's—"

"Hey, boss," Liam interjected. "Security says someone's here."

Stan looked to his right. Chairs sat around a table with no obvious hiding place, save the underbelly of a low sitting couch along the wall. His eyes returned to the weed, weighing the places to hide, evaluating how difficult it would be to maintain the bud on the folder in each place. Stan glanced down, realizing he could sit behind the desk and crawl under it, but the spacing created by legs holding the desk up, rather than the frame continuing to the floor, allowed for someone who was searching to notice something amiss. If they paid attention to even the smallest detail, that is.

The janitor grabbed his Maglite from the cart, trying to steady his heart pumping the blood through his body and his weak wobbling knees. Filling his nostrils with a reassuring sigh, the janitor controlled his breath, stepping over his tipped bucket. He picked it up carefully to prevent any noise.

Mad Dog scurried to the door of the warehouse to determine what disturbed his interrogation. A familiar black luxury car sat at the security gate. Though he could not see through its tinted window, Thomas knew the occupant was Faust.

"Take her somewhere out of sight," Mad Dog commanded his men.

They took action immediately. Sarahn followed her capturers down a long corridor, if only to make it easier for her escape attempt. They led her to a dark office in the back of the warehouse. The McDaniels brothers guarded the entrance of the doors in the hallway.

Stan's eyes reverted to the green dispersed across the folder. Scooping it up, he made a quick break for the corner of the bookcase. Facing the wall with his grass cupped by the folder, he hung his head back, shifting his hat to disguise himself as a coat rack.

The janitor stepped into the room; a musky smell hung in the air. Slowly making his way over to the desk, he tried to make out what looked like dirt thrown about on the surface. Stan watched over his shoulder as the janitor approached the debris field of bud. Using this moment, Stan quickly slipped out of the room, while the door slowly closed behind him. The sound frightened the janitor. He spun around to face the door. Stan ducked below the first available secretary desk.

The luxury car rolled from the security gate to a staging area in the front of the warehouse. Mad Dog stared with contempt as the vehicle came to a complete stop. The driver jumped from his seat to open the door for his employer.

"I got my own Stephens and ev'rything now." Faust smiled at his childhood friend as he stepped out of the black car onto the black top where Mad Dog stood. "What do you think?"

"A man living his life in comparison to others will never be fulfilled, Faust." Mad Dog took a long drag from his ashen cigarette before growling. "What do you want?"

"Oh, come now, Tommy," Faust jostled. "We both know you're all bark and no bite."

The janitor opened the door to check for anyone in the common area of the offices on this floor and saw nothing but empty desks. Stan, cradling his weed delicately, hid breathlessly behind the first secretarial desk.

The janitor turned back into the office to further examine the scene left behind. Stan made a break for the elevator but slipped on the soapy mop water on the floor. Stan's stash clung to the folder with inertia, *and the prominence of its stickiness,* but the folder slipped from the tips of his fingers. Determined to not even allow God himself to separate him from the flower of bliss, Stan focused his adrenal gland on claiming his prize while heroically sacrificing his body for the salvation of his sacred pile. He came crashing against another desk, then down on the floor.

Sarahn finally loosened the knots holding her wrists.

"Somebody's into BDSM," she mumbled mockingly. The thief looked around her cell. Small vents allowed circulation of what she correctly assessed from the inventory diagrams posted on the wall to be the warehouse foreman's office. "Damn, how old is this building?"

"This is it, huh?" Mad Dog snarled. "This is where our roads led us, and we're right back here."

"You seem surprised," Faust replied.

"Just be honest with me for the first time in our lives." Mad Dog grunted through his gnashed teeth. "Has it been you, standing in my way at every turn?"

Faust smiled.

Busy compiling the intruder's remnant debris, the janitor heard the crash. His eyes traced to the door, then to the weed piled together with his pinkie, back to the door.

Stan gathered his poise, smashing the button for the elevator. Slowly, the doors began to slide open; when it widened enough for him to slip through, he jostled for position. Securing his stash, he toggled the close door button.

Sarahn liberated herself from her rope shackles, the dark of the room settling to the limited light received by her eyes. Books were stacked and covered with dust on the ornamental shelves. An old Gibson guitar hung on the wall by its neck.

Rummaging through the drawers of the desk, the captive thief searched for anything she could use to gain the upper hand. In fatigue, she sat back into the chair. Her eyes fell upon a lone picture frame.

"It didn't have to come to this." Faust smiled. "Had you never cut me out, my resources could have been yours."

"If I hadn't cut you out," Mad Dog retorted, "you would have taken everything!"

"I know about the Maglev, Tom."

Mad Dog stood stunned; his words failed to form on his tongue.

"I know what's on it," Faust continued in response to Mad Dog's deafening silence. "And I know what it means. I want in."

The janitor opened the door just as the elevator doors slid closed. His eyes caught sight of a tattered gray trench coat through the crack. He made his way to the elevator doors, knowing he would never catch the intruder by taking the stairs. It would be much quicker to wait on the elevator. He voraciously bombarded the down button.

Sarahn twisted the picture frame to see it better in the dim light. It was a family. A happy family—the father, the mother, and their two children: a son and daughter. Her eyes traced the children's smile when she recognized the son's snub nose. "It's Mad Dog." She examined the desk she sat behind. The dust-covered mess reminded her of Stan's office, but the dust was much older. She rubbed her finger across the dust on the name placard next to the old intercom, revealing the name, James Killian.

The elevator doors opened on the main floor. Stan stepped to cross the threshold when the doors violently tried to shut around him, startling Stan and forcing him to almost lose his stash. The doors reopened, jostled by Stan's mere existence, barely giving him time to react before attempting to close again.

After a few seconds of fighting with the door about whose atoms would occupy what space, Stan heard the click of a lock turn. He thought to himself, *"Shit, the jig is up!"* Resigning himself to the metaphorical and literal doors of opportunity closing around him, a pillar standing near the elevator door caught his eye.

Mad Dog retrieved his key from the lock on the door to his office building. His guttural growl mirrored every breath.

"I'm glad you're starting to come around, Tommy. It'll be good to work with you again," Faust continued.

The light from the warehouse reflected off the window of the door. Thomas checked their reflection in the window. His bowler cap was reflected by Faust's. Thomas's suit jacket complemented Faust's green eyes. Beneath Faust's graying trench coat Mad Dog saw the gun nestled in his old friend's holster. He opened the door for Faust.

"I would've never done to you the things you've done to me," Thomas lamented. "My father loved you like a son, and I trusted you like a brother." They marched into the lobby illuminated only by the dwindling light shining through the closing elevator doors they approached. "And now you come back to extort me."

Stan stood next to them in the shadows bewildered, no idea what to do next. Without thinking, he reached out, tapping the elevator button for his arguing acquaintances.

"Extort you?" Faust rebutted, turning to thank whoever opened the doors but found no one there to express his gratitude. "Th-Why I'm not here to extort you. I'm here to help you."

"Oh, another 'Gentleman's Deal'?" Thomas stepped into the elevator. "Perhaps, this time, you won't skim off the top and take a share as well?" The elevator doors shut in front of them.

The janitor stood, frantically slamming his thumb down hard on the button to call the elevator.

Maybe he should have just taken the stairs.

Finally, the elevator responded to his command, rising to the second floor. The doors slid open, revealing his uncle and a man he had not seen in years.

"Tommy, you wouldn't understand," Faust pleaded, unaware of the elevator stopping on the second floor. "There were mitigating circumstances—Lil Tom?" He interrupted his own train of thought. "What the hell are you doing here? Wow, have you grown."

Faust was about to remark about how much he resembled his mother, but Mad Dog interrupted his train of thought before it reached the next station.

"Go home, boy." Mad Dog spat, looking at the mess in his bullpen.

What the hell does he pay you for?

"But Uncle Tom, someone was—" His eyes caught sight of Faust's graying trench coat. "Was it you? I guess that explains the weed."

"Was what me?" Faust grunted.

"Ah, doing a little late-night espionage," Mad Dog snarled. "Getting your own hands dirty when I have your little thief." Moving to press the close door button on the elevator, he stopped to repeat to his nephew. "Go home, boy."

The janitor stood there perplexed as the elevator doors closed. What just occurred?

He turned around to the mess the intruder made of the bullpen. Important papers spread over the floor, soaking up the water his bucket spilled.

The secretaries were sure to blame him.

He listened to his uncle's order, collecting the remnant debris left on Mckinney's desk, stowing it in a sack in his book bag. Situating his headphones in his ears, he started the next song on his playlist. Another cover by Clapton. He entered the elevator and lowered himself to the first floor.

The janitor clocked out at the time clock by the door he exited. His eyes caught the shimmer of light reflecting from a trench coat dancing across the property. He turned about-face, running to the elevator. He had to tell his uncle.

Stan escaped the building, only to find himself battling gusts of wind trying to rob him of his weed. Folding the folder every which way, he tried to prevent the wind from disrupting it as he danced from the office building to the security gate. The private investigator noticed the security officer talking to another man by the warehouse, seizing this moment to slip into the security room.

The investigator noticed there weren't any cameras in the office building; he saw a lot of Killian's employee's standing as if on guard of something as his eyes flicked from camera to camera. The last monitor, labeled "James" with an old piece of masking tape, was shut off. Stan quickly remedied the situation.

There she was, mounting her great escape, illuminated by an infrared camera, the singular prize Killian's men were guarding— Sarahn. Below the monitor was an old intercom button. Stan pressed it, watching Sarahn jump at the sound of the feedback on her end.

BZZPT. "Hey." Sarahn heard the familiar voice of her former paramour vibrate through the intercom. "I think I know the answer already, but do you want some help to get out of there?"

Sarahn scrambled to the dusty intercom on the desk, turning the volume down.

"Shh," she hushed his voice over the intercom. "Be quiet. You always make things worse. Just go away."

"Well, all right." Stan shut of the intercom, standing straight to marvel at her ingenuity through the monitor. She pushed the desk to block the doorway and added a small table atop that. Leaning forward, he flipped a switch to comment, "You know, I would have never thought of using the false ceiling."

Immediately, the guards at the door turned and attempted to enter the office used as Sarahn's cell. Stan looked at his hand on the switch he thought matched the office Sarahn was within; however, it belonged to one labeled hallway.

Stan watched Sarahn shake her head and flip the bird to the cameras. The guards battled the door barred with furniture. Leaping to the desk, she made her escape through the ceiling tiles.

The elevator doors slid open, revealing Faust and Mad Dog.

"And you?" the foul, raised voice erupted from Faust. "What would you do then?"

"I'd be more cautious who I threaten," Mad Dog marched to his office, Faust following closely behind, "especially when casting the threats toward someone with as much past as we have, Victor."

Faust calmly smiled. "I haven't heard that name in years."

Thomas spoke from the chair of his desk with the flickering light of a forgotten post perched within the alleyway Thomas's office overlooked. "I wouldn't barge onto the property of an old friend, when darkness has taken the day and there are no others to see your strife!" Thomas's voice decrescendoed to a grumbling growl.

Faust stood in front of the wide-open doorway. Mad Dog watched Faust draw his gun from the holster inside his jacket. "So that's it then? Threats of darkness to make a man feel alone? As if the years meant nothing. My imprisonment meant nothing! You brought us here, Thomas!"

Thomas, idle, rested further back into the chair. Faust's gun remained pointed toward him. "Let's settle this, then. Father would have never broken you off, save an outright betrayal, of the like he's lucky he never had to see." He lifted his leg to cross the other. "But I did. I lived to see the man I trusted to run a part of my business, OUR business, skim from me. Here and there, little by little, you put your filthy fucking hands all over the company I worked so hard to build!"

"If I tried to explain it to you…you'd never understand…" Tears welled in the eyes of Faust; his top lip wrestled the lower one, gnawing and biting for it to stay still for a moment. "I never would have hurt you, your family, or the company! I swear it!" He beckoned, the gun trembling in his hand pointedly at Thomas.

"Ah. So you're Robin Hood, and I'm the Sheriff then?" Thomas inched closer to the desk, his fingers lingering over a gun fastened to the bottom of the desk. "See, the problem with that analogy is I was fucking BROKE FAUST!" His free hand crashed on the table. "You thought that it was okay to steal from me, my family, my Gracie." Thomas shuddered at the utterance of her name. "I thought it would be okay to cut you out of the deal entirely this time. What is it you offered to our arrangement after you made your return on your investment?"

"Beer kegs." Faust whimpered, attempting to use his sleeved arm to wipe the tears from his face. "I know the company."

Thomas sat in bewilderment. "What are you talking about?" But his eyes knew the answer before it left Faust's lips.

"I know the trucks. The drivers. The kegs. Everything except the new drops but a quick look at the books." Faust's eyes fell to Thomas's desk in between them. "And I'll know all of it. I'll know where you hide it, how, where it'll go, and who it'll be going to. I will blow the..." Faust trailed off, the tears covered his face, and snot running from his nose. "You brought us here! I'll blow the whole fucking operation, Tom!"

Thomas filled with fear, then solitude, ending in anger.

"Let's just do the old Gentleman's Deal! You don't understand! I have to make this work!" Faust cried his demand. He stepped backward, feeling for the door to Thomas's office with his free hand. The gun quaked in his hand. "More than you realize depends on this!"

"You call this a Gentleman's Deal." Mad Dog stood from his desk. He could sit for this insolence no longer. "You standing there brandishing your gun in my face."

"Don't make me do this. Don't make me replace you!"

Similar to the horizon of a black hole, Mad Dog found himself encircled in a moment of time, standing still, devoid of progression, absent regression. Void of sound, except the beat of his heart thumping in his ears, time shattered and bleakness swallowed a broken man.

The crash of a water bucket disrupted Faust; fear struck in his spine, and he turned his head for a short, distracted moment. The moment his eyes deviated from Thomas, he heard a shift at the desk, a quick movement. He vaulted himself backward into the door.

The seconds preventing the existence of "now" passed long enough to cause the bullet fired from the gun Mad Dog drew from beneath his desk to pierce the cotton fibers and shatter the button of Faust's coat, resulting in nothing more than a mere missing button. Beyond the intended...a command was heard from the next room over. "Stop right there!"

The audible world faded away, and a boy, the becoming of a young man, lay bleeding out. The floor was just beginning to dry; the remaining suds and water combined in the pool of blood welling from the unknowing, *undeserving*, and frightened janitor.

Faust watched the pain take hold of the man, knowing he had been extinguished from all thought. Mad Dog was no longer concerned with Faust.

He considered shooting him then and there, and perhaps he should. Faust replaced his gun in its holster.

Perhaps the hell of man's creation is worse than the one that awaits him.

Faust watched Mad Dog inch toward his nephew. Falling to his knees, then hands, he crawled to the boy, struggling to catch a breath, trying his best to reach out to his uncle, soaked in bloodied suds.

"No," Mad Dog whispers, crawling closer to his nephew. Over and over, he repeated himself, as if nothing or no one was around. He felt the weight of his heart drop below what his physiological body could know.

"I saw him." His nephew spat blood out, sputtering to finish the sentence. "The man in the trench coat." His body began to seize. A tremor took him into the long night.

"Saw who?" Mad Dog cried as he grabbed the face of his passing nephew. "Trench coat?" A grief struck him with a fierce anger, raging with an unforeseeable void of malcontention toward the world.

Faust had escaped when Thomas returned to the moment; he looked around the darkened office. "It won't be for nothing, boy. I promise you that." He gleamed into the eyes of his departed nephew and thought toward why he began this path. Turning back now would be allowing his death to mean nothing. It would mean Gracie giving up the life he earned for her. The broken brow and warped heart earned over the years of toiling for his company would all be for naught. No. He would fight. He would not just win. There would be no competition left to stand, and anyone who did anything to get in his way or hurt those he loved would meet such an end.

"Who got away?" Thomas thought. *"Who killed my nephew?"*

Foreword, or Backword?

Stan watched the Killian's employees trying to coax Sarahn from the rafters, to no avail. A loud noise exuded from the office building; Stan took this as his sign to leave, scurrying his way to the road with his back hunched over and appearing very frightening to anyone considering picking up a stranger this late in the evening. Seeing a car approaching, he waddled into the road with both hands, holding the folder to protect his weed, forcing the car to stop.

The lights of the car blinded Stan, standing in the middle of the road, lowering his head, allowing his hat to block the light. The driver must not have seen him until the last moment as Stan listened to the brakes screech to a halt. "Can I please get a ride back into town?" Stan pleaded to the car as if it were the pagan god of roads. His hands were trying to balance the folder to maintain what remained of his pile.

"You sure can, baby," a familiar voice answered. Through the bright headlights, Stan could not tell who it was at first. Approaching the passenger side of the car, he realized it was his bus partner a few weeks ago. "Go ahead and hop in, hun."

Stan carefully got into the car, making sure not to spill any bud. "I thought people that rode the bus didn't have vehicles." Stan used a tone sounding more like a question than a statement.

"Honey, you need to get yourself a car. I just ride the bus to work and home," she said, smoking a cigarette with the elegance of a queen and the cares of a hooker. "It saves me from dealing with rush-hour traffic, and I get to meet new friends." She winked at Stan and caressed his thigh.

Stan began to consider the thought of having a car again. They hit a rather large hole in the road, the outskirts of the city, and the folder bounced in the air, landing on the dash, but as Stan watched his bud fly, time felt condensed. Each second felt like years, stretching his arms out, trying to catch the folder before it came tumbling down. His eyes widened with dilated pupils, his fingers touching the underside of the folder but failing to grasp it.

To his luck, the folder landed perfectly on the dash, and none of it was lost. "Seems to me that stuff might be more than just a hobby for you, babe. Ever think you should slow it down a bit, hmm?" she asked with a reminiscent coy bite of the lip, arousing and confusing him as she gave him a quick glance.

Pulling the folder back into his lap for safety, he started wondering whether he'd developed a dependence. After a short ride back into town with some much-needed conversation in a more pleasant tone than he'd become accustomed to as of late, they arrived at Stan's place. "Thanks for the ride, uhm…"

"Michelle, dear. I expect our next date you'll know me by name." She smiled, her eyes glittering.

Stan smiled in return and prepared to exit the vehicle. "Excuse me." She laughed. "I think a goodbye kiss is appropriate for a second date. Wouldn't you say so?"

The fear and joy clouding Stan's eyes left him in a further state of confusion than normal. He obliged.

He climbed the steps of Draper's Properties, his attention fervent on the manila envelope in his hands. Very little of his bud vanished in transport; he would be damned to lose it all now. After successfully dodging a late-night Edna, he approached his doorway with disgust, glaring into the hole of the cracked windowpane.

"Dominick's going to be pissed." The private eye carefully searched his pockets for his keys and unlocked the door. A noise from his neighbor's apartment erupted Katie from their door. She looked at him through panicked eyes.

"A kid's been shot. There was a burglary at the old Killian's building!" she said, nothing more, and simply turned and ran down the hallway and stairs.

Entering his apartment, he dropped the folder onto his desk and gave a huge sigh of relief as he collapsed into his chair.

Stan felt his breast pockets for his packet of papers. He retrieved a gummed rolling paper with haste. Fatigue settled in for the day, and his surgeon-stable hands began to shake as he piled the bud into the fold of the paper.

After rolling it sufficiently tight, Stan searched himself for his new matchbook he snagged from Dirty Vegas, but it was nowhere to be found. Rummaging his desk, he found an old, worn matchbook, also from Dirty Vegas, hidden beneath a stapler.

Striking the match, Stan lit his joint. From the same drawer he found the matchbook, he retrieved a labeled mason jar. He stood from his chair, the joint clasped in his lips, emptying his pockets onto his desk, searching for all of his caches of bud hidden on himself.

He pooled his supply into the jar and returned it to the drawer. Stan stretched out his back, taking a deep breath through the tubular structure of the joint. A cloud of smoke released from his lungs as he removed his coat, draping it on his coat rack.

Stan stumbled across his office to his couch, removing the cushion and pulling out his foldout bed. In his lethargy, the tired investigator lay out in his bed, crossing his feet to remove the pressure in his lower back. He knew he would pay for this in the morning, but for now, it felt amazing. He tipped his hat over his eyes to blot out the impending sun.

"Potstow's best investigator."

East of Potstow

A well-postured man stood alone on the sidewalk outside the offices of Book and Associates, eyeing his wristwatch; his face was drenched with anxious sweat. The light-blue suit contoured to his body, creating the illusion that he was even slimmer than he already was. Turning his head to his left, he stared down the road as far as his eyes could observe. Then he checked his right. Cars inhabited both lanes of the road, though the man wasn't satisfied with the sight reflecting from his pupils. His eyes averted back to his wristwatch before he changed hands with his briefcase, restarting the process from the beginning.

A few more frantic cycles passed, and finally, the balloon of anticipation burst. Looking to his left once more, his eyes perceived a familiar black, four-door sedan approaching with its blinker ablaze. The sedan came to a halt in front of him. He opened the back door.

"Come," a rough voice grunted from the back seat of the car, "get in."

The well-postured man did as he was bid and took a seat next to the man with the rough voice. "So what's the urgent business, Faust?"

Faust's green-and-yellow teeth shined from the darkness, his silhouette encompassing the shadows. "The day of reckoning is almost upon us."

The car pulled forward, Faust tilting his face into the light.

"My informant from Killian's Distribution has been…disposed." His gruff voice continued after he took a swig from his hip flask. "I need somebody to go in and find out what Mad Dog has planned. He has finances going into a project, but she couldn't get eyes on it."

"I'll get my finance guy on it immediately. He's a master at finding hidden money, and I—"

"No, there's nothing on the books," Faust interrupted, lighting a blunt with his zippo. "We're going to have to get someone on the outside to get close."

"Do you have someone in mind?" asked the man in the light-blue suit.

"Well, my informant." Faust took a hit, offering some to his guest, who waved him off. "She said there's this dick in town." He puffed again. "He's been hoverin' around the guy she was stealing information from."

"His name's Dick?"

"No, no…" Faust paused, smoking his blunt once more. "Well, maybe." He laughed a cold, hollow laugh. "Honestly, I forget what his name was, but you'll find him there." Faust pointed out the window to a three-story building sitting ahead on the corner of the street.

"Why don't you just go hire him? My rates aren't cheap. You know this."

"I can't be found anywhere near any of this, you hear me." He blew his smoke into the man's face, dropping two envelopes in the man's lap. "Just bring me whatever you can find on Project Díoltas."

"Okay." The man placed the envelope emblazoned with his name into his briefcase.

The car came to a stop in front of the building. "Get out." The man, again, did as he was bid, closing the door behind him.

Turning to walk into the building, the window rolled down behind him. Faust called after him. "If he fails, kill him."

"Okay." He turned to walk away again, conflicted with his order.

"Of course, if he succeeds," Faust called out to him once more as he rolled up the window. "We'll have to kill him eventually, anyways."

The man in his light-blue suit entered the double doors beneath the sign for Draper's Properties. Adjusting his cuff links, he walked up to the manager's desk, ringing the little bell sitting upon the counter.

The head belonging to a short, portly man stuck out from behind the office door. "Yes, how can I help you?"

"Yeah, I'm looking for a Dick, I—"

"Third floor."

"Well, honestly, I'm not even sure—" the man rebuked.

"Third floor." The manager spat a rude rebuttal shortly, slamming the office door behind him.

"Right." The man spoke to himself in response. "Well, I guess I go to the third floor."

Pivoting his step, he gazed at the stairs. He and his snazzy suit mounted the staircase, beginning his journey. Above him, he could hear the rumbling of a thundering herd bounding. Carefully, the man took each step, dripping with the anxiety of what he'd gotten himself into, surmounting with every step forward to perdition.

"Here, kitty, kitty, kitty, kitty." An old lady's voice carried down the stairwell the man ascended. When she saw the man, she said, "Excuse me, sir, have you seen my cat?"

"I-uh," he stammered. The man was unprepared for this line of questioning.

In his line of work, that does not happen often.

"No, I haven't seen any cats, ma'am."

"Well, do keep your eyes out." She scowled before continuing, "That dick upstairs refuses to look for him."

"So wait," the man gasped, "is his name Dick or…?"

The old lady spun around as if she did not hear a word. "Here, kitty, kitty, kitty, kitty," she called out, shaking a can of cat treats. Meows from her other cats echoed inside her apartment; little paws poked through the gape beneath the door. She was ignoring any attempts the man made toward clarification, interrupting with her repetitive "Here, kitty, kitty, kitty, kitty" call.

He turned to make his way up the stairs once more. The old lady's call echoed from behind, the drywall and ceramic tiles carrying the sound throughout the building. Stepping onto the third-floor landing, he looked down the left hallway, a single door allowing the sun to shine through its broken window.

A mumbled conversation grew as he approached the door.

From the door, the man heard a female voice yelling, "GET! YOUR SHIT! TOGETHER!" She opened, then slammed the door behind her.

"Excuse me." Surprised, the man stammered to ask the buffalo if he was heading in the right direction, but she shrugged him off with a surprisingly gruff noise. He watched her trot down the hallway to the stairs, simultaneously approaching the door she exited to deliver a light and respectable knock, followed by a stern but gentle, "Hello, may I come in?"

"Jesus, I suppose so," a voice replied from the other side of the broken window in the door.

The door squeaked open, glass shaking from the pane and falling to the floor. The well-dressed man stepped from behind the door to enter the well-lit studio apartment. He truly wished it had not been.

"Huh." The jaw of the man in the light-blue suit slacked in discovery, taking in his surroundings, forgetting to read the lettering upon the door.

A realization occurred to him when his eyes circled back toward the other man across the desk. The man donning the light-blue suit said, "You must be Dick."

"It's Stan!" Stan rebutted, dropping what seemed to be a roach from the stale stench inhabiting the room.

"Guess that explains it then," the man said ecstatically to finally have clarification. "They must have been calling you a dick."

Stan sported a smug look on his face and grumbled, lowering himself to his hands and knees, searching the floor in desperation; the man assumed Stan was looking for the roach he dropped.

Stan sobbed, slumping himself in the chair behind his desk, and searched its drawers. Retrieving a mostly empty jar labeled "Sticky-icky," Stan twisted the lid from the top, releasing the pungent odor into the air.

"You know, I've been in this town since the very beginning, but I'm still not used to seeing it everywhere."

"They don't call it 'The Town Pot Built' for nothin'." Stan emptied his jar on a manila folder; random papers and other files the man assumed were from Stan's past cases lay strewn across the desk.

The man felt sorry for their poor, lost faces, each exhibiting their own bits and remains of debris left from long-forgotten packed pipes and hand-rolled cigarettes.

Stan kicked his feet up on the desk, packing the remains of his pile into the exquisite meerschaum pipe. "What can I do you for?"

The man watched the lost faces trickle to the floor, displaying the filing system of a knuckle-dragging Neanderthal. The man shuddered at the thought of living in such decrepit filth. Stan, however, showed no sign of worry or care or comprehension of the papers shuffling to the floor.

"Ah, straight to the point, my kind of guy. My name's Jimmy Book." The man made a quick glance at the fallen files, instantly recognizing the faces of the late Craper and Montey children. He raised a single eyebrow to Stan. The well-postured but nonthreatening man outstretched his hand to shake Stan's with a smile, entirely forced.

The sleuth stared at the hand blankly, then cashed the long pipe into his hands. Jimmy watched Stan casually rub the ashes into his thigh, ignoring his hand. Jimmy quickly took the hint, resting his hand back on his briefcase. "Right, well…" he paused to gather his thoughts, "I'm looking for a man that can be discreet, and I'm told you're that man."

"They apparently said I'm a dick too." Stan struck a match across the strip of the Dirty Vegas matchbook and took a long draw from his pipe.

"At this point, I'd say that builds credibility more than anything," the man rebutted, sitting in the dust-covered seat across from Stan, uncomfortably crossing one leg over the other with his begrudging smile. His insides cringed imagining the dust collecting on his pants and suit jacket.

"Hmph." Stan smirked, taking the pipe out of his mouth. "All right, so what's the gig then?" He chuckled, putting out the match.

"I'm on this case—"

"Case?" Stan perked. Jimmy knew he had him hook, line, and sinker, and he probably would not retrieve the hook.

"Yes, a case," Jimmy answered quickly. "I'm a lawyer. A client I'm working for believes there is a local distributor that he suspects of questionable business practices." A long look filled the attorney's face. "But nothing can be found on the books."

"So," Stan grunted, leaning forward, grabbing Jimmy's attention, "you'd like me to utilize some questionable business practices so you can prove someone else's questionable business practices?" The lawyer wiped the smirk he'd been forcing since his entry from his face.

"No, I don't need that kind of trouble…" Stan trailed off. Jimmy could tell there was something at the door catching the host's attention. The mail slot opened to have a bright-pink envelope shoved through. Jimmy noted the look on Stan face—as if his testicles just descended for the first time—and the sensation both surprised and pained him.

Quickly reaching for the matchbook and the pipe once more, Stan crossed the room to grab the envelope.

Jimmy watched Stan limp in a slow tension across the floor of his apartment. Stan glared at the envelope on the floor in utter distaste, bellowing an overture to himself.

Jimmy knew those bright-pink envelopes from his office all too well. He could see the envelope radiating with malcontent the words "Final Termination Notice" between Stan's fingers, stamped in red on the front.

"It seems to me you could use a bit more of this trouble, you know, to pay your bills," Jimmy said as though dropping his ace on an all-in hand where the grand prize was a detective who could barely spell the word clue but still managed to solve cases, at even his own surprise.

Stan gaped at Jimmy with disgust. He tore open the envelope as he planted himself back into his chair.

"What's the pay?" Stan tossed his legs back onto his desk, knocking the manila folder he broke the last of his bud from his desk. The folder fell and opened facedown among the files to fall formerly.

Jimmy watched Stan's eyes search the pink paper from the envelope for the fiscal damage.

"You'll be compensated for your discretion, of course. How does…" Jimmy thought for a moment: the size of the apartment, the bimonthly frequency, Stan's likelihood to stretch his money as far as he could before he would pay his bills, "…five hundred fifty sound?" By the look Stan gave him, Jimmy figured he was off by about fifteen, maybe twenty dollars. "Appropriate?"

"One thousand, plus expenses. So I'd say about fifteen hundred should get the job done."

"Odd." The defender of the law gave the investigator a mocking look, thinking it amusing the private eye asked for so little. "You calculated expenses with little knowledge of the job." His smile returned to his face. "But fine. I expected you to be a dick about it after speaking with them." Jimmy stood from the dusty chair.

"Who are 'they' you keep referring?" Stan asked, sounding exceptionally annoyed.

"It's of little consequence." Jimmy pulled the second envelope Faust gave him, void of name, from his inner coat pocket. "There's two grand in here. I'm sure you'll find that to be enough. I'll be in contact."

He simpered. "I see certain supplies in need already." The lawyer glanced toward the almost-empty mason jar. "See you tomorrow." Jimmy buttoned his light-blue suit jacket. He wiped off the dust that accumulated on his pants. He crossed the room to take his leave.

The building remained quiet as he walked down the first flight of steps. He passed a black cat with intensely green eyes that pulled your focal point from the white spot on its chest. She watched him pass in bleak silence, and Jimmy was glad for it. From his inner coat pocket, Jimmy pulled out his phone, searching his contacts to dial his secretary, Barbara.

"Yes, James?" Barbara's annoyed voiced answered the line.

"I need you to find all the information you can about Killian Distribution." Reaching the first-floor landing, Jimmy focused on the registrar. He examined the lettering of "Private Eye" behind the glass.

"Anything else?" asked the secretary over the phone line.

"Yeah," Jimmy spoke, "I need you to find me everything about this dick named Stan Greene—who he is, where he comes from, who he had for twelfth-grade English. I need everything."

Barbara coughed and laughed.

"Who the fuck is this dick, Stan Greene?"

Letter in "Janitor" provided by Chancy Glance.

Created by: Cydney Taylor

Special Thanks

Ed Hauck	Jason Meyer	Alex Lawyer
Maydelin Jofre Tejeda	Wendy Hanna	Robert Hanna
Pete Dantinne	Drewboo Smith	Chris Wilson
Kaitlin Davis	Tj Rogers	Jaiden Rogers
Candi DeGroff	Tim Rogers	Twyla Rogers
Jon DeGroff	The anointed princes and princess	Kimmie Pearcy
Michael "Hj" O'Connor	of "Turd head" Mountain	Jonny Brava
Ben Swiger		Evan Cole
Chris Wiley	Cydney Jackson	Craig DeBastiani
	Craig Phillip	Paul Nguyen
	Bruce Lane	Jeff Summerfeld
	Rob Heater	Andy Patel (R. I. P)
	Joshua Hanna	
Stephen "Steve" Martinez	Jessica Martinez	Josh Lucas
Joseph "Broseph" Martinez	Alyssa Weaver	Jordan Wean
Will "Poobauer" Neubauer	Mitchel Mayle III	Sean Cochran
Dan "Stemp" Stemple	Andrew Drain	Neil Wallace
Jim Rogers	Lois Hibbs	Rob Hawkins
Elaine Rogers	Jim Hibbs	Ethan Earl
Mel Walton	Jaclin "Poonanny" Hall	Dan Arthur
Jeeeeell Huffman	Allison Stine	Nicco Mills
Jack Saunders	AJ Riggenbach	Noah Mills
Leslie Forquer	Richard "Squirrelly" Caners II	Corey Nesselrotte
Justin Channell	Courtney Studley	Joseph "My Peter" Studley
Dina Hudson	Zach Fowler	Tim Pelligrin
David Bohon	Aaron Aites	Donna Carpenter
Andrea Hubbard	Sue Travis	Terry Carpenter
Rick Satterfield	Richard Satterfield	Jessica Satterfield
Robert Abel	Dan Abel	Garrison "#21" Scarberry
Tim "Butter Butter" Matthews	Melissa Middleton	Jayme Ferguson
Shihan Tom Stowers	Amber Shuck	Jackie Bavely
Lea Morris	Steven Cook	Daniel Facemire
Dylan Garza	Michael Stewart	Daniel "Horseweinie" Orsini
Justin "Scrum" Yates	Destiny Holmes	Jamar Turner
Brenda Satterfield	Becky Markley	Justyn Boyers

About the Author

Shawn Amick and Terry Rogers met reluctantly while working in a small wireless retailer. The pairing developed into a partnership that extended beyond the workplace. Terry had been developing the world of Dick, Stan Greene as a graphic novel for many years. Meanwhile Shawn had been learning to write to allow immense worlds to become an escape for readers; as they both did as children.

By day Terry finds himself working for a local pizza franchise in small town West Virginia. Shawn continued his path of retail and reached upper management in hopes of being able to run his own company. More than anything, they both desire to be their own bosses and help cultivate a world for others to believe and become engaged.

This book is the culmination of many fights consisting of the authors screaming and berating one another. All the while knowing that the other was trying to make the book the best it could be. It is mutually recognized that this would never came to fruition any other way. With any book or project they may start, prepare yourself for suspense brought from the furious minds of two men jaded by the status quo.